Aside from the corpses near his feet, most of the available space was given over to rows of theatre seats, all facing a raised stage. The leading edge of the acting area jutted out into the seating, like the down-stroke of a letter T. Across this, more than a dozen figures in elaborate make-up and the flimsiest of costumes were engaged in numerous sexual couplings and muscular ménage à trois.

"Bojemoi!" Dante stared at the stage in disbelief. "What do you call that?"

Oh my, the Crest replied. *Kabuki porn.*

Six ninja dived through the paper wall above Dante's head and landed on the seating in front of him, their weapons already drawn and ready to attack.

Sex and violence, the Crest sighed. *You should feel right at home.*

NIKOLAI DANTE

IMPERIAL BLACK

David Bishop

BLACK **FLAME**

For Simon, who first transformed Dante from words into pictures

A Black Flame Publication
www.blackflame.com

First published in 2005 by BL Publishing, Games Workshop Ltd., Willow Road, Nottingham NG7 2WS, UK.

Distributed in the US by Simon & Schuster, 1230 Avenue of the Americas, New York, NY 10020, USA.

10 9 8 7 6 5 4 3 2 1

Cover illustration by Simon Fraser.

ISBN 13: 978 1 84416 180 5
ISBN 10: 1 84416 180 3

A CIP record for this book is available from the British Library.

Printed in the UK by Bookmarque, Surrey, UK.

PROLOGUE

*"The hero does not think of death in
battle, but of victory."*

– Russian proverb

"2070 AD: The Siege of the Winter Palace and the
Battle of Rudinshtein were the final conflicts of the
war between Tsar Vladimir Makarov and the
House of Romanov. A war begun by a murder
ended in atrocities and genocide. Even now, many
years later, a visit to either location evokes the horror and suffering endured. You can almost hear
the screams, see the clash of troops and smell the
blood in the air. After the war, the Winter Palace
was left in its ruined state; a mute testament of
what happens to all who dare challenge the Tsar's
rule, and as lifeless as the nearby Romanov
Necropolis. Rudinshtein was not so fortunate.

After the war's momentum had abruptly
switched to the Imperial forces, the Romanovs
regrouped in Rudinshtein before retreating to
their Winter Palace. Only two members of that
noble dynasty stayed behind to defend the poorest city in the empire – Andreas Romanov and his
illegitimate half-brother, Nikolai Dante. Four years
earlier, Dante had rescued Rudinshtein from sub-
jugation and its people proclaimed him a hero.
But heroes are not enough against the Imperial
Army.

The Tsar's second-in-command, Count Pyre, directed the Battle of Rudinshtein. The 33rd Imperial Artillery Division initiated a relentless bombardment that all but demolished Rudinshtein's ramshackle defences within an hour. In the aftermath of the war, Vladimir the Conqueror denied responsibility for the city's destruction. Tsarist officials claimed it was Pyre's vendetta against Dante – who had killed the count's lover five years earlier – that accounted for the acts of genocide that blackened the Imperial victory. Certainly, it was Pyre who denied the surviving civilians safe passage from the city, but it was General Ivanov who prosecuted that order.

Vassily Ivanov, a brilliant warrior of unequalled savagery, led the Imperial Black, a regiment whose mere mention was enough to void the bowels of most foes. Officially, his thousand-strong force took its name from the jet-black uniform that was proudly worn by the regiment's soldiers. But most believed the sinister sobriquet had been inspired by the horrific conduct of the murderers and rapists that filled the Imperial Black's ranks. The regiment was the hammer that crushed the life from Rudinshtein, both in battle and during the following three years.

Rudinshtein fell upon the third assault. A tide of blood flooded the city as Imperial forces surged forward, cutting a merciless swathe through decimated rebel ranks. A spirited final defence took place around the grounds of the Governor's mansion, but even the Hero of Rudinshtein could not save the city he had once ruled.

On the last night of the battle, Dante walked among his men, sharing a final drink with those still alive from his rabble of conscripts known as the Rudinshtein Irregulars."

– Extract from *Tsar Wars*, by Georgi Lucassovich

Nikolai Dante sat in front of the ruins of the Governor's mansion and, with two double vodkas inside him, thought about life and death.

Since the war began, he had killed more men than he could remember. The blood of hundreds, perhaps thousands of enemy soldiers was on his hands. He did not enjoy killing. It gave him no pleasure beyond knowing that the act preserved his own life. At the beginning of the conflict, Dante had entertained the notion that each Imperial soldier he slew brought him one step closer to killing the Tsar. Now he recognised just how fanciful that notion had been. Each death provided carrion for the crows that haunted battlefields across the empire, nothing more.

Around him, the civilians trapped in the ruins did their best to ignore the stench of rotting flesh and burned bodies. In a province all too familiar with poverty, the mansion had once been a building of rare grandeur. Now it was a bombed out wreck. The rubble was useful only as a hiding place for those who had not escaped the doomed land in time.

Tired hands clutched thin clothes around malnourished bodies. Faces smeared with soot and despair stared hopelessly past each other. Some civilians huddled round burning barrels of oil, which provided the sole illumination. Others tried to sleep, their slumbers made fitful by the pounding of Imperial artillery, a barrage so constant it had become merely a dull thudding at the back of each mind. Mothers sought to comfort children or nurse their babies. The few male civilians were cripples and geriatrics, those unfit to fight. Any able-bodied man had long since been sacrificed upon the altar of Romanov ambitions, sent to war against the Tsar, sent to fight and to die.

Barring some miracle, their families would be joining them in the hereafter before the next dusk.

A few days ago these people had looked at Dante with hope, believing he would find some way to save them, however unlikely. He had done it before, could he perform another miracle? Their faces no longer registered his presence among them. Such a thin line separated life and death, Dante thought. Tomorrow, they expect to cross that line, he sighed, and so do I.

Rouble for your thoughts, a patrician voice asked inside Dante's mind.

"I'm surprised they're worth that much to you, Crest."

I was being generous, the voice replied archly. *Besides, it's hard to find exact change on a battlefield.*

Dante rolled his eyes. Being bonded with a Romanov Weapons Crest was not without advantages. The sentient battle computer was a repository of vast knowledge and wisdom, and it could access and override any computer in the empire. It massively enhanced Dante's natural healing abilities; and it enabled him to extrude cyborganic swords from his fists, providing formidable weapons in close quarter combat. But living with the Crest in his thoughts at every waking moment was akin to having a supercilious servant occupying your mind day and night – useful when you needed it, an almighty pain in the brain the rest of the time. "If you must know, I was wondering how drunk I have to get to shut you up."

Finish that bottle and you should find out. But I doubt even an inveterate drunkard like you wishes to die with a hangover.

"Good point," Dante conceded. "If I die tomorrow–"

Which seems the most likely outcome.

"If I die tomorrow," Dante persisted, "what happens to you? Do you die too?"

I will cease to function soon afterwards, if that's what you mean. We are symbiotically bonded, so my status is dependent upon yours. It is possible that a gifted surgeon, with the correct tools and expertise, could retrieve some of my mechanism from your corpse, but such talents are rarely found on a battlefield.

"So we both die together."

I am a battle computer, Dante. I do not think in terms of life and death, but of success and failure.

"So if I died..."

That would be a failure. I am programmed to mould you into a potential emperor. However hopeless a task, that is my mission. If you perish before that happens, I have failed. I would experience regret, or its machine equivalent. So, if you could find some way to remain alive, that would be preferable.

"Thanks for the encouragement," Dante muttered sourly and swallowed another mouthful of bathtub vodka, the clear liquid searing its way down his throat. He threw the bottle into the darkness, but the expected smashing of glass never came. Instead, a stench like boiling cabbages and day-old pus fouled the air, assaulting Dante's senses and making his eyes water.

"You and the missus arguing again?"

Dante did not need to peer into the shadows to know who had spoken. The man's voice was a lecherous rasp, born of the sewer, raised in the gutter. Such gruff words and revolting smell could mean only one thing: Spatch-cock was approaching. Sure enough, a hunched figure emerged from the darkness clutching Dante's discarded vodka bottle, his foul-smelling form clad in the soiled uniform of a Rudinshtein Irregular.

"The Crest might be bonded to me, but we aren't married," Dante replied.

"You argue like you are." Spatchcock drank gratefully from the bottle before offering it to his commanding officer. "Sure you don't want any more, captain?"

Dante shook his head. "It's all yours."

"Cheers." The lice-ridden conscript swallowed the last of the vodka before belching mightily. His face strained for a second, then an explosion of wet noise burst from between his buttocks. "Oh, that's better."

"Diavolo," Dante winced. "We could use your ass as a biological weapon against the Imperials."

"Bit late for that now," Spatchcock said with a shrug. He peered towards the enemy forces encircling the Governor's mansion. "D'you think they'll attack again before dawn?"

"Probably not. They'll want to finish us off in daylight, savour the moment."

Spatchcock nodded grimly. He had been a prisoner in a Romanov gulag when the war began, incarcerated for being a pickpocket, poisoner, forger and an all-purpose purveyor of filth. Offered a choice between execution and fighting against the Tsar, he had chosen conscription. He was no soldier, but his murderous skills had been put to good use under Dante's unconventional command. Spatchcock jerked a thumb towards a case of Imperial champagne lying unopened on the ground. "You ready to inspect the men, captain?"

Dante sighed and nodded. Ever since the assault on St Petersburg, he had made a habit of walking among his troops on the eve of battle, sharing a drink and a few tall tales with them. It was his way of saluting their loyalty, a reward for following him into certain death. It would be the last time. Everyone knew that. The end was coming and it was dressed in an Imperial uniform.

Spatchcock threw the empty bottle back into the shadows and was rewarded with a dull thud and a cry of pain. "Oh, I say," an aristocratic voice protested. "You could have had my eye out."

Rai chewed on his fingernails, his teeth gnawing at the corners of each cuticle. It was a nervous, childhood habit that he'd never quite outgrown, despite repeated thrashings from his father. One day you will be this village's leader, the old man had raged – how can they respect anyone who still chews their nails? Since joining the Romanov forces, Rai had bitten his fingernails down to nothing and beyond. He liked to think his father might understand. When you lived on a constant knife-edge, you needed some way of relieving stress. Most of the other soldiers smoked or drank, or went with whores in the long moments of boredom between battles, anything to distract themselves from the inevitability of what lay ahead. Rai chewed his nails; as a vice, it was cheap and harmless. There was little in the war about which you could say the same.

He glanced at the others who were sprawled around him, dozing fitfully in the dark. Most were Russian or from the Balkans, a few came from further away. Like him, most had been released from an Imperial prison that was overrun by the Romanov forces in the early days of the conflict. Offered the chance to join what was the winning side at the time, they had eagerly volunteered. There was no hiding place from war. Besides, most of those in Rai's gulag had been political prisoners of the Tsar's regime, so it was a chance to put their principles into practice. Only a handful of those liberated from the prison remained.

"Deep in thought?"

Rai scrambled to his feet and snapped to attention when he realised who was approaching. "Captain Romanov. Sorry, I was just–"

"Relax, private, relax. This isn't an official inspection. And my name's Dante, not Romanov – not anymore."

Rai studied the face of his superior. The captain was perhaps thirty, but looked older in the light from a fire that was dying nearby. His black hair was cropped close to the skull, while a ragged beard and moustache masked much of his face. There was weariness about the captain's eyes, as if they had seen too much, witnessed more than anyone should.

"I don't understand," Rai admitted.

"I was born a Dante and I'll die a Dante," the captain replied. "Besides, most of my so-called noble family has left us here in the lurch. They can take their damn name with them." He called over his shoulder. "Flintlock, where are you?"

"Here, captain," a harassed voice replied in the cut-glass accent of a Britannia aristocrat. A tall, middle-aged figure with tousled, blond hair and a bruise that was forming under one eye, hurried into view carrying an armful of champagne bottles. He stopped and offered one to Dante. "Here you go."

"They're for the men, not for me," the captain hissed.

"Oh, rightio." Flintlock offered one of the bottles to Rai.

"No, thank you. I don't drink."

"Really? Oh well, all the more for the rest of us." Flintlock smiled and raised the bottle to his lips, but it was snatched from his grasp by the captain.

"You've had plenty already," Dante snarled. "Go help Spatch give out the remaining bottles to anyone who wants it. Soldier or civilian, I don't care which."

"But I–"

"Go!" A swift punt in Flintlock's posterior sent the protesting private away.

Dante smiled at Rai. "There's no need to stand at attention for me, you know. Sit down, relax and take it easy."

Dante sank to the ground, resting his back against the ruins of a stone wall.

"Yes, sir." Rai sat opposite him, resisting the urge to resume chewing his nails. He noticed the captain's fingers were just as careworn.

"What's your name?" Dante asked.

"Rai."

"Where did you join us? You don't look local."

"I'm from the Himalayas. My people live in the mountains, an area we call the roof of the world."

"That explains your appearance. We don't get many people with brown skin and Oriental eyes in Rudinshtein. You're a long way from home. Why?"

"I was arrested shortly before the war began, for protesting against Tsarist oppression in the Himalayas. For centuries one regime or another has been trying to lay claim to the mountains, hoping to exploit them and the native people – my people. I decided something had to be done about it."

"On your own?" Dante asked, a note of disbelief in his voice.

Rai nodded. "I thought I was being brave. My father thought it foolishness."

"You were both right."

"Perhaps." Rai could feel Dante's eyes examining him.

"So you were arrested and…?"

"Brought before the Tsar. I told him to desist any and all incursions into the Himalayas, or else he would suffer the consequences."

"Consequences?"

"My people believe that in the time of greatest peril, our living goddess the Mukari will strike down forces intent upon destroying us, our way of life."

"And you told the Tsar this?"

Rai grimaced. "Once he'd finished laughing, he marked me for execution as a political subversive. But then the war broke out and–"

"The Imperials decided to concentrate their fire upon Romanov forces."

"Yes. We were left to rot in prison, until your men found us."

Recognition crossed Dante's face. Rai could feel the captain staring at him, some inner calculation being made behind those piercing eyes. Finally, Dante spoke again, his voice a low whisper, his face grim and serious.

"Rai, I've been moving among the men tonight, talking to them one by one, looking for someone special. I think you could be that someone."

Rai shifted uncomfortably on the ground. He'd been afraid of this: first the bribe of alcohol, then the proposition. He hadn't expected it from the captain, who was reputed to be a womaniser of great enthusiasm, but war did strange things to men. "Captain, I'm flattered, of course, but I'm not really like that."

Dante gazed at Rai, bewilderment evident on his features. "Sorry?"

"No, I'm sorry, honestly I am. If I shared those sorts of feelings then I'd be more than happy to oblige you, but I don't. If you see what I mean."

"Rai, I'm looking for somebody brave enough and foolish enough to lead a group of civilians out of here at dawn."

"Oh."

"What did you think I meant?"

"I…" Rai couldn't think of how best to explain his mistake and decided not to try. "I'm not really sure, sir. My mistake."

"How do you feel about it?"

"About…?"

"Leading the civilians out."

"Fine. Not a problem. I'm your man. For that job, I mean."

"You sure? This isn't an order. Andreas has said he will take one group of women and children out, but I need more volunteers to take the others. The Imperials have made it clear they'll slaughter anyone who tries to escape, soldier or civilian. In all probability, what I'm asking you to do is a suicide mission."

"We've all got to die sometime," Rai said firmly. "It might as well be for a cause we believe in, right?"

Dante didn't reply. "I'd take the civilians out myself, but the men need me here to lead them. We'll begin a diversionary attack before sunrise. Try and draw the Imperials away from your route. That should give you a chance."

Rai nodded.

In the distance, sounds of a brawl could be heard, two men shouting over a spilt drink. Rai recognised the higher pitched voice as Flintlock, while the other man could only be Spatchcock, judging by the odour souring the air. The scuffle stopped briefly as a bottle broke, before the thud of fist on skin and a muffled sob of pain concluded the conflict.

"If those two spent as much time fighting the Tsar's forces as they do each other, we'd have won the war by now," Dante muttered. He stood and stretched, twisting his neck from side to side. Joints clicked and popped. Overhead, the first glints of light were colouring the early morning sky. "It'll be dawn in an hour. I'd better get the civilians ready."

"Captain?" Rai said, as Dante turned to leave. Dante paused and looked back at him.

"Yes, private?"

"What were you planning to do after the war?"

Dante shrugged. "Hadn't thought about it much, to be honest. I'd like to get back to being me – a rogue and a renegade, the lover not the fighter, always looking for a good time. Why, what were you planning to do?"

"Find my sister. We're twins. I haven't seen her for years, but I know she's still alive somewhere. I can feel it."

"You're lucky. I can't feel anything anymore," Dante said, before going. "I'll call you when it's time."

"Yes, sir," Rai replied. He looked at his fingernails and sighed. *I wonder if it's true that they keep growing after you're dead?*

General Ivanov watched as the first rays of sunlight stained the clouds red over the Governor's mansion. The battle to seize Rudinshtein from Romanov control had taken far longer than should have been necessary, thanks to the unconventional tactics of the opposing commander, the tenacity of his troops and the stubborn attitude of Ivanov's superior. Count Pyre had left orders that the pleasure of killing Captain Nikolai Dante should be his and his alone. The general argued that Dante should be assassinated, either by a sniper's bullet, or strategic air strike, whatever would do the job best. Once the Rudinshtein Irregulars' charismatic leader was dead, the remaining forces would be smashed within a day and Rudinshtein taken.

But Pyre was adamant that Dante must die by his hand and no other. So Ivanov had pressed his men into service elsewhere along the frontline. The Imperial Black inflicted more damage on the peasant army than all other infantry units combined. The men's uniforms were still glistening hours afterwards, wet with the blood of slain enemies, such was the ferocity of the regiment's attacks. Ivanov smiled to himself, pleasure creasing his cruel-looking features. The pincers were closing around the last stronghold. Soon, the final pocket of resistance would melt like a candle in a firestorm.

Then there would be a reckoning, the general had decided. For every day he had been forced to tarry in the godforsaken province, he would revisit that misery upon Rudinshtein a thousand-fold. For every wound sustained by one of the Imperial Black, a thousand people would be maimed. For every member of Ivanov's regiment that died, a thousand citizens would be executed in front of their families. For every hour the general was forced to remain, he would inflict a thousand hours of torture upon any civilians who survived the coming onslaught. And Ivanov would rejoice in the experience, savouring their suffering and their terror. It gave him a thrill so complete and a joy so satisfying, he wished the war would never end. He was a born warrior and the prospect of peace was like approaching purgatory.

Ivanov removed the black, peaked cap from his bald, polished pate and mopped his scalp with a monogrammed silk handkerchief. Just thinking about the delights that were still to be savoured was arousing him. His thumb stroked the livid scar that ran down the length of his face, a souvenir from the first woman he had ever killed. A hellion from Mongolia, she had sliced his face open like a peach with her fingernails, as Ivanov crushed her windpipe. He was a captain back then, sent into the east to subjugate a minor rebellion. The ringleader proved to be a woman, but Ivanov had not flinched from giving the order for her execution. That was when she attacked him and he had found the delight of mixing pleasure and pain.

Watching the life slowly fading from her eyes, Vassily discovered just how much he enjoyed inflicting pain. Not satisfied with a single victim, he had personally throttled every adult living in the ringleader's village to make an example of them. His superiors had been appalled by his bloodlust, but it made him a better soldier, propelling him through the ranks in record time. An Imperial psychologist, tasked with assessing Ivanov's mental fitness for command, had once accused him of being a sadist with homicidal tendencies. That diagnosis was confirmed by the time Ivanov finished torturing the psychologist, but the poor man was in no state to file his assessment, having recently choked to death on his own, severed genitalia. When the Tsar heard about the incident, he rewarded Ivanov with command of the Imperial Black.

Approaching footfalls attracted the general's attention. He replaced the moist handkerchief in a pocket and glared at his second-in-command. "Report."

"Sir, our scouts have spotted two sets of movement, one striking out northwards from the Governor's mansion, the other heading toward the south-west."

"Excellent. And which one is led by Captain Dante?"

"The strike to the north, sir. The other is mostly made up of civilians."

"No doubt the captain seeks to create a diversion, drawing our focus away from those hoping to elude our wrath. Very well. Inform Count Pyre his quarry is heading directly towards him. Since our glorious leader is so intent on killing Dante personally, he can have that pleasure. Instead, we will gorge ourselves on the civilians. They shall bear witness to the fury of the Imperial Black!"

"Yes, sir." The second-in-command saluted crisply before leaving to carry out the general's orders. Ivanov smirked. Already he could feel the excitement coursing through his veins, that familiar thrill of a forthcoming kill bulging the crotch of his black uniform. His fingers twitched for a weapon. Let them come, let them all come, he thought. I shall bring them pain and death as they have never known it. I shall bathe in their blood and be reborn, for I am righteous.

Rai led the cluster of civilians across the wasteland, away from the Governor's mansion. Less than a hundred of them were making the journey, the others too frightened or infirm to leave their refuge. Three other Rudinshtein Irregulars were helping him escort the civilians. Judging by their faces, they were almost as scared as him, Rai thought.

Vast tracts of land across Rudinshtein had been sown with a bitter crop of mines and serpent wire so, even if they somehow eluded the Imperial forces, there was little hope of escaping. Of the three possible deaths to encounter, Rai favoured stepping on a mine – at least that would be quick. Being captured by the enemy was worse as they liked to torture prisoners before executing them. But serpent wire was what all soldiers feared most.

A semi-sentient form of barbed wire, the murderous weapon responded to any movement. Touch it and the wire would bind itself round you, digging into skin and flesh. Fight to free yourself and the wire simply cut deeper, slicing through sinew and bone, feeding upon your pain and terror. Serpent wire was banned by all international protocols of war, but such treaties meant little in a conflict so bloody and brutal.

To Rai's left, a woman carrying an infant stifled a cry of pain as her legs gave way. It was not serpent wire, but sheer exhaustion that caused her to stumble. To Rai she looked less than twenty, but her hair was streaked with grey, and black rings encircled her eyes. "Here, let me take the child," he offered. The woman smiled gratefully and handed over her infant.

Rai clutched the bundle, pulling back the blankets to look at the baby within. "Is it a boy or a girl?" he asked. But he noticed the infant's face was still and lifeless, a bullet hole in the centre of its forehead, like a third eye.

"I couldn't leave him behind," the woman said. "I've lost everyone else, I couldn't lose him too."

Rai nodded his understanding. He was crouching down to comfort her when the first bullets strafed the civilians, otherwise he would have died instantly. Metal punched through flesh and bone, killing and maiming. Then came the cries of the attacking soldiers, charging towards them.

Rai pushed the dead baby back into its mother's hands, but she did not notice. She and the baby were both dead. Rai drew his weapon and began shooting as a swarm of soldiers in black uniforms grew closer.

Ivanov was disappointed to find so few of those trying to escape had survived his men's first onslaught. The fugitives had been mostly women and children, but they could have offered something better in the way of sport, couldn't they? I shall miss this war when it's over, the general decided, not for the last time.

"Over here, sir." The familiar voice of Ivanov's second-in-command summoned him across the wasteland to examine the single enemy soldier still alive. Curiously, his skin tone was a deep, warm brown, while hooded eyes that slanted upwards at the edges offset his broad nose. Most of his teeth were missing and crimson spilled from several wounds, but he was definitely still alive. Ivanov smiled at the prospect of what lay ahead.

"What kind of mongrel are you?" he began, spitting into the captive's face.

"Himalayan."

"I swear the Romanovs let any scum fight for them," the general snarled, his men laughing heartily along with him. "Himalayan, eh? You're a long way from home, my little mountain goat. Tell me, do you have any family back there, patiently awaiting your return?"

The prisoner nodded, a movement made harder by his dark shoulder-length hair being clenched tightly in the fist of an Imperial Black sergeant.

"Then tell me your name," Ivanov commanded, "so I may find your family to tell them how you died screaming and cursing their names."

"Rai."

"Is that your first name or your last name?"

"Does it matter?" Rai replied, glaring at the bulky figure leering over him.

"I suppose not," the general agreed. He dropped to one knee in front of the prisoner, taking Rai's chin in his grasp. "Do you enjoy pain, Romanov whelp?"

Rai smiled, then spat a mouthful of blood into the general's face.

Ivanov did not flinch. He waved away the soldiers who were ready to stab the prisoner with their bayonets for inflicting indignity on their commanding officer. "Nobody touches him but me!" Ivanov turned back to his captive. "When I've finished, he'll wish I had let you kill him." The general leaned closer, whispering into Rai's left ear like a lover. "I'm going to spoil your pretty face forever. You're going to beg for mercy and then you'll beg for death. How does that sound?"

The prisoner hissed an obscenity at Ivanov.

"I won't have you hearing such language," the general whispered. He closed his teeth tenderly around Rai's ear-lobe, then ripped the succulent pendant of flesh and skin away from the captive's head.

Dante was crawling towards the Imperial lines when he heard the sound of a man screaming in agony. The noise was unnatural, both human and animal at the same time. In war such screams were all too common, but Dante had never got used to them. He scanned the horizon for the source. "Crest, where's that coming from?"

Behind and to your left. Your other left, it prompted a moment later.

Dante swivelled round and peered across the battle-scarred landscape littered with broken metal and splintered corpses. "I can't see anything."

Try using the sight on your rifle, the Crest suggested with a supercilious sigh.

Dante brought his Huntsman 5000 upwards, pressing one eye against the sight atop the long barrel. He swept the weapon from left to right, scanning the horizon, until he located a group of men in black uniforms gathered round a single, kneeling figure. From this distance only three things were obvious: the crimson jacket of a Rudin-shtein Irregular on the prisoner's chest, the blood pouring from a wound to his head and the colour of his skin. "That's Private Rai," Dante realised. Around the captive lay the bodies of those civilians that had tried to escape.

I sense Imperial forces closing on our position, the Crest warned.

"I can't leave him to die," Dante replied. "He's out there because I asked him."

He volunteered. He knew the risks. You have to withdraw – now.

"No," Dante insisted. "I won't abandon him."

If you don't pull back to the Governor's mansion in the next thirty seconds, you will be killed or captured yourself. Is that what he'd want?

"Fuoco…" Through his rifle's sight Dante could see an imposing, bald figure with the markings of a general standing over Rai. The general gestured to one of his men, who came forward carrying a large metal box. The soldier gingerly placed the container in front of Rai, releasing the catches that held the lid in place before hurriedly retreating. Already the lid was being to open and strands of silver metal crept out from within.

Fifteen seconds until this position is overrun, the Crest insisted.

"They're going to torture him," Dante replied. "I can't leave him to die. You know what serpent wire does. Nobody deserves that, Crest."

Yes, but–

"But nothing! At least this way he'll die quickly." Dante's finger tightened round the trigger mechanism of his rifle. "Forgive me, Rai…"

ONE

"Vice is not bad, it has a bad reputation."
– Russian proverb

"For centuries in Japan, the geisha (literally translated 'a person of the arts') was a female performer skilled in many traditions of that land such as dance, music, flower arranging, poetry and the tea ceremony. It took many years of study for a maiko (trainee) to become geisha, attaining the high social status that accompanied such a career. But the number of geisha steadily declined after Japan's defeat in the twentieth century's Second World War, until fewer than a thousand remained. The geisha tradition was dying, becoming part of history.

Some seven hundred years later a much-bowdlerised incarnation of this revered profession was to be found at *Okiya*, the Geisha House of the Rising Sun. In essence a Japanese brothel, this establishment had pretensions to something grander and indulged these by staging pornographic versions of the art forms once practised by geisha. Thus clients could have their needs serviced while savouring the delights of ikebana (flower arranging) or listening to singing accompanied by the three-stringed instrument known as the shamisen. The okami (headmistress) of *Okiya* was Kissy Mitsubishi, a woman with the distinc-

tion of having worked in both the Empire's most
famous brothels: the House of Sin and Famous
Flora's Massage Parlour in St Petersburg.

Constructed on a vast pontoon and powered by
solar energy, the *Okiya* sailed the Empire, offering
a taste of the Orient to all who could afford its
exorbitant prices. Alas, the Makarov-Romanov war
came close to bankrupting this unique endeavour
in the annals of professional sexual services.
Within three years it had become a honey-trap,
infamous for turning tricks into dupes with cus-
tomers forced to pay for fake divorces or face
public shame and disgrace. The end came in 2673
when the Geisha House of the Rising Sun was all
but destroyed by a devastating enemy attack. No
group ever claimed responsibility for the surgical
strike, but many suspected the paramilitary wing
of the puritanical, sex-hating Church of
Skoptzy…"

– Extract from *MacCoy's Imperial Sex Guide*,
2677 edition

Waking up with a hangover was an all too familiar sensation for Dante. Since puberty he had been a prodigious
consumer of alcohol, his intake increasingly dramatically
since bonding with the Crest. Having enhanced healing
abilities enabled him to recover far quicker than most
from the debilitating effects of inebriation, but even that
was not enough to ward off the worst of hangovers. This
time, he decided, either his skull had shrunk in the night
or his brain had doubled in size, such was the vice-like
pain clenching his cranium. Plus someone had replaced
his tongue with a furry flap of roadkill and his eyes felt
like pinpricks in a frozen potato.

"Bojemoi," he whispered feebly, not daring to look
around. Better to stay still and try to get his bearings by
other means.

He was lying between silk sheets on what felt like a waterbed, the mattress offering gentle undulations in response to any of his movements. The scent of jasmine and cinnamon mingled in the air like lovers savouring the afterglow of a particular vigorous bout of lovemaking. The sound of voices murmuring nearby was audible, along with the lapping of water. A curious *plink-plonk* tone in the distance nagged at the senses, at once familiar and foreign. None of that answered the most pressing question in Dante's mind. "What did I drink last night?"

More to the point, what didn't you drink? The Crest's voice was akin to a sudden creeping barrage of explosions in Dante's brain, each syllable a dull detonation across his synapses. *Not only did you sup your way to oblivion, you anaesthetised my systems so completely the last twelve hours are missing from my memory.*

"Please, don't shout," Dante whimpered, nursing his thumping head in both hands. "I'll do anything you ask if you'll just stop shouting."

You'll give up drinking for a week?

"When I said I'd do anything, what I meant was–"

I ASKED IF YOU'D GIVE UP DRINKING FOR A WEEK, the Crest roared.

"Yes, yes. Anything, anything!" Dante cried, his face stricken with agony, desperate to stop the cacophony in his mind.

Very well, the Crest replied, its voice now back to a murmur. *Is that better?*

"Yes, thank you."

Good. May I suggest you find some more suitable clothing while I analyse the surroundings. You could be in imminent danger, and your present attire offers little protection against the slings and arrows of outrageous misfortune.

"What's wrong with what I'm–" Dante's words stopped once he'd opened his eyes and looked downwards. "Interesting. Very interesting."

A more accurate description would be obscene.

Dante was stark naked but for two items of what could charitably be termed clothing. A garter belt of red silk was strapped tightly around his left thigh, while a whisper of cloth covered his crotch. This miniscule triangle of black silk was encrusted with crimson sequins embroidered into the shape of a heart. The legend "GET IT HERE" spelled out by more sequins within the heart. Two tiny straps led away from the crotch and round his hips. Dante could feel them knotted together behind his back, joined by a third strap rising from between the cleft of his buttocks. The size and shape of the g-string suggested it had been designed for female use, as it struggled to encase any of his genitalia. "Perhaps I should have asked for a Brazilian before swapping underwear?"

My sensors are coming back online, the Crest announced. *Beginning analysis of the surroundings.*

"Good." Dante sank back on to the bed. "Let me know if you find something significant. I'll be busy concentrating on lying very still and wishing I was dead."

You should consider yourself fortunate inebriation did not disable my subcutaneous defence mechanism.

"Anytime you want to speak in words I can understand, just let me know."

Subcutaneous – beneath the skin. That's why I'm not currently visible.

Dante checked his left arm. The area below the shoulder was bare; normally the Crest was visible as a circular tattoo resembling the double-headed eagle symbol of the Romanovs. But when Dante was rendered unconscious, an automatic defence mechanism hid the Crest from view.

There's someone approaching this room, it warned. *Be on your guard!*

Dante looked round for an escape route or a weapon. The room was sparsely furnished, just the bed, a small wooden cupboard to one side and a stack of white towels atop that. The only light spilled in from a circular porthole above the bed, while an assortment of oriental paintings and tapestries decorated the white walls. A white door on the far side of the room was the sole exit.

Five seconds…

Dante groped for his Huntsman 5000 rifle under the bed. He habitually hid it there before falling asleep each night, within easy reach. The footsteps were rapidly getting closer as his fingers closed around a heavy cylindrical object on the floor. He snatched it out from under the bed and aimed one end at the door while groping for the trigger with his right hand. But instead of a firing mechanism he found himself pressing a button near the end of a three-foot long rubber phallus. It began vibrating in his grasp, accompanied by a gentle humming.

That's certainly offensive, the Crest observed, *but I doubt it'll make much of a weapon. Perhaps you could use it as a flexible truncheon?*

Dante was still clutching the double-ended dildo when the door swung open to admit an Oriental woman clad in a red, silk kimono that scarcely covered her crotch. She had dark hair, scarlet lipstick to match her kimono and a hungry look about her. Her eyebrows rose at seeing what was clutched in Dante's hands. "You like that, Quentin? I love you long time, but I try anything once if you want."

Realising his actions were being misinterpreted, Dante quickly threw the still-vibrating phallus to one side. "No, no, no, I didn't mean–"

The woman advanced on him, her hands reaching for the sash that kept her kimono closed. "Or maybe little Quentin too tired? For five dollar I wake him, yes?"

"A generous offer, I'm sure, but I've never paid for sex yet," Dante replied, scrambling his way off the bed.

Not with money, the Crest agreed, *but in plenty of other ways you have.*

"You said you'd shut up!" Dante protested.

No, I simply agreed to stop shouting – not the same thing.

The woman looked perplexed, since she was only hearing Dante's half of his conversation. "You want me shut up? I have rubber gag and blindfold in next room, but you pay extra for that, Quentin."

"No, no, I wasn't... I didn't mean–"

"You want me put gag on you instead?"

"No, I was talking to... Look, it doesn't matter." Dante sat down on the bed, all too aware of the g-string strap that seemed intent on garrotting his rectum. He patted the mattress, motioning for the woman to sit down beside him. The bed gently rippled beneath their weight. "Now, could anybody tell me where I am?"

I can, the Crest replied. *My sensors are now fully functional. You are on a floating platform some three hundred nautical miles from the oceanic city-state of Pacifica. I detect close to a hundred people in the surrounding rooms.*

"You on our bed, Quentin," the woman said in broken speech. "You no remember?"

Dante bashfully shook his head. "Sorry, no. I drank too much last night."

That's putting it mildly.

"We celebrate. You too happy," the petite woman agreed.

"In fact," Dante admitted, "I drank so much I seem to have forgotten your name, Miss...?"

"Sang Gen."

"Miss Sang Gen."

I've heard that name before.

"But now I will be called Mrs Durward."

It's all coming back to me now. Oh dear. Dante, I have good news and bad news. Which would you like to hear first?

"Really? Did you get married recently?"

Sang Gen punched Dante playfully on the arm. "Don't you remember, Quentin? It was big wedding. You very generous man."

"Well, I don't like to be a tightwad."

No, you just like getting tight. The good news is this minx believes you are the entirely fictitious Quentin Durward. You must have used that old alias last night while drinking yourself into a stupor. If you'd been using your real name, this little gold digger would have already handed you over for the multi-million rouble bounty on your head.

"And the bad news?" Dante asked.

"Now is time for honeymoon, yes?"

I believe you may have married this woman.

"Honeymoon?" Dante spluttered. Beside him, Sang Gen's smile broadened even further, revealing a mouthful of golden fillings.

"You drink too much last night, you no perform for Mrs Durward. But now you all better, you make me much happiness, yes?"

Dante, better make your excuses and leave, the Crest suggested, urgency apparent in its tone. *Now. While you still can.*

Sang Gen was sliding one hand inside his g-string while her other retrieved a rolled document from within her kimono. She firmly clasped the contents of Dante's underwear while unrolling the sheet of paper to reveal what was written on it. "We husband and wife now, yes? You make me happy." Sang Gen clenched her fist around Dante's testicles, making him gasp in pain and dismay. "Or else you be very unhappy. You understand, little Quentin?"

Five rooms away, Lord Peter Flintlock was having a perfectly dreary time. It was more than twelve hours since Dante had disappeared and, to Flintlock's way of thinking, even the finest houses of ill repute began to pall if you stayed within their walls too long. Savouring the delights of the Orient's finest courtesans was all very well, but eventually you became sated both in body and in spirit, no matter how gargantuan your sexual appetite. You reached a point where you had seen and experienced enough – any more was, quite literally, an anti-climax.

Dante had brought him and Spatchcock to the *Okiya*, the Geisha House of the Rising Sun, after a particularly successful piece of piracy. The freebooting threesome had intercepted an Imperial cruiser bound for St Petersburg that was heavy with wealthy passengers but light on security. Having stripped the Tsar's allies of their possessions, Dante gave his two accomplices the choice of where to celebrate their good fortune. It was Spatchcock who wanted to visit the *Okiya*. "I had a cousin who had such a good time there he ended up in hospital. It took the surgeons three hours just to get the smile off his face."

So Flintlock had spent several tumultuous hours in the arms of a creature calling herself Fragrant Lotus Blossom. But when he emerged from her bedchamber, with a blush on his face and a spring in his step, his two partners in crime were conspicuous by their absence. Dante's vessel, the *Sea Falcon*, was still moored nearby, but the brothel's okami could offer no clue about where Flintlock's friends had gone. Exhausted from his exploits, the man from Britannia hired a private room for the night, paying double for the privilege of sleeping in it alone.

Alas, whoever was responsible for the *Okiya*'s interior decor failed to realise using rice paper for the walls was not a sound idea. It gave the place a veneer of Japanese antiquity, but also meant you could hear everything happening in the adjoining rooms. Flintlock had spent the night trying – and failing – to get some sleep while being aurally assaulted by the comings and goings of innumerable clients, their hostesses screaming with feigned pleasure in a dozen different Oriental tongues. "I'll never eat sushi again," the exiled Brit muttered as he rolled off his unforgiving futon in the morning. He found a wash-basin filled with ice-cold water beneath a mirror and splashed the liquid on his face while contemplating his reflection.

There was a haughty, almost arrogant aspect to his features, no doubt a product of his aristocratic origins and severe upbringing. A loveless childhood and fifteen years of schooling with regular thrashings in various boarding institutions – no wonder the upper classes of Britannia favoured a stiff upper lip. Born a lord of the realm, Flintlock had fled his native land for certain offences he preferred not to recall. He still had a full head of hair and all his own teeth, but time was leaving its mark around the corners of his gimlet-eyed expression. Flintlock rasped a hand across the greying stubble on his chin and jowls. What I wouldn't give for a straight razor, some shaving foam and a badger's hairbrush, he thought wistfully. A female scream from outside the spartanly furnished room got his attention. "I know that voice," he muttered and strode to the door.

He looked out in time to see Fragrant Lotus Blossom sprinting past, a hand towel clasped over her groin, an expression of pure disgust curdling her pretty face. "You bad man. You nasty! I hate you. I tell the others. You no joy here!"

"I say, steady on old girl. What seems to be the matter?" Flintlock inquired politely, but the woman had already dived into another room, slamming its door shut behind her. "Dash it, what could have repulsed a woman of her experience so? I'd have thought there's little she hasn't seen or done in her time here."

The answer appeared from the opposite end of the corridor: Spatchcock, stark naked, his clothes clutched in one hand. "Your lordship! You haven't seen a pretty girl go past, have you? Smelly Local Flower was her name, I think."

"No, sorry, I haven't." Flintlock averted his eyes hurriedly, taking care to breathe through his mouth instead of his nose. Spatchcock might be the closest thing he had to a friend, but Flintlock would rather have his own scrotum bitten off by a ravenous rodent than gaze upon the vile little man's repulsive privates. As for the stench... the only times Spatchcock came close to washing was when he fell into rivers or oceans by mistake.

The odorous runt cursed loudly, his face scrunching with frustration as he picked lice from his crusty armpits and popped them in his mouth. "Shame, I thought we was getting on quite well. She didn't scream once when I undressed."

"A remarkable woman," Flintlock agreed. "Perhaps you should think about putting some clothes on. Don't want you catching your death of cold, do we?"

"Suppose not." Spatchcock began getting dressed again, a cloud of dust escaping each garment as it was pulled on. "You seen the boss this morning?"

"Last time I saw him, he was face-down in a bowl of sake with a cunning little vixen admiring the size of his wallet. Why, do you think he's in trouble?"

Spatchcock shrugged, pausing to scratch his pimple-ridden posterior. "He's always in trouble, isn't he? That's why we stick with him. Life with Dante might be dangerous, but it's never dull."

"Durward. He said we should call him Quentin Durward, remember?" Flintlock hissed, glancing along the corridor to ensure nobody was listening to their conversation. "If the staff here found out there was a fifty million rouble bounty on his head, they'd kill him and claim the reward without blinking."

Spatchcock nodded. "Alright, alright, keep your wig on, your lordship."

"I do not wear a wig."

"Sorry, I meant toupee."

Flintlock's eyes narrowed. He knew Spatchcock took great pleasure in antagonising him, but he refused to let such baseless accusations pass. "I do not wear a wig, a toupee or any other kind of follicle enhancement. My blond hair is all my own, thank you very much."

"You sure? Then why can I see–"

Their bickering was cut short by another scream, which was distinctly male. "That was Dante's voice," Flintlock said, already running in the direction from where the scream had emanated.

"I thought we were supposed to call him Durward," Spatchcock replied, racing after the gangly Brit.

"Shut up, you stupid guttersnipe!"

Sang Gen released Dante's testicles, satisfied she had his attention. "You read!" she snapped, thrusting the marriage certificate into his hands.

Don't bother, the Crest advised. *I've already scanned the Imperial Net for data about this woman. Sang Gen is a notorious extortionist who calls the Geisha House of the Rising Sun home. She gets rich young fools drunk, stages a fake wedding ceremony and then demands they pay an exorbitant fee for a quick annulment. I tried to warn you last night, but you were more interested in the contents of her g-string. Perhaps I should have warned her instead. You're certainly a fool, but not so young anymore. And as for riches…*

"Will be you be quiet?" Dante hissed. "I'm trying to read."

Sang Gen looked round the bedroom in bewilderment. "Who you talk to? Me? You tell me to shut up?"

"No, I was just talking to my…"

Better half?

"…Talking to myself."

"Time for talk is over, husband. You listen now," Sang Gen said. "Me your wife. You make me rich or you make me happy. You choose."

"Look, for a start, we can't be legally married. I wasn't conscious when the ceremony took place, so how can I be your husband?"

Sang Gen's face folded into a determined scowl. "You no want me wife?"

"I'm sure you'll make a lovely bride for somebody one day."

Only after hell freezes over with this harridan.

"But I'm not the marrying type, okay? This has all been a terrible mistake."

Sang Gen folded her arms. "You want no marriage, yes?"

She has a delightful knack for tautology, doesn't she?

Dante grinned sheepishly. "Well…"

"You want no marriage, you pay for no marriage."

"I would, but I seem to have mislaid my belongings: my jacket, my trousers, my rifle, my money pouch. I don't suppose you'd know where they are?"

"You want them back, you pay for them too."

"But how can I pay for them when I don't have any money?"

Dante's new wife smiled like a barracuda. "You can pay in other ways."

I have a bad feeling about this.

Sang Gen gave a sharp whistle and the door opened to reveal a mountainous man waiting outside. Balding, bearded and barrel-chested, he was wearing nothing but a black leather throng and a crooked smile of lust. "This is Genghis. He like it when boys scream," Sang Gen explained sweetly.

Genghis had to duck his head to step into the bedroom, his massive bulk blocking the exit once he was inside.

I imagine that hangover must seem the least of your worries now.

Dante was already on his feet, careful to keep the bed between himself and Genghis. "I'm open to any brilliant suggestions, Crest."

You could try playing hard to get.

"I don't think that's going to be enough!"

Perhaps not. But use your cyborganic weapons and they'll soon realise your true identity. You need to find another way out of this.

"So you be my husband," Sang Gen asked, "or you be Genghis's wife?"

Dante shook his head. "Decisions, decisions..."

The sleek, silver flyer skimmed, only a few feet above ocean's surface. Keeping close to the water enabled the aircraft to escape all but the most sophisticated defence systems, slipping unnoticed past Pacifica. In the cockpit the navigator located their quarry. "The *Okiya* is dead ahead. We should be above it in three minutes."

In the flyer's cargo hold the overhead lighting switched from red to amber, a signal that the drop-zone was close. A dozen figures clad head-to-toe in black rose in unison from their seats, checking weapons and making adjustments to equipment. Only their eyes were visible through a slit in the black cloth wrappings that shrouded their heads. A single command from the smallest of the twelve brought the others to attention. The leader inspected them briefly before giving a curt nod to the one standing nearest the cargo door. He pulled it open, wind and light flooding into the confined space from outside.

The leader leaned out to look at their fast approaching target. From this distance the Geisha House of the Rising Sun resembled the love child of an aircraft carrier and a jade pagoda. It hovered close to the water's surface, sunlight glinting on the raised corners of its elaborate exterior. A dozen smaller vessels were moored around the *Okiya*, but they did not matter. Few witnesses would be left alive, and those that did survive would not be able to identify their attackers. Get in quick, find and neutralise the target, then get out.

Satisfied, the leader withdrew into the cargo hold and examined the display on a tiny computer strapped to his wrist. All was as expected. "Our target is still on board the *Okiya*," the leader announced, shouting over the roaring wind. "We have a lock on the signal from his Weapons Crest. Remember, the corpse of Nikolai Dante is worth fifty million roubles, but the Tsar will pay considerably more than that if he is captured alive and presented at the Imperial Palace. Make sure we take him alive. Is that understood?"

The men nodded their assent.

"Good. Anybody who gets in the way is collateral damage, nothing more, nothing less. Shoot to kill if necessary. Once we have Dante, the *Okiya* will be destroyed. If you are wounded, we will leave you behind to die. Stand by."

The hold's interior lighting switched from amber to green. "Green signal! Go, go, go!"

TWO

"The aftermath of the war proved more savage and more brutal than many of the atrocities committed during the conflict. The Tsar celebrated his victory over the Romanovs by sending Purge Squads to mercilessly take revenge against those whom he felt had betrayed him. Noble houses guilty of switching loyalties to the Romanovs, when it seemed the Makarov regime was doomed, felt the full force of the Tsar's wrath. Most were destroyed and new ones created from the ashes, their future loyalty assured by the Tsar's limitless tyranny.

Nikolai Dante, the so-called Hero of Rudinshtein, somehow escaped capture and execution by the Imperials. The corpse of Count Pyre was discovered after Rudinshtein fell, apparently murdered by his nemesis. The name of Nikolai Dante became accursed across the Empire, with the Tsar putting a massive bounty on the Romanov renegade's head. But what of the people left behind in Rudinshtein by their former leader?

Despite Dante's apparent desertion, the civilians who survived the war still believed in their hero and hoped he would return to save them. Rudinshtein may have been the poorest city in the Empire, yet its people proved most resistant to the reinstatement of the Tsar's rule. The job of crushing their rebellion was given to the most feared regiment of all, the Imperial Black, led by General Ivanov. It was during the next three years he earned the name Ivanov the Terrible, a reference to the oppressive regime of Russia's first Tsar, Ivan the Terrible.

Given an entire province as his plaything, Ivanov set to work with relish. He appeared to revel in the pain and suffering of others, personally supervising interrogations, torture sessions and punishment beatings. He authorised his men to use rape and murder as weapons of terror, herding innocent citizens into camps for the most brutal of subjugations. The general announced anyone who dared to say Dante's name out loud was signing their own death warrant, and offered massive rewards to those collaborators who would inform against their family or neighbours. After enjoying one of the most enlightened leaderships before the war, Rudinshtein now suffered beneath the most savage."

– Extract from *After the Tsar Wars*, by Georgi Lucassovich

Jena Makarov hated having to play hostess for butchers like Ivanov. She had willingly fought and killed for her father during his war against the Romanovs, but that didn't give her any liking for the military or its leaders. The generals were men – and they were all men – who made a living from institutionalised murder, yet wished to dress it up as somehow respectable by adopting the notions of duty and honour. Honour be damned, Jena thought to herself before grimacing. Sounds like the sort of thing Nikolai used to… No, I'm not going to think about him today. Just once I'd like to get through a day without wondering where he is or what he's doing.

Three years had passed since the end of the war, when she had let him escape the ruins of Rudinshtein. Since then, Dante had led his would-be captors a merry dance, eluding all attempts to claim the bounty on his head. Despite herself Jena kept tabs on her former lover's latest escapades. He was an itch she couldn't scratch.

A few months earlier she had rejoiced in using Dante as a pawn to thwart a scheme hatched by one of her father's allies. Now she found herself waiting to welcome a man sworn to destroy Dante.

Jena had encountered Ivanov twice during the final days of the war in Rudinshtein. The bloodlust in his eyes and the sour milk stench of his breath were equally repulsive. She had no wish to ever encounter the general again, but disobeying a direct order from her father was tantamount to treason. So she waited at the Imperial Palace's aerial docking bay, cold arctic air from outside ruffling her auburn curls. In one ear a tiny comms device informed her that Ivanov's flyer was making its final approach from the south-east. "Very well," she replied. "Once the access code is confirmed, lower the energy screen and let him in."

Vassily Ivanov had been waiting for this moment all his life. The personal message from the Tsar, the invitation to step inside the hallowed halls of the Imperial Palace, the fact his contribution to the war and all his efforts since were to be acknowledged and praised by the Tsar himself... These were the moments that made all the sacrifices of the past three years worthwhile.

I must savour every second, the general told himself as he watched his flyer's final approach from behind the pilot's shoulder. I must remember every detail, every element of the experience. I shall want to relive this day many times in years to come.

The flyer sped towards the Imperial Palace, already well under the mighty shadow that the grand structure cast. The Tsar's home resembled a huge, ornate egg hovering about the city of St Petersburg. Fashioned in the style of a Fabergé jewel, the palace was a hundred metres high. Set into one side was a vast entry port, its surface buzzing with luminous energy. As the flyer drew closer the energy faded, a clear window opening to allow access. Ivanov's aircraft swept inside the docking area and automatic systems guided the vessel to its berth.

Satisfied with the nature of his arrival, Ivanov made his way back into the main cabin, surrounded by a phalanx of Imperial Black troops and a single figure that sported the insignia of a major. "Stand easy," Ivanov commanded and his men obeyed in a heartbeat. "Sadly, I must ask you to remain here – the Tsar allows only his personal bodyguard to roam the hallways of the Imperial Palace. It seems our reputation has preceded us." The soldiers, except the major who kept his own counsel, responded with an appreciative laugh. "But whatever honour I receive from our leader, I will share it equally with you. We are all brothers under our uniform, bathed in the blood of our enemies, forged in the heat of battle. Where one of us goes, all of us walk. For the glory of the Imperial Black!"

"For the glory of the Imperial Black!" the soldiers responded fervently.

Ivanov smiled at them benevolently. "Very good. Major, if you'd accompany me outside, I believe the Tsarina is waiting for us."

"Yes, sir." Like the other soldiers, the major was clad in the black uniform of his regiment, but his helmet included a full facemask, tinted to hide the features behind its surface. Only the bottom of his jaw line was visible, and that was a horrific mass of scar tissue. The major strode to the flyer's main doorway and activated the ramp. Once that had extended out to the docking bar walkway, the flyer's outer door slid sideways.

Waiting on the walkway was a beautiful woman in a trouser suit of emerald green. Her face was pale and unlined, with perceptive green eyes framed by her auburn hair. A pert, slightly upturned nose gave her an aristocratic look, as did the way she stood.

Ivanov smiled at seeing her again. He strolled along the ramp towards Jena, his right hand reaching forward to grasp hers. "Tsarina. A pleasure, as always, to see you."

"General Ivanov," she replied curtly. There was no warmth in her face.

Ivanov stepped aside to introduce his second-in-command. The major was more than a foot taller than Jena, his imposing physical bulk and ominously blank face-mask created an oppressive presence. "And this is my strong right hand, a man known simply as the Enforcer." The major nodded to Jena, who appeared grateful at not having to shake his hand as well.

"My father bids you welcome to the Imperial Palace and says he will see you shortly. I am to escort you to the Map Room."

"So be it," Ivanov replied smoothly, quickly falling into step beside Jena as she strode away. The Enforcer followed, three paces behind. "If I may ask, what occupies the Tsar this morning?"

"You may ask," Jena said icily, "but you should not expect an answer."

The general arched an eyebrow, keeping his rage hidden beneath an otherwise serene face. You snotty-nosed little bitch, he thought. What I wouldn't give for the chance to make you cry. I imagine your face would be almost beautiful when bathed in tears, christened by sorrow, chastened by fear. I could make you fear me, Tsarina. How would that suit you?

Jena led the two men down numerous corridors and through many doors within the palace. Along the way she nodded her head towards the glowering form of the Enforcer. "Is he the strong, silent type, or does he speak for himself?"

Ivanov smiled warmly. "The major only talks when he has something important to say. For most of the time, he lets his actions speak for themselves."

"I've read about your actions in Rudinshtein," Jena said. "I'm not sure they are anything of which to be proud, general."

"We have broken the rebellious spirit of the natives, as your father ordered. To a soldier, there is no greater honour than following orders," Ivanov growled, struggling to keep his temper under control. "I would have thought you of all people should understand that, Tsarina."

She did not reply, but the look of anger and disgust that crossed her face spoke volumes. Yes, I would very much like to make you weep, Ivanov decided.

Jena stopped outside a pair of double doors, their surface covered by an ornate design in gold leaf. She gestured and the doors opened to reveal a vast chamber, the height of three normal rooms. The walls were lined with leather-bound volumes, while a large holographic globe hung above a priceless antique rug on the floor. Reading tables and armchairs were scattered about the chamber, while a musty odour characteristic of libraries hung in the air. "This is the Map Room. It contains a copy of every atlas or cartographic document published in the past thousand years. The globe shows the current status of the Empire's terrestrial endeavours. You are welcome to study any of these items until my father arrives."

Ivanov and the Enforcer watched her leave, before accepting the invitation to enter the Map Room. Its double doors glided shut behind them.

Minutes later, the doors re-opened to admit the Tsar, flanked by four heavily armed guards from the Raven Corps. Ivanov and the major instantly dropped to one knee and bowed their heads, prostrating themselves before their commander-in-chief. The Tsar dismissed his bodyguards, telling them to stand outside and ensure he was not disturbed. Two metres tall, the Tsar was powerfully built with broad shoulders, a formidable face and fierce, flinty eyes. The Ruler of all the Russias was swathed in his crimson and gold Imperial robes. "Forgive my clothes," he said, after beckoning the two soldiers to stand upright. "Normally I wear a military uniform to meet members of my armed forces, but didn't have time to change after sitting in the Chamber of Judgement."

"There is nothing to forgive, sir," Ivanov said.

"Indeed. Well, general, I have much to thank you for. Rudinshtein's people were a rebellious rabble when I placed you in charge of them three years ago. From all reports they are now a shattered remnant, their spirit crushed beneath the boots of the Imperial Black, their former bravado broken."

"These reports speak true, sir," the general replied, unable to keep the glee from his face. "I have taken much pleasure in enforcing your will. There is not one among the survivors who challenges your rule."

"If all parts of the Empire were that compliant."

"Indeed, sir. If I may be so bold, I believe that in Rudinshtein we have developed methods of torture equal to any you have at your disposal here. I have tried to emulate your own flair for the creative and the cruel."

"Hmm." The Tsar approached Ivanov's second-in-command. "Major, it is a severe breach of palace protocol for visitors to wear facemasks in my presence without express permission. You would be wise to remove it immediately." The Enforcer leaned forward, slipping the helmet from his head. When he straightened up again, the Tsar blanched at the horrors that had been hidden behind the facemask. "Now I understand," the Tsar eventually said. "What creature did that to you, major?"

"I did," Ivanov interjected. He got a glare of disapproval from the Tsar, but still continued his explanation. "The major once challenged my orders. I was forced to discipline him. Ever since he had been the most loyal of all my men."

"Very well." The Tsar gestured for the Enforcer to put his helmet back on. "Now, I have a new mission for you and the men of the Imperial–"

"Forgive me, sir, but I understood you had summoned us here to reward our efforts in Rudinshtein. I had hoped you might consider appointing me as your second-in-command, bearing in mind–"

A mighty fist smashed against Ivanov's face, cracking his head to one side. The general staggered and coughed blood, but did not lose his footing. The Enforcer took a step forward to intervene, but was waved back by Ivanov. The Tsar moved to within inches of the general's face, his own features red with fury. "You dare interrupt me, your commanding officer? You presume to suggest how I should reward those who fulfil what little I expect of them?"

"Forgive me, sir. I... forgot myself."

The Tsar seethed, sucking in breath between clenched teeth, his chest rising and falling. "Forget yourself again and you shall learn exactly how creative and cruel I can be. The acid enema may not be a new innovation in the world of torture, but I think you would find being on the receiving end of such a treatment must instructive in the difference between pleasure and pain!"

Ivanov did not dare meet the Tsar's eyes, keeping his own gaze fixed upon his dazzling black leather boots. "Yes, sir!"

The Tsar turned away after a pause that felt like a lifetime to the general. Vladimir the Conqueror gestured toward the holographic globe floating in the centre of the Map Room. The topographic illusion slowly rotated on its axis. As the raised mountains of Tibet and surrounding areas came into view, the Tsar pointed at that section of the globe. "As I was saying, I have a new mission for you and the men of the Imperial Black, a task of utmost importance. Consider it your reward for the good work done in Rudinshtein. I wish you to find and secure the fortress known as the Forbidden Citadel."

The general almost spluttered in disbelief, but quickly bit back his words of derision. "Yes, sir. And why do we seek this... goal?"

The Tsar smiled, apparently amused at the care with which Ivanov was choosing his words. "For the past three years Imperial interrogators have questioned the Romanov family retainers that were captured during the war. They proved resistant at first, many willing to die rather than betray the confidences they kept, but recently two of them began to weaken. One revealed the Romanovs had a special link with the Forbidden Citadel, and the other confirmed the fact when placed under sufficient... duress. Analysis of flight manifests and pilots' logs captured from the Winter Palace proved the Romanov patriarch Dmitri made several journeys to the Himalayas during the war, one of them at a time when his presence was urgently required elsewhere." The Tsar swivelled round from the globe to glare at Ivanov once more. "I want to know why he went there and you will discover that for me. Use any and all means necessary. My daughter will brief you further. That is all." He abruptly turned away and strode to the double doors. They opened automatically and the Tsar swept out, four of his bodyguards falling into step behind him.

Ivanov only spoke once the Tsar was out of earshot. "That bastard! He's sending us to the ends of the earth, just to satisfy his own curiosity."

The general did not notice Jena appearing in the doorway of the Map Room. "I suggest you speak about my father with a little more respect, general. He does not tolerate insubordination twice in one day, let alone from the same man."

"Forgive me, Tsarina. I did not realise you were there."

"Plainly." She walked into the Map Room, the doors closing silently behind her. "Tell me, general, what do you know about the Forbidden Citadel?"

"Very little," Ivanov admitted. "As far as I am aware, it is a myth, a legend. A supposedly impregnable fortress, hidden in the Himalayas – a fanciful notion."

"Perhaps. But as with many myths, there is a grain of truth hidden within the legend. Our analysis of the Romanov archives suggests the patriarch of that family first discovered the Forbidden Citadel some thirty years ago." Jena strolled across the room towards the holographic globe. "How he found it we do not know. According to legend the citadel may only be seen by those who have been within its walls before. A contradiction, but a useful defence mechanism if true."

"You have a precise location for this fortress?"

"No," she replied. "We know it must be high up in the Himalayas, for the flight logs of Dmitri's personal pilot show several trips to that area. Unfortunately, this is one of the few regions within the Empire that has defied meaningful investigation. The harsh terrain, remote location and lack of strategic value meant there was no reason to waste significant resources on such an investigation."

"But now you want me to lead the Tsar's most feared fighters, the Imperial Black, into this area to find a mythical fortress that may not even exist?" Ivanov asked, unable to keep the exasperation from his voice.

"Precisely." Jena smiled at the general. "If the legends are to be believed, the Forbidden Citadel is home to a religious sect blessed with special abilities, supposedly a mark of their closeness to God. This sect guards the citadel jealously, because it holds a secret so powerful any man who looks upon that secret goes blind."

"A weapon?"

She shrugged. "That is for you to find out. If the Romanovs did have a secret weapon hidden there, your orders are to claim it for the Tsar and bring it back here to the Imperial Palace. If for whatever reason you cannot remove this weapon, you are authorised to destroy it and the citadel. Better it be the property of none than fall into enemy hands." Jena folded her arms. "Any questions?"

Ivanov glared at the holographic representation of the Himalayas as it rotated past him on the globe. "I am a warrior born, I do not believe in myths or fables. Why did the Tsar choose me for this quest?"

"You are an ambitious and dangerous man. Such energies are always welcomed within the Imperial forces, but they can become misdirected if ambition overwhelms reason or judgement. My father says you can be guilty of overstepping your responsibilities, of taking more than is your due."

"I suppose I should be honoured that he takes me so seriously."

Jena laughed. "To my father, you are like the flea that bites an elephant – a minor irritant, but one that can still draw blood. Nothing more, nothing less." She made to leave, but stopped herself. "The Tsar gave me a parting message for you. Take one thousand men as your army. Cost is no object. Succeed in this difficult mission and you will be amply rewarded, Ivanov. Fail in your task and you need never return."

The general contemplated all she had said before nodding in agreement. "Very well. It will be winter soon. No military commander in seven hundred years has been foolish enough to launch an offensive into such hazardous terrain during winter. The major and I will return to Rudinshtein immediately. It will take several days to select and equip my men for the mission, but we will make ready for the mountains with all possible haste. We have but a few weeks to succeed."

"Good luck," Jena offered, before turning away from him. "You'll need it."

THREE

"Rush not at a knife, if you don't want to get cut."
— Russian proverb

"Kabuki is a form of traditional Japanese theatre that dates back more than a thousand years to the early seventeenth century. Early kabuki featured both male and female performers, but the plays became so immodest that women were banned from taking part. Instead, male actors took on the onna-gata (female roles). Over the centuries this style of theatre became increasingly stylised, with elaborate costumers and make-up, the actors speaking in a slow, monotonous tone. Popular plots involve historical events, moral conflicts and love stories. Trap doors and rotating stages were commonplace, enabling rapid changes of set. By the twenty-seventh century, kabuki was forced to diversify to retain an audience, but the use of all-male casts was retained – sometimes with unexpected results..."
        — Extract from *Japanese Theatre 1600-2673*,
                            by Floyd Kermode

"This place is like a rabbit warren," Flintlock complained, pausing to catch his breath. He and Spatchcock had been running from room to room in search of Dante, bursting into bedchambers and startling the *Okiya*'s clientele in the midst of some impressively deviant acts.

Twice Flintlock had been forced to drag his libidinous lackey away from those unscheduled peepshows.

"The guests certainly hump like rabbits," Spatchcock agreed. "But we still haven't found Dant... Mr Durward. We still haven't found Mr Durward."

Flintlock rubbed his chin thoughtfully, looking up and down the white-walled corridor. "I was certain his scream came from down here."

His ruminations were cut short by the sound of tearing paper. The body of a naked brute flew horizontally between Flintlock and Spatchcock, before smashing through another rice paper wall. He came to rest, face-down in a bubbling Jacuzzi, a long rubber object protruding from between his buttocks.

Spatchcock studied the unconscious figure with amusement. "Is that what I think it is?" he asked, thumbing at the offending item.

"Brings tears to the eyes just thinking about it," Flintlock agreed. The two men turned to the gaping hole in the wall from which the unfortunate hulk had abruptly appeared. Through the shredded paper they could see Dante standing over an Oriental woman, demanding the return of his belongings.

"You've seen what I did to your friend Genghis," he warned. "Unless you want the same treatment, I suggest you fetch my clothes and rifle. Now!"

"Yes, Mr Durward," the woman replied meekly, bowing deeply as she backed away from Dante towards the door. "Me fetch them now, husband."

"And the honeymoon's off too!" Dante shouted after her. He noticed Flintlock and Spatchcock peering in through the hole in the wall. "You took your time."

"You and her married?" Spatchcock asked.

"Not exactly."

"Just good friends?" Flintlock offered.

"No," Dante said firmly. He stopped speaking, cocking his head to one side like a dog hearing a far-off, high-pitched whistle. Dante's expression darkened, souring into a grimace.

Flintlock recognised the signs – Dante was hearing the crest's voice in his mind. That usually meant only one thing: trouble.

"We're not alone," Dante announced.

"We know," Spatchcock agreed. "There's laughing boy in the jacuzzi, for a start. Once he comes round, I doubt he's going to see the funny side of things."

"He's the least of our worries. The Crest has detected a stealth flyer hovering nearby with twelve new arrivals on board."

Flintlock shrugged. "That doesn't make them a danger to us. Could be high profile people, trying to make a discrete visit to the geisha house."

Dante shook his head. "Somebody has locked on to the Crest's presence here, they're using it to track my movements. That only means one thing – enemy action. The Crest has been forced to shut down temporarily, but we've got to get off this floating cathouse right now." He held out his hands as his skin changed colour, its natural pigment draining away to be replaced by slithers of silver and purple. The shape of each hand mutated as the hilts of cyborganic swords emerged from the discoloured flesh and bone, stretching outwards into metre-long blades. "No need to maintain the pretence of being Quentin Durward anymore. Somebody already knows I'm here!"

The dull thud of an explosion shook the *Okiya*, accompanied by the rattle of gunfire. Dante and his partners in crime sighed. "So much for a quiet night of Oriental culture and copulation," Flintlock observed.

A low rumble of fury got his attention. The trio swivelled round to see the naked brute emerging from the Jacuzzi, his face flushed with rage and agony.

"Meet Genghis," Dante said. "He tried to rub me up the wrong way."

"But you got to him first?" Spatchcock asked. Genghis charged at the three men as another explosion shook the *Okiya*. "I think he's coming back for more!"

The strike team burst through the skylights of the geisha house's roof, dropping to the reception area below, weapons cocked and ready to fire. The *Okiya*'s madam was first to die, cut down by a hail of bullets as she emerged from her office. Two of her personal bodyguards followed within moments, slumping back into the chairs from which they had begun to rise. The strike team's leader studied blueprints and floor plans for the *Okiya*, plotting the best way forward. Four fingers gestured at double doors leading into the eastern section of the structure, sending four black-clad insurgents scurrying forwards to the bedchambers. Four more fingers pointed at the madam's office door, which led into the staff's private quarters, so another group went that way. The remaining three commandos waited as their leader consulted the tiny computer display. Where a blinking light had shown the Crest's location, there was now nothing. It must have detected the signal lock. That didn't matter now the trap was sprung. There would be no escape for Nikolai Dante.

The leader nodded to the other members of the strike team, sending them through the final internal doorway that led to the geisha zone, where traditional Japanese activities like ikebana and kabuki took place. The leader remained in the reception area, guarding the main exit in the unlikely event that Dante had made it that far. Satisfied with these tactics, the black-clad figure dropped into a lotus position on the floor and began to meditate, listening to sounds of battle spilling through the brothel's paper walls.

Spatchcock stuck out a foot and tripped Genghis as the brute charged past, intent on attacking the man who had so humiliated him. But Dante danced around the brute's clumsy lunge, at the same time slicing one of his cyborganic swords across the top of the bed. Genghis tumbled into the mattress, his arrival displacing a cascade of water that drenched the room. A dripping wet Dante admired his handiwork. "I didn't know the *Okiya* offered watersports."

"I think his scuba-diving days are behind him," Spatchcock added.

"Didn't you say we should be leaving?" Flintlock asked.

"Good point. Crest, what's the best way out of...? Crest?"

"You told it to shut down."

Dante grimaced. "Guess we'll have to find our own way off this love boat." He stepped through the hole in the wall created by Genghis and pointed to his left. "This way, I think."

But Sang Gen was waiting for them at the end of the corridor, wearing Dante's jacket. She was aiming his rifle at the trio, one finger closing around the trigger. "You want no marriage, you pay for no marriage!"

Dante gestured for Sang Gen to lower the long-barrelled weapon. "You can't use that against me. It's a Huntsman 5000, keyed to my DNA. If anybody but me fires that rifle, the bullets will make you their target."

"You lie!" Sang Gen shrieked. "Just like you lie about name. You no Quentin, you Nikolai Dante! Tsar offer big reward for you!"

"Pull that trigger and you'll never turn another trick."

"You lie about name, you lie about gun too!" Sang Gen fired the rifle, a grim look of satisfaction on her features. A second later she was dead, the bullet having entered her forehead and removed the back half of her skull.

Dante walked over to Sang Gen and crouched down, quickly retrieving his jacket and rifle from the dead woman. "I tried to warn you," he said sadly. At that moment half a dozen discs of spinning light flew past Dante's head, slicing through the paper wall beyond him. He glanced up to see four black-clad figures running towards Spatchcock and Flintlock. "Look out! Behind you!"

The two ex-convicts twisted round just in time to see another handful of spinning discs flung at them. Spatchcock dived across the corridor, his shoulder slamming into Flintlock's stomach. The Brit was driven backwards into one of the *Okiya*'s bedchambers, his breath still whistling out from between his teeth.

In the corridor Dante threw his hands in front of his face, the discs deflecting off his swords, taking chunks of flesh and blood with them. Taken by surprise, Dante screamed in pain. His cyborganics were all but invulnerable against most weapons. What the hell were these guys throwing at him? Before he had time to wonder any further, the first of the four was upon him, brandishing a short-bladed weapon in each hand. Dante parried the thrusts of both blades, then flashing his own swords outwards, sliced off the attacker's hands at the wrist. The black-clad figure went down screaming, blood spurting from each wound in a wide arc. Dante dived away from another shower of spinning discs, taking cover behind a corner.

"Flintlock! Spatchcock! Are you alright?"

He pulled on his jacket while waiting for a reply, but none came. "If you can hear me, get back to the boat. I'll meet you at the *Sea Falcon*."

The insurgents' leader studied the team's progress on his wrist computer. One of the twelve lights representing the location of each member stopped blinking, indicating they were dead. Three more were gathering on the spot where their colleague had fallen. The leader activated the comms unit in their ear. "Target has been found in the eastern section. Converge on that area, find and disable the target. Do not, repeat, do not eliminate the target. Aim to wound."

"Have they gone?" Spatchcock peered back over his shoulder, bracing one arm against Flintlock's throat to get leverage. The gangling Brit gasped in protest, his arms flailing weakly at the rancid creature on top of him.

"Get... off of me... you pestilent... oik!"

Spatchcock realised why Flintlock was choking and rolled off. He crawled over to the wall and peered out into the corridor. Dante and his attackers were gone, except for a handless corpse on the floor.

Flintlock was still coughing and complaining from where he had fallen. "What in the name of all that's holy were you playing at?"

"Saving your life, your lordship," Spatchcock replied. "You almost got sliced in two by a fistful of laser shuriken."

"Laser *what*?"

"Old martial arts weapon, new twist. Throwing stars made out of pure light. Can slice through almost anything. Nasty."

"Not as nasty as your body odour," Flintlock whined, his face curdling at the smell on his clothes. "It'll take a week of washing to get your foul stench out of my garments!"

"Stop your bleating for once," Spatchcock snarled. "Dante needs our help."

"You heard him, old boy. 'Get back to the boat!' For once in my life, I intend to do as I'm told. I suggest you do the same." He joined Spatchcock by the wall. "Have those chaps in the black pyjamas gone then?"

"They're called ninja, martial arts warriors. The black clothes help them blend into the shadows. They know more ways to kill you than I've got diseases."

Flintlock smirked. "Impressive. And certainly less offensive than your odour." He stepped out into the corridor. The sound of fighting and death could be heard from the left, where the ninja had gone in pursuit of Dante. The Brit turned to his right. "This way, I think. You coming, Spatch?"

"We shouldn't abandon him. He's saved our necks plenty of times."

"Discretion is the better part of valour, old boy." Flintlock strode away, Spatchcock reluctantly following him.

Dante sprinted round another corner, then slammed himself against the wall, intending to use it as a hiding place from which to surprise his pursuers. The thin white surface gave way behind him and Dante fell backwards into a darkened room. "Fuoco!" he cried out, tumbling head over heels. He came to rest against a row of seats, his head smashing against a wooden support strut. Blackness closed around him for what seemed like a few seconds, but when his eyes opened again three of the hunters had surrounded him. They were only visible in silhouette, the room pitch dark but for the light spilling in from a hole high in one wall created by Dante's arrival.

"Child's play," one of them said in an accent Dante did not recognise. "Why did the Parliament send a dozen of us? Anyone could bring this fool back alive."

"There's more to this fool than meets the eye," Dante replied, slicing his left hand horizontally through the air. His cyborganic blade cut across the knees of the three ninja, neatly disabling the trio with a single blow. They crumpled to the floor in agony, cursing in several languages. Dante scrambled to his feet, one hand rubbing the bump on his head where it had hit the wooden strut. "Now, who's going to tell me about this Parliament? Who is it, and why do they want me captured?" He rested the bloody tip of his left blade against the throat of the attacker who had spoken. "Start talking or start dying, your choice."

"So be it," the ninja replied. He ground his teeth together, creating a faint popping sound. Within seconds white liquid began to seep through the cloth masking his face. The other two men followed his example, their eyes squinting with pain before the pupils rolled back into their skulls.

"Suicide pills," Dante realised. "They killed themselves, rather than be captured or forced to reveal who sent them." He staggered away from the corpses, feeling his way along the row of seats. "Where the hell am I, anyway? Crest? Crest, I need you to reactivate." Dante closed his eyes to concentrate, summoning the battle computer out of its standby status.

You called?

"Finally. I need you to check if there are any more of these goons nearby."

Beginning scanning.

"And could you point me towards the lights?"

There's a switch on the wall to your left, about chest height. Turn that on, it should illuminate your location.

"Thanks." Dante was hitting the switch when the Crest spoke again.

But I'm not sure you're ready for what you're about to see.

The chamber was bathed in light, momentarily blinding Dante. He covered his eyes, squinting to take in his surroundings. Aside from the corpses near his feet, most of the available space was given over to rows of theatre seats, all facing a raised stage. The leading edge of the acting area jutted out into the seating, like the downstroke of a letter T. Across this, more than a dozen figures in elaborate make-up and the flimsiest of costumes were engaged in numerous sexual couplings and muscular ménage à trois. Men dressed as women were pleasuring other men dressed as women, while their actions were appreciated by yet more men who appeared most intent upon pleasuring themselves.

"Bojemoi!" Dante stared at the stage in disbelief. "What do you call that?"

Oh my, the Crest replied. *Kabuki porn.*

Six ninja dived through the paper wall above Dante's head and landed on the seating in front of him, their weapons already drawn and ready to attack.

Sex and violence, the Crest sighed. *You should feel right at home.*

Dante dived behind the seats to avoid a fresh flurry of laser shuriken. His sprawling hands grasped a familiar shape on the floor. A mischievous smile crossed Dante's face as he pulled the Huntsman 5000 closer. "Diavolo!" he cried. "You bastards, I'm bleeding to death!" Two of the ninja broke cover to check his condition and were quickly dealt with, but the others stayed back. "Seems I've got an advantage over you," Dante announced. "You have to capture me alive, but I can kill as many of you as I want. Kind of evens up the odds, doesn't it?"

He stuck his rifle over the top of the theatre seats and fired a volley of shots towards where his hunters had been lurking. He was rewarded by several cries of pain, but when Dante peered over the top of the seating the ninja were nowhere in sight. However, most of the all-male Kabuki porn cast was advancing towards him, brandishing various sexual implements as weapons. The rest were still on stage, tending the actors wounded by Dante's unfriendly fire.

"Oops."

One thing's for certain, the Crest noted as Dante ran for the nearest exit, pursued by the naked actors. *They know you don't fire blanks.*

Spatchcock and Flintlock burst into the *Okiya*'s reception area to find three ninja waiting for them. "Don't hurt us," Flintlock whimpered. "We're innocent."

The tallest of the warriors regarded them with suspicion. "Nobody is innocent in a whorehouse."

"True," Spatchcock agreed, his face curling into an innocuous smile. "But we're more innocent than most of the people in here. If you see what I mean." The warrior glanced at the smallest of his colleagues, looking for guidance. Spatchcock realised the strike team's leader was a woman. All her attention was focused on a device strapped to her left wrist, while her right hand was pressed against one ear.

"Fall back, let him come to you," she hissed. Only her eyes were visible but they displayed her anger eloquently. "Remember, we're to take him alive. I don't care how enraged the porn actors are. If they catch up with him, you'll have to intervene." She noticed the tall warrior trying to get her attention. One glance at Spatchcock and Flintlock was all she needed to decide the pair's fate. "They are of no consequence, let them go."

Spatchcock pushed the quivering Flintlock forwards, but somehow tripped over his own feet and bumped into the nearest ninja. "Sorry, sir, sorry, begging your pardon, sorry," he said, bowing apologetically as he hurried towards the *Okiya*'s front doors. Once outside, Spatchcock scurried to the nearest hover-shuttle and jumped in. Flintlock was still standing on the dock, looking back at the brothel.

"What about Dante?"

"You couldn't wait to leave before, and now you're worried about him? Get in!"

Flintlock did as he was told. "I know Dante can look after himself but... did you see who was in charge of those ninja? A woman."

"I know." Spatchcock twisted the wheel of the hover-shuttle, sending it scudding away from the geisha house dock and towards the nearby *Sea Falcon*.

Flintlock was still watching the *Okiya*. "Nikolai always falls for a woman."

"They've been ordered to take him alive. I doubt even Dante can overcome all of them. So when they leave, we can follow."

"How? We don't know who this lot are or where they're going." Spatchcock retrieved something from his pocket and tossed it to Flintlock. The exile studied it, not comprehending. "What's this? A wristwatch?"

"Dante said they found him by locking on to the Crest. That's one of their tracking devices. I lifted it off that ninja when I bumped into him."

Flintlock smiled appreciatively. "Spatch, old boy, I could almost kiss you!"

"I'll want be wined and dined first, your lordship."

Dante burst from the kabuki theatre to find the four ninja waiting for him outside. He shot two before they could move, ducked beneath the lunge of another and smashed an elbow into the last one's face as he ran past. By the time his attackers recovered, the enraged and mostly naked porn cast was pouring from the theatre in hot pursuit. The resulting confusion gave Dante enough time to sprint away along the corridor. But the far end was also a dead end, with no doors or windows. Looking over his shoulder, Dante could see the angry mob hurrying towards him. He flung the butt of his rifle against the nearest wall, which ripped apart after a single blow. A sickly sweet, intoxicating scent billowed out from within, dizzying Dante with its alcoholic fumes.

"Fuoco, I remember that smell," he said, choking back the urge to vomit. "Whatever is causing that is how I got this hangover!"

Sake, the Crest observed, *an alcoholic beverage made from fermented rice, and traditionally served at a temperature of between forty and fifty degrees centigrade. Congratulations, you've found the chamber where they warm the liquid in bulk before distributing it throughout the* Okiya.

Dante looked through the torn paper wall. The chamber beyond best resembled a long swimming pool, its liquid contents stretching from wall to wall in all directions. A hatchway at the far end offering his only means of escape. "You're suggesting I swim through a tank of hot sake?"

Either that or take on two deadly ninja and a mob of murderous thespians from an all-male porn troupe.

Dante slung the rifle over his back and dived headfirst into the pool.

The strike team's leader could not understand how a single man had succeeded in escaping her insurgents. She cursed the survivors via her comms earpiece and set off with the two remaining team members to intercept Dante on the far side of the sake tank. "If you want something done properly, do it yourself," she muttered beneath her breath, sprinting through the *Okiya's* corridors.

Dante was halfway when he heard several splashes behind him. *Don't worry*, the Crest reassured him, *that's the kabuki cast after you. The ninja are finding another way round.*

"Easy... for you... to say," Dante gulped, in between mouthfuls of air and warm alcohol. "You're... not the one... being chased... by frustrated sex fiends!"

Now you know how most women feel about you, it fired back. *Try not to swallow so much. You'll be too drunk to open the access hatch.*

Dante spat out a long stream of sake and concentrated on swimming, but his attempt at the breaststroke was rapidly descending into doggy-paddle. When he reached the other side, his hands slipped on the side of the tank, whereby he sank down into the warm liquid. Frantic kicking got him back to the surface, by which time the actors were almost upon him. The nearest dived down and grabbed Dante's waist, fingers clawing at the thin strands holding the borrowed g-string in place.

Powerful arms plunged into the sake and grabbed hold of Dante's flailing limbs, pulling him up and out of the intoxicating liquid. He scrambled through the access hatch and kicked it shut behind him. The lock automatically slotted into place, trapping the actors on the other side.

"I made it," Dante spluttered disbelievingly. "Remind me never to drink again."

Stay alive long enough and I might have the opportunity.

"We have orders to capture you alive," a female voice announced. The smallest of the black-clad figures stepped forward to confront Dante. "However, there is nothing in our instructions about delivering you unhurt. So far you have killed or disabled seven of my colleagues. For that you must pay a price."

"I'd offer you cash," he slurred, suppressing a hiccup, "but I seem to have left my money pouch somewhere. Don't suppose you've seen it, have you?"

The woman lashed out savagely, the back of her hand slapping Dante's face with the power of a whip cracking. He winced and rubbed his cheek.

"I'm guessing I should take that as a no."

The woman slapped him again, first to one side with her palm, then the other way with the back of her hand, repeating the treatment until Dante grabbed hold of her wrist with surprising speed for someone so drunk.

Try not to antagonise her, the Crest warned.

"The last time a woman hurt me that much, we were in love," he hissed.

I despair of you sometimes, I really do.

Dante's attacker glanced down at his crotch, the sake-soaked genitals rapidly shrivelling in the cool, air-conditioned atmosphere. "There's not much of you to love," she said, her lips curling in disgust.

"I've never had any complaints," Dante maintained, ignoring the Crest's protestations in his mind. "I could give you a demonstration, if you like?"

She wrenched her hand free, her dark eyes sparkling with anger. The lithe woman stepped aside and signalled for the others to take over. "Hurt him, but do not kill or cripple. I leave the rest to your imagination."

Dante braced his back against the access hatch, trying to concentrate enough to will his cyborganic swords into place. But the effects of his swim across the sake tank were taking hold, turning his attackers into eight men, then a dozen. "Now boys," he slurred, "you wouldn't fight a man without trousers, would you? Besides, I can't fight all of you at once. Be patient, there's plenty of me to go around, you know..."

The fight was over in less than a minute.

When the men were satisfied with their work, they stepped aside to let their leader look at Dante's bloody and bruised body. She removed the fabric masking her beautiful face and shook her long, black hair free.

"I should kill you now," she spat at Dante. "It's no more than you deserve."

FOUR

"The Tsar's Purge Squads did much to exterminate any visible opposition to the Makarov dynasty after the war, but undercurrents of resistance remained. Many were those among the Empire's noble houses who spoke of their loyalty to the Tsar in public, while fostering discontent and resentment in private. But few were willing to act upon their feelings while the threat of reprisal hung heavy in the air. One of the rare organised attempts to foment was the short-lived Parliament of Shadows."
        – Extract from *After the Tsar Wars*,
                by Georgi Lucassovich

Dante woke with another splitting headache and the stench of stale alcohol on his breath. All around him was darkness, the air heavy with dust and neglect. A faint luminescence struggled to illuminate his surroundings. When he tried to move, pain shot through every muscle and tendon in his body. "Bojemoi," Dante gasped. "How many elephants trampled on me?"

You've been beaten bloody, drugged and you nearly drowned in a tank of hot sake, the Crest replied. *But at least you've got some clothes on now.*

Dante peeled back a black, skin-tight top to discover a patchwork of bruises on his skin, the purple and yellow contusions showing he had been unconscious for more than a day. Tight grey trousers covered his lower half, preserving his dignity. "Shame. I was getting rather fond of that g-string. It's always good to feel the sun on your cheeks."

Dante, you wear a g-string on your crotch, not your face.

"I didn't mean those cheeks." Wincing in pain, he sat up. The floor felt smooth and solid, while the air around him was still. Directly overhead a circular glimmer of light offered the only hint of a way out. "So, where am I this time?"

Inside an oubliette.

"That's not some kind of whale, is it?"

Dante, just once I wish you would resist the urge to say or do the first thing that enters your head. Life would be easier if you didn't always act on instinct.

"Yeah, but it'd also be a lot more boring. Beside, you wouldn't get the chance to scold me, or give one of your lectures about things I don't understand."

The Crest snorted derisively. *An oubliette*, it said archly, *is a dungeon with the only exit out of reach overhead. They are frequently circular or oval in shape.*

"Like being stuck inside a gigantic egg?"

Must you always reduce everything to the simplest possible example?

"If I want to piss you off, yes." Dante peered about his confinement. "No sign of my rifle. But they'd have to be pretty stupid to leave me with a weapon."

Like your cyborganic swords, for instance...

"Yeah! I could use those to try and cut my way–" He stopped, realising the Crest was teasing him. "I would have thought of that without your help, you know."

Of course you would.

"I didn't ask to be bonded with you!"

Instead of trying to escape, why don't you argue some more?

"All right, I–" Dante bit his bottom lip, not trusting himself to say anything more. Instead he concentrated on recreating his cyborganic blades. But try as he might, the silver and purple circuitry failed to appear from his hands.

You've obviously been injected with a neural inhibitor that disables your cyborganics, the Crest observed.

"Pity it didn't shut you up too," Dante muttered. Before the Crest could reply, the glimmer of light overhead began changing, becoming first a crescent, and then a complete circle. A metal ladder descended until it stopped in front of Dante's face.

"Climb out," a stern female voice commanded.

"What if I don't want to?" he asked.

"Then you can rot down there."

I suggest you do as you're told – for once.

"Nag, nag, nag." Dante grabbed the lower rungs of the ladder and hauled himself upwards, his arms and shoulders protesting each movement with fresh stabs of pain. "Fuoco, you're worse than my mother." He emerged from the dungeon into the beams of numerous spotlights. The same female voice as before commanded him to push the ladder down into the oubliette and close the entrance. Dante followed her instructions, all the while squinting around himself, trying to get a grasp of where he was.

He stood in the centre of a large, six-sided chamber. The floor was covered by a pattern of black and white checks that stretched out to the corners. High on the surrounding walls were five platforms that jutted out over the floor. The spotlights were mounted on the edge of these, but Dante could make out two figures standing on each platform. Their shapes were silhouetted in front of open doorways behind them. None of their faces were visible, as each figure was wearing a hood. A familiar scent hung in the air, teasing Dante's senses. What was it? Lavender? Heather? He knew he had smelled it before, but couldn't recall where. His mind was still a drugged muddle.

"Welcome." The voice was male, deep and booming. Dante thought he detected some St Petersburg in the accent, but couldn't be certain.

"Err, hi," he replied, warily.

"Welcome to the Parliament of Shadows," the voice continued. Dante thought it was coming from the middle platform, but the resonant walls bounced sound around in circles, creating echoes upon echoes. "This is our council chamber, where we meet to discuss future strategies and interrogate those who have information useful to our goals.

"Any chance you could turn down the lights?" Dante asked hopefully. "I'm guessing you got me here for a reason, but I won't be much use to you blind."

"These beams help shield our identity. We are a cabal intent on overthrowing the Tsar. Each one of us represents a different noble house, a dynasty that would dearly love to see the Makarov regime swept away and an end to all tyranny. As such, we must protect ourselves from the Tsar's spies and informants. That is why we call ourselves the Parliament of Shadows."

"Uh-huh." Dante scratched the side of his face while smiling broadly up at his captors. "Crest, what's a cabal?" he hissed under his breath.

A secret plot, a conspiracy. Don't you know anything?

"That's your job," Dante muttered.

No, my job is to teach you, mould you into a potential Emperor.

"Good luck!"

"I don't believe we have your full attention," the booming voice interjected. "Perhaps this will enhance your concentration."

There was a clicking sound and Dante felt as if his feet had caught fire. Sparks of electricity were dancing across the surface of the floor and Dante was dancing with them, involuntarily bouncing from foot to foot, trying to keep himself airborne. Whenever his flesh touched the floor another jolt of electricity surged through him, jangling his teeth and wits together.

Another click and it was over, the black and white checks no long alive with the sound of sizzling skin. Dante collapsed to the floor, cursing loudly at the Parliament's leader. He pulled his feet towards his face and blew on them, one hand trying to waft cold air over the scorched soles.

"When you've quite finished feeling sorry for yourself," the voice said, "we will lower the intensity of our lights a little. Consider it a gesture of goodwill."

No sooner were the words spoken than the beams softened slightly, allowing Dante to look at the figures around him without squinting. He stood and folded his arms. "What do you want of me?"

"This is not about you, Dante – this is about the future of the Empire. The noble houses we represent all had covert alliances with the House of Romanov during the war. Like your father, Dmitri, we believe that if anybody has a right to claim leadership of the Empire, it is the Romanovs. Your family can trace its claim to rule over all the Russias back almost a thousand years. We wish to restore the Empire to Romanov rule, rid ourselves of the Tsar once and for all."

"The Romanovs are all dead, or haven't you been paying attention?" Dante sneered. "They got their asses kicked during the war."

You would do better not to antagonise your captors, the Crest advised.

"I don't give a damn what you or anybody else thinks," Dante continued. "The Romanovs are dead and I want nothing more to do with them. I renounced that name during the Battle of Rudinshtein. End of story."

Another click and a fresh dose of electrocution was the reply. The Parliament's spokesman continued once Dante had recovered. "Yes, most of the Romanovs are dead, but not all of them. Young Arkady is now a ward of the Tsar, kept close beside the Makarov despot. Lulu remains at large, intent on waging her own one-woman war against the Empire. And there are even rumours that Lady Jocasta survived the final onslaught at the Winter Palace, although we have no proof of that, nor knowledge where she might be."

"I told you, I don't care about my so-called family anymore. They left Rudinshtein to the Imperials, abandoned the civilians while trying to save their own skins. I hope they all rot in hell together!"

"And then there is the bastard offspring of that noble dynasty. The roguish renegade known as Nikolai Dante."

"That's my name, don't wear it out," Dante spat back.

Such sparkling repartee, the Crest groaned. *I've told you before: never engage anyone in a battle of wits, Dante. You're not equipped for such a fight.*

"Your Crest is correct," another voice added from the shadows. "Shut up and listen to its advice, you might get out of here alive."

Dante spun round, trying to deduce who had spoken. He recognised the voice as the woman who had summoned him up from the dungeon, but where else had he heard her? "Hey, how do you know what the Crest is saying? It only talks inside my thoughts. Nobody else can hear it."

"I can read your mind, so I am also privy to what the Crest tells you," the woman snarled. "Now be quiet, for once in your life."

Ooh, I like her, the Crest said admiringly.

"Will you listen to our offer, or must we subject you to more shock treatment?" the Parliament's spokesman enquired, with a hint of menace beneath his calm words.

"You've got an offer? Fine, I'll listen," Dante replied casually.

"Have you heard of the Forbidden Citadel?"

"Can't say I have."

"That is unfortunate."

The Forbidden Citadel is a legendary fortress in the Himalayas, the Crest interjected, *supposedly invisible to the eyes of outsiders.*

Dante smiled. "I once went to a restaurant called the Jade Citadel. Or was it the Forbidden Pagoda? Could have been the Shirley Temple, now I come to think about it. Anyway, that place did a wonderful wonton soup."

"Your flippancy will be your downfall," the Parliament's spokesman warned.

"Yeah, yeah. What's your point?"

"The citadel is home to a secret weapon once jealously guarded by the Romanovs. We believe that weapon will enable us to overthrow the Tsar. Normally only those who have been within the citadel can see it from outside. But we have discovered it can also be found by those bearing a Weapons Crest."

"I should have known," Dante sighed.

"As we speak, the Tsar is sending an army of a thousand men into the Himalayas to find and take the Forbidden Citadel. That mission cannot be allowed to succeed. We want you to lead a small expedition into the mountains. You must reach the citadel first and retrieve the weapon."

"Why should I?"

"Would you rather the Tsar had the use of this device?" the Parliament's spokesman demanded. "We know little about the nature of the weapon, except that your father was keeping it as a last resort in his war against the Tsar. Such was the rapid reversal of fortune against the Romanovs, he never had a chance to deploy the weapon in battle. How would you feel if it was tested on Rudinshtein and its people, for whom you profess such affection?"

"Everything you've said is full of 'ifs' and 'buts'. Admit it, you don't know whether this weapon even works, do you?"

"No, but we do not dare let the weapon fall into the hands of the Tsar!"

"I understand that," Dante shouted back. "I'm not stupid."

All evidence to the contrary.

"Why should I go on this mission? You people don't even have the guts to show your faces, let alone take on the Tsar in the open!"

The woman standing in the shadows near Dante replied to his accusation. "You will go because you know you must. You will go because there is nobody who can go in your place – that's why you were brought here. And you will go because if you do not, I will murder you where you stand." She stepped out into the light to confront Dante. He recognised her as the same women who had supervised his capture on the *Okiya*. She was beautiful, with long, dark hair framing Oriental features and nut-brown skin. Her build was athletic but, to Dante's eyes, it curved outwards against her skin-tight garb in all the right places. Most striking were her eyes, anger overlaid on sadness, a flash of recklessness about their expression. Dante had met a few women like her in his life. She seemed dangerous, passionate and utterly implacable. Every time he'd fallen like a stone for them, and every time it had ended badly. *I'm in trouble here,* he decided.

"Yes, you are," she replied. "I can read your thoughts, remember?"

Dante's face switched from consternation to bafflement in moments, before settling into mischievous. A vicious slap wiped the smile from his features. "Keep your mind off my arse," she warned.

Sound advice, the Crest added.

"Don't you start," Dante muttered.

"You accused us of lacking the courage to show our faces," the Parliament's spokesman said. "Very well, then. I shall reveal my face to all those present, so there can be no doubts about my belief in this cause." He deactivated the spotlight that was mounted on his platform and stepped forward so everyone could see him. With slow, deliberate movements, he pulled back his hood. Beneath was a middle-aged man with receding red hair and a prominent nose. "I am Zachariah Zhukov, leader of the House of Zhukov, and I challenge the rule of the tyrant Vladimir Makarov. Who else will step forward and identify themselves, show their courage?"

One by one the other members followed his example. Finally, Zhukov turned to Dante. "Well, we have risen to your challenge, Dante. Will you rise to ours?"

Spatchcock led the way through shattered gravestones and broken memorials, Flintlock hurrying nervously along behind. The ground was frozen by frost, each blade of grass a tiny slither of ice and green. None of the inscriptions on the masonry were legible, having been systematically vandalised by some previous visitor. "Cheery sort of place, isn't it?" Flintlock whispered, hoping Spatchcock would think the cold was causing the tremors in his voice. He rubbed his hands together for warmth and clouds of steam issued from his nostrils as he breathed.

"Dante's close," Spatchcock muttered, all his attention focussed on the stolen tracker strapped to his left wrist. "The signal's strongest over there." He hurried on, clambering over a stone angel whose wings had been shattered.

Flintlock moved more awkwardly, despite his long legs. Spatchcock scuttled like a spider over all kinds of terrain, whereas the exiled aristocrat still felt it beneath himself to be furtive. A lifetime of training for greatness did not prepare him for low company and low life. He tripped on the wingless angel, tumbling face first into a freshly dug mound of soil. "I say, I'm most dreadfully sorry," Flintlock spluttered, his mouth full of dirt.

Spatchcock glared back at him. "Will you stop buggering about, your lordship. We're trying to–" He stopped abruptly, noticing the earth beneath Flintlock. "What's that doing there?"

"What's what doing where?" the Brit replied. "Give me a hand, Spatch."

But the little man ignored his fallen comrade, preferring to dig his hands into the dirt. "This shouldn't be here. The ground's frozen, hasn't been touched in months, but somebody's dug this over recently. Probably today."

A low rumble of machinery startled them both. They scrambled clear of the dirt mound as it descended into the ground, revealing a concrete staircase hidden below. "That must be the way in," Spatchcock realised.

Flintlock was about to comment when he felt a small, hard circle of metal jab into his back. "Spatch, old boy. I think we've got company…"

"Don't worry, we'll wait until they've gone, then nip down the stairs."

"I don't think that's going to work," Flintlock ventured, peering over his shoulder at the cluster of armed guards standing behind him.

Dante was still arguing with the Parliament of Shadows when Spatchcock and Flintlock appeared from a concealed doorway, striding purposefully into the centre of the chamber. "There he is. What did I tell you, Spatch? My nose for a brigand never fails me. It's that bounder, Nikolai Dante. The Tsar will pay a pretty penny for this rapscallion."

"Who are you two?" Zhukov demanded from his platform, unhappy at the interruption.

"Begging your pardon, sir," Spatchcock replied, bowing grandly. "We are Spatchcock and Flintlock, bounty hunters extraordinaire. We have tracked this fugitive halfway across the Empire and may we thank you all for keeping him detained. Now, we shall relieve you of this burden and take him to face his crimes before the proper authorities."

Dante rolled his eyes. "I hope this isn't your idea of a rescue mission because it doesn't exactly inspire confidence."

Flintlock performed an elaborate mime that suggested there was nothing to worry about, or else he was planning to take up belly dancing; Dante wasn't sure which was the more accurate description. "My learned friend is correct," Flintlock announced, turning back towards Zhukov. "We hereby claim Dante as our captive and will be removing him into our custody."

The woman guarding Dante pulled a weapon from a holster strapped to her thigh and aimed it at the new arrivals. "Lord Zhukov, these men are known accomplices of Dante. They were with him at the *Okiya*." She stepped towards Spatchcock and ripped the tracker off his wrist. "They must have followed him here, after stealing this device from one of my men."

"In that case, they shall share Dante's fate, whatever he decides."

"Spatch, old boy, I don't think they're falling for the bounty hunter story," Flintlock muttered quietly.

"We'd have gotten away with it if you'd kept your mouth shut." Spatchcock looked at his former commander. "What's this decision you've got to make?"

Dante smiled, despite himself. "Either all three of us are executed here..."

"Right," Spatchcock said, his face thick with concentration. "No, don't like the sound of that much. What's the second option?"

"...or we can embark on an impossible quest to find a legendary fortress that probably doesn't exist so we can steal a secret weapon of terrifying power."

Flintlock was busy winking lustily at the beautiful, gun-wielding Oriental woman nearby. Spatchcock elbowed him in the ribs. "I say, what were the options again?" Dante repeated them for the Brit. "Well, I think the impossible quest sounds more my cup of tea, don't you?"

Spatchcock nodded his agreement. Dante gave a thumbs-up signal to Zhukov. "I've just got one question. What's the pay like for suicide missions?"

FIVE

"Be a rogue, but be kind."
– Russian proverb

"The so-called Russian rogue is, in fact, a thief, a brigand and a philander for whom the opposite sex is merely a way to provide him with physical pleasure and visual stimuli. Dante's notoriety is well known across the Empire, but the circumstances of his first significant brush with the Imperial authorities are remarkably illustrative of the renegade's salacious behaviour. He was arrested in St Petersburg in 2666, after being found in the bedchamber of Lady Zoya, an Imperial seductress employed by the Tsar's own hussars. Dante made a cowardly attack upon a captain of the hussars, then fled the scene in terror for his life.

Not content with having besmirched the good name of Lady Zoya, he conspired to steal her jewel-encrusted eroticostume as some tawdry souvenir of his sexual exploits. The thief was captured trying to sell the garment at the Tsyganov black market. He was brought before the Tsar on charges of banditry, fraud, deceit, unauthorised duelling and seduction for the purposes of financial gain. The fact that Dante offered no defence for his crimes speaks volumes about his character. It is regretful the Tsar did not have this vile creature executed immediately. Such action would have spared the Empire from Dante's subsequent displays of carnality, lawlessness and cocksure bravado."

> – Extract from *Nikolai Dante: A Character Assassination*, various contributors

Once they had agreed to undertake the Parliament of Shadows' mission, Dante and his comrades found themselves being treated like honoured guests. The trio were escorted to private quarters for their ablutions, before being offered a hot meal. Spatchcock had little enthusiasm for washing, heading straight for the food table in the adjoining room. "I haven't had a square meal for three days," he said. "Anyway, every time you wash, it invites fresh bacteria on to your body. I like the bacteria I've already got."

Dante and Flintlock manhandled the odorous ex-felon into a bath full of hot water and bubbles, holding his head beneath the surface until Spatchcock agreed to bathe. "If we're supposed to be racing the Tsar's men to the Forbidden Citadel, I don't want your lack of personal hygiene giving us away," Dante said while Spatchcock washed. "One bath a year won't do you any harm."

The trio emerged to find fresh clothes laid out for them, form-fitting tops and trousers in stretch fabrics, plus numerous outer layers for insulation against the mountain cold. Beside these were a selection of boots and climbing equipment, while hooded jackets in white and silver were hung on the wall.

"White? Not very flattering for somebody with my fair complexion," Flintlock complained. "I'll look terribly washed out."

"That's the point. They're camouflage to hide us in the snow," Dante replied. He was pleased to find his rifle lying among the equipment, restored to his possession again. The Huntsman 5000 was made by the same alien technology responsible for the Romanov Weapons Crests. The rifle created its own ammunition internally and so never needed reloading, a useful quality in the sort of fire fights Dante encountered all too frequently. He patted the weapon appreciatively, then settled down to dinner with the others. "I could eat a horse."

Flintlock stopped chewing, a forkful of sausage frozen in front of his lips. "You don't think this is horse, do you? I've had some dubious dishes since leaving the old country, but I've no urge to eat equine."

"I don't mind a good haunch of horse," Spatchcock said happily, smacking his lips. "Can be a tasty bit of meat, especially if you marinade it first. Some red wine, a few capers, handful of freshly chopped herbs..."

"Arsenic, cyanide, strychnine," Dante added mischievously.

"I never mix cooking with the concocting of poisons," Spatchcock protested.

"With your cooking it's hard to tell the difference," Flintlock interjected.

"Well, if you lifted a finger to help, your lordship, I wouldn't have to do all the cooking. But you're so high and mighty, I doubt you could boil water."

"The only boils I associate with you, Spatch, are the ones on your arse."

Dante didn't bother trying to referee his two comrades' argument. They bickered worse than him and the Crest. Only a well-matched couple could argue so much and still stay together. He smiled and continued eating, happy at his unholy being trinity back together again. *If only I could escape the nagging feeling I'm being watched, like someone itching the back of my mind,* he thought. Then he remembered the Oriental woman, how she was able to hear the Crest speak inside his thoughts. *She could be watching me through my eyes right now...*

Dante closed his eyes and thought of the most repulsive sexual scenario he could imagine. His mind was flooded with images of the telepathic woman, himself, a bathtub full of jelly and a game of hide the sausage. The presence at the back of his thoughts abruptly vanished. "That's better. Now I can enjoy my meal in peace," Dante announced. His bickering companions looked at him as if he'd suddenly sprouted an extra head. "Don't mind me," Dante replied, happily shovelling another forkful of meat into his mouth.

Lord Zhukov came to bid them farewell in the morning, after the trio had snored through the night in a private dormitory. Dante and the others met Zhukov in the meeting chamber with the black and white checked floor, but now the spotlights were off and the mood much less threatening. On his raised platform Zhukov had seemed powerful, almost magisterial. In person he was small in stature, only a few inches taller than Spatchcock. His eyes flickered around the chamber nervously, as if he expected Imperial troops to burst in at any moment.

"Forgive my unease," Zhukov said. "This is the first time the Parliament of Shadows has taken action against the Tsar."

"We're the ones doing the dirty work," Spatchcock muttered darkly.

"True, but even meeting with the likes of Dante is an offence punishable by death. To conspire against the Makarov regime is to invite severe retribution. Our noble houses would be ruthlessly exterminated if word of this endeavour reached the Imperial Palace." Zhukov explained how the trio would be transported to the foot of the Himalayas in a stolen flyer, before continuing their quest on foot. "We have arranged for a native of that region to act as your guide within the mountains. They will get you close. The rest is up to you, Nikolai."

Dante nodded. It was much as he had expected. "Who's going to be our guide dog then? Some crusty old Sherpa with fewer teeth than wits?"

Look who's talking, the Crest chipped in. *A man with fewer wits than teeth.*

"I will be your guide." The voice was female, the tone severe. Dante didn't need to look round to know who had spoken. It was the same woman who had wished him dead in the Geisha House of the Rising Sun; the same woman who had threatened to execute him in the same room the previous day; the same woman who had been reading his thoughts since he got here. "Correct," she replied.

Flintlock watched Dante and the new arrival glower at each other. "You'd almost think these two used to be lovers," he whispered to Spatchcock.

Dante heard the comment and smiled. He let his eyes wander down over the woman's body, mentally removing her from the skin-tight jumpsuit. She rewarded him with a slap across the face.

Dante cried out, nursing his wounded cheek. "Diavolo! At least take your jewellery off before you hit me like that."

She retaliated with a smile. "I was only using your own emblem against you." She held the ring in front of her face, a smear of blood visible on the metal band. Fixed into the gold was a tiny yellow circle with a double-headed eagle inside – the symbol of the Romanovs.

"Where did you get that?" Dante demanded.

Uncertainly clouded the woman's beautiful features. "I don't know."

"Crest, can you identify the origins of that ring?"

No. I've never seen its like before.

"But that is the Romanov symbol, yes?"

Yes. Beyond that, I can tell you no more.

"You'll have plenty of time to talk about this en route to your destination," Zhukov said. "Your flyer will be ready to leave within the hour. Might I suggest gathering your equipment and then all meet back here? Mai Tsai will escort you back to the dormitory, gentlemen."

The beautiful Oriental strode from the room, Spatchcock and Flintlock hurrying after her, both with their eyes fixed on the bounce of her pert buttocks. Dante followed, still rubbing the side of his face where the Romanov ring had grazed his skin. He waited until they were all in the dormitory before speaking, a wicked glint in his eye. "Forgive me, I missed your name when Lord Zhukov said it before. What did he call you?"

The woman's eyes narrowed as she replied. "Mai Tsai."

Dante couldn't keep the smirk from his face. "Your name is My Sigh?" He winked at Spatchcock and Flintlock. "I'll make her sigh alright."

Another slap resounded against his cheek. "Fuoco, I wish you'd stop doing that!"

"And I wish you'd stop insulting my intelligence and drooling over my body," she snapped back. "At least with your two colleagues I can choose to ignore their lecherous expressions and furtive glances, I don't have to listen to their thoughts as well. I lack that option with you."

Spatchcock frowned. "Hang on... You can read his mind, but not ours?"

"Correct."

"So if I thought of the most disgusting, perverted thing I can imagine..."

"Nothing out of the ordinary then," Flintlock commented, getting a glare from Spatchcock for his interruption.

"...you wouldn't know what I was thinking?"

"I only see into Dante's mind," Mai replied. "Crawling through the sewer of his thoughts is bad enough. I have no wish to sample your cesspit as well."

"Ah, Spatch. You've only just met and already she knows you so well."

Dante and Mai went outside while Flintlock and Spatchcock's argument descended into a frenzy of hair pulling and verbal abuse. Dante closed the door on his comrades. "Ignore those two," he said. "They fight like cats and dogs, but their hearts are in the right place. Mostly."

Mai nodded. "They followed you halfway across the continent. That shows great loyalty. It is a useful asset for where we are going."

"How well do you know the Himalayas?"

"I believe I was born there."

"You believe? Don't you know?"

"There are many gaps in my memory, things I do not understand or cannot explain." Mai twisted the gold band on her finger. "The origin of this ring is one such example. My ability to read your thoughts is another fact I cannot explain. I believe this journey may help find answers to these and other questions that trouble me."

Dante nodded and smiled. "Well, it shouldn't take long. I mean, how hard can it be to find the Forbidden Citadel?"

Explorers and treasure hunters have been searching for this lost fortress since before Mount Everest was conquered, more than seven hundred years ago. Nobody has found it. At least, nobody has found it and come back alive to tell the tale.

"Ah, I see."

Nothing ever easy with you, is it Dante?

He looked at Mai and smirked. "Some things are harder than others, if you know what I mean."

She lashed out at his face, but Dante caught her wrist and held it firmly. "I was goading you deliberately that time, to see how you would react. Unless you learn to control that temper, you're liable to get all of us killed in the mountains. Understand?" Mai nodded and he let go of her arm. "You don't have to like me, but we have to work together, okay?"

"Don't worry," she snarled. "It's my job to keep you alive long enough to find the citadel. But the moment you've outlived your usefulness, I'll take the greatest of pleasure in executing you, you murdering bastard." Mai marched away, leaving Dante utterly perplexed.

"I'd never met this woman until a few days ago and now she wants me dead already. I wonder why?"

A good question, the Crest agreed. *Most women need to spend a week in your company before becoming homicidal.*

The door to the private quarters swung open and Flintlock tumbled out, trying to appear relaxed, his bag of climbing equipment being thrown out after him. "I say, is it time to go yet?"

Spatchcock emerged with a smile of satisfaction. He looked around. "Where's her ladyship gone? Don't tell me you've scared her off already."

"Apparently she's planning to kill me once I've outlived my usefulness," Dante replied. "She didn't specify a particular reason."

"Business as usual then," Flintlock said, getting to his feet. "Shall we go?"

General Ivanov savoured the exquisite torment of his cat-o'-nine-tails as it flailed through the air. He had once heard an adage that "the first cut was the deepest." Nothing could be further from the truth with the lash. The first taste of leather upon skin, it was the most shocking, yes, but that was only the beginning of a long, seductive process that took place during a whipping. Repeated blows dulled the nerve endings beneath the skin, until the skin split open. As always, that moment brought tears, the pain almost unbearable for whoever was receiving the brutal treatment, as an involuntary cry for mercy would colour the air. The blow after the skin gave way – that was the deepest, when the steel-tipped ends of each leather strand bit into the exposed flesh. Everything after that was an anti-climax; painful, yes, but more akin to a blow upon a bruise. Each successive impact had less effect than the last. To continue was useless.

A rapid knocking took Ivanov's thoughts. He let the lash slip from his grasp to the floor, its leather tails stained crimson with blood. His face was bathed in sweat, such was the effort of his latest thrashing, but it had given him little satisfaction. "Come," he shouted, wincing at the effort.

His second-in-command entered, stood to attention and saluted briskly. "General, the men are ready for your inspection."

"Very well," Ivanov replied. "I've done all I can here."

"Yes, sir."

"Major, I'll need you to administer the final step of the punishment."

"Of course, sir."

The general gestured to a large jar of white crystals beyond his reach. "The salt is over there. I want you to pour it into the wounds. Don't stop until the jar is empty, no matter how much the subject may cry out."

"Yes, sir." The Enforcer strode to the glass jar and removed its lid. He picked up the salt container and approached the general. "Now?"

"Go ahead." Ivanov tensed himself, preparing for the screams that would fill the room.

The Enforcer positioned the jar above the bloody back and began pouring, tipping every grain of salt over his superior officer's writhing body. Ivanov howled with rage and fury, his eyes bulging out in their sockets. Finally, when his self-inflicted punishment was complete, he gave a quiet shudder of delight.

"Very good, major. I will be out to inspect the men once I have finished cleaning myself up. We leave for the mountains at dawn, so I expect to see everyone with all alpine kit and equipment, is that clear?"

"Yes, sir."

"Very well, dismissed." Ivanov watched his second-in-command leave, before rising from the whipping stool. He picked up the cat-o'-nine-tails and held it lovingly against his face, inhaling the pungent, metallic odour of blood and sweat that had soaked into the leather. "You know how to treat me, don't you, my love? You know how I feel about you, your caress upon my skin, your pleasure and my pain. You know it all, don't you, my sweet?" Ivanov kissed the cat-o'-nine-tails, then laid it tenderly inside a specially made box of sandalwood, lined with red velvet and inlaid with his initials in gold lettering. "You rest now," the general whispered, his voice soothing, like that of a lover. "You rest, my beauty."

Spatchcock and Flintlock were first to emerge from the Parliament of Shadows' underground headquarters, finding themselves back in the frozen graveyard. Mai bounded up the steps into the cold air of morning, following them outside. She scanned their surroundings with practiced ease, her sidearm ready to fire, while the two men joked with each other. "Back in the cemetery again," Spatchcock noted. "Hope this doesn't become a habit."

Dante was last to emerge, a hefty backpack laden with climbing equipment slung over his shoulders. As he glanced about for their transport, a chill of recognition crossed his face. "I know this place. Crest, isn't this...?"

The Romanov Necropolis, it confirmed. *It's the final resting place for generation upon generation of your adopted, noble family.*

Dante had been here only once, before the war. The Romanovs had gathered for a hunting party, a tradition among the Russian aristocracy for centuries. It was supposed to be a way for families to get closer, bonding through the butchery of innocent animals. For Dante the experience had been a sobering one. He found himself acting as bodyguard to the Romanov matriarch, Lady Jocasta, when three hired assassins tried to kill her. The hitmen died in the effort, but Dante learned two cold, hard facts that day. All his siblings had been the product of an incestuous relationship between Dmitri and Jocasta, albeit one consummated by science, not between the sheets. Sickening as that was, Dante was more disturbed to discover it was Dmitri who hired the assassins to kill Jocasta. She was a barrier to the ruthless ambition of the Romanovs, as well as its progenitor. From that moment Dante had known he could never truly be part of such a family. That was a few years ago. So much had happened since then. So much pain, so much suffering. He had returned to the graveyard of the Romanovs once again and he felt no different. For the most part he was glad they were dead.

"How can you feel that way?" Mai demanded. "I would give anything to have my family back."

"Do you have to eavesdrop on every thought I have?" Dante demanded angrily. "Bojemoi, it's bad enough having the Crest is my brain all the time–"

Charming!

"I don't need you in my mind as well!"

Mai strode towards him, shaking her head. "You think I want to be inside that slime-infested rat hole you call a brain? Every whim, every notion that passes through your perverted cranium gets transmitted into my mind too."

"Well, try keeping your comments to yourself then," Dante suggested through gritted teeth. "The last thing I need for the rest of this mission is you imposing your morality on me, okay?"

"Morality? You don't know the meaning of the word."

Spatchcock and Flintlock exchanged weary looks of resignation. "I guess we're not leaving just yet," the Brit muttered out the corner of his mouth.

"You think they want to be alone?" the smaller man asked.

"Not yet. They too busy hating each other at the moment," Flintlock replied. He sat down on a nearby tombstone, Spatchcock following his example.

Dante and Mai were still arguing, their voices getting progressively louder. "Don't lecture me on right and wrong," Dante snarled. "You know why I'm half-Romanov? Because my father raped my mother and I was the result. They called me the bastard of the family, but I couldn't hold a candle to the rest of them."

"Didn't stop you taking their name during the war, did it?" Mai snapped. "Didn't stop you claiming Rudinshtein as your own private fiefdom, did it? Didn't stop you abandoning its people and those who tried to defend them?"

"Were you there?" he hissed. "Did you fight on the frontline? Did you experience one moment of that battle?"

"No," Mai admitted, "but my brother did. And he died because of you, you murdering bastard!" She burst into tears, slumping to the snow-covered ground.

A long, painful silence was eventually broken by the sound of an approaching flyer. Spatchcock stood up and smiled. "Well, I think it's time we were going."

Flintlock nodded. "Absolutely. Nothing like a crying woman and an angry Dante to make any journey fly by." He started towards the flyer, which had landed on a nearby hilltop. "You two coming with us or not?"

Dante looked down at the sobbing woman on her knees in front of him. She's only a girl, he realised. She's eighteen at most. I didn't think–

"You never think," Mai replied, wiping her face dry with one sleeve as she stood. "You blunder in, causing chaos and hurting more people than you help. But when the going gets tough, you run and hide. That's who you are, Dante." She picked up her rucksack and hurried after the others.

A little harsh, but not entirely inaccurate, the Crest added.

"Don't you start," Dante spat. He ran after Mai, Spatchcock and Flintlock, catching up with them as they boarded the sleek, silver flyer. It rose into the crisp air and made a slow circle of the hills surrounding the graveyard. Inside the cabin Spatchcock took the opportunity to do some sightseeing.

"Hey, what's that over there?" He pointed through a window at the remains of a mighty tower. Its structure was torn apart as if ravaged by a ferocious attack in the past.

"The Winter Palace," Dante replied, his words without feeling. "It must have been destroyed during the last days of the war." He looked at Mai, who kept her gaze fixed out the opposite side of the flyer. "And that wasn't the only thing..."

Beneath the graveyard, Lord Zhukov watched the flyer's departure on a screen. Satisfied Dante, Mai and the others were gone, Zhukov ventured out on to his platform overlooking the council chamber. The other members from the Parliament of Shadows were gathered on the black and white floor below, nervous faces betraying their fear. "You will be happy to know Dante and his comrades have left safely for their mission."

One of the members stepped forwards to address him. Lady Nikita was the House of Zabriski's matriarch. She was a stern-faced woman in her fifties who normally shared the leader's platform with Zhukov. "Would you mind telling us what is going on? We were informed you wanted to speak with all of us before we left. Why have we been herded on to the chamber floor like subjects for interrogation?"

Zhukov smiled at her. "Ah, Nikita. I knew I could depend upon you to step forward and confront me. For months you have coveted my position as leader of this assembly. Your ambition for power will be your undoing."

"What are you talking about?"

"All of you are just as guilty," he continued, addressing the other members. "At least she has the courage to challenge me."

"You haven't answered my question," Lady Nikita said, refusing to be ignored. "What is the purpose of this gathering, Zhukov?"

"Why, to make it easier for the Raven Corps to kill you, of course." He smiled at her like a benevolent parent explaining a simple truth to an obtuse child. "The soldiers will be here within minutes. They have orders to execute all of you. The manner and means of your deaths is up to you. Those who co-operate fully, providing the names of other treasonous conspirators against the Tsar, will be slain in as quick and painless a manner as possible. Those who refuse to help will suffer all the torments and agonies we can inflict before their bodies give in."

"The man's gone mad," Lady Nikita muttered. "Come down here this instant and explain yourself."

"I don't think so."

"In that case I will come to you." She strode to the nearest door. As her fingers touched the metal handle, electricity surged through Lady Nikita's body. White sparks danced across her and her face contorted into a mocking grimace. Lips pulled back from her teeth as if to smile. After several seconds, her fingers let go of the handle and her body fell backwards to the floor, still twitching and jerking. Then she laid still, a wisp of blue smoke rising from her corpse, a pool of urine slowly spreading out from beneath her.

The effect on the other members was all too apparent. Several screamed, others took to praying and sank to their knees, sobbing uncontrollably. Once Lady Nikita was dead, her colleagues turned to face Zhukov one by one, compelled to see his response. Their leader was smiling broadly.

"Simply shocking," he said, a slight giggle of hysteria betraying his words. Zhukov cleared his throat before continuing. "I regret to inform you all that the Parliament of Shadows was a trap, a ruse to flush out dissident elements within the Empire's noble houses. The clue was in the name. You see, this gathering was an elaborate shadow play to lance the boil of petty ambitions and conspiratorial discontent within the aristocracy. Left unchecked, such sentiment could one day have become sufficiently organised to create a significant threat to the Tsar. So he asked me to create the means for such a movement to find its voice and even provided the funding to create this underground headquarters beneath the Romanov Necropolis. Quite appropriate, don't you think? You will all die beneath the graves of those you would resurrect as rulers of the Empire. I can't think of a more fitting epitaph for the last pocket of resistance."

Another of the parliament's members dared to speak up, his face pale and perspiring, his hands nervously rubbing together. "If we co-operate, do you promise to let our families live?"

"No. Why should I? The reprisals against your kin, your noble houses and all you hold dear will be as savage as they are swift. All you can be assured is the manner of your own passing will be briefer if you help us. That is all traitors such as you deserve." Zhukov looked down his nose at the man who had spoken. "It will probably be of no comfort for you, but the Tsar had not expected the venture to bear fruit so soon. He was prepared to play the long game and let your trust in me build until you were ready to reveal your identities. It was his idea that the Parliament should meet in secret, so that none of us knew each other's faces. Happily, the arrival of Dante gave me the chance to force events along."

"So, he was part of this conspiracy?"

Zhukov snorted at such a notion. "His hatred of the Tsar is even greater than yours. No, Dante was merely a pawn, a means to an end. His mission to the Himalayas is a fool's quest, an errand that shall lead inevitably to his death. Just as his appearance here has led, inevitably, to your deaths."

The sound of marching became audible, heavy footfalls growing louder and louder, echoing around the council chamber.

"Ah, that will be the Raven Corps. Right on time." Zhukov smiled. "I would like to say it's been a pleasure knowing you all, but I consider each member of this so-called Parliament of Shadows a disgrace to the Empire. None shall mourn your passing, nor should they. Goodbye, ladies and gentlemen."

SIX

"The heart hath no window."
– Russian proverb

"Most people have only the slightest knowledge of
the Himalayas. Fewer still possess any first hand
experience of this remote region of the Empire.
Ask any citizen in St Petersburg or New Moscow
and they will know it is a mountainous area. To
them the Himalayas are a vague concept, a far
away place made up of snow-capped peaks and
little else. They might have heard of the Sherpa, a
people of Mongolian origin who live on the mountain slopes and are much sought after for their
climbing prowess. The region in which they live
has been fought over for centuries and remains
one of the few unspoiled parts of the Empire.

The Himalayas are actually a vast mountain system in South Asia, extending one and a half
thousand miles from Kashmir, in the west, to
Assam, in the east between the valleys of the
Rivers Indus and Brahmaputra. This system covers
most of the lands once known as Nepal, Sikkim,
Bhutan and the southern edge of Tibet. The
Himalayas are the highest mountain range in the
world, with several peaks over twenty-five thousand feet."

– Extract from *Secret Destinations of the Empire*
by Mikhail Palinski

The girl sat alone in her room, listening to the world beyond the windows. She was allowed to leave the temple-residence a few times a year, as part of the key religious festivals observed by the followers of her religion. But even then, she was not permitted to play with other children her own age. She was special. Those who looked after her could not risk her to be injured. Besides, she was forbidden to laugh or even smile in public, as it was believed it would bring great misfortune upon the country. Her family were a distant memory and the laughter of other children in her village barely an echo in her thoughts.

She sat on a throne of exotically carved wood, with clusters of cinnamon-scented candles alight on either side of the raised dais. Lamps burned yak butter for illumination, adding to the heady aromas in the room. Discarded nearby was a plate laden with fresh fruit, while a carved wooden elephant rested alongside, its trunk pointing up to the wooden beams criss-crossing the ceiling. The room was filled with the richest treasures: statues of elephants and lions made of pure gold; glittering gemstones and bejewelled icons; tapestries with the most intricate designs and finely woven fabrics, the most impressive of which, a simple white material interwoven with threads of gossamer-thin silver, hung on the wall behind her throne. The effect of the design was so subtle, it was only apparent when seen from precisely the right angle. Otherwise it was close to invisible – a nagging peripheral vision. The girl knew that design well. She knew its significance better than anyone alive. Such was her burden, one of a thousand she had to bear.

Like the walls around her, the girl was dressed in red and gold. Her long, black hair was held back from her face by a golden tiara. It was merely the frontispiece for a grand headdress, made of the finest plumes and spun gold, encrusted with stones of crimson and black. Painted on her forehead was a vermilion third eye, on a black backdrop of mustard oil and soot. The monks had told her that this was the divine eye that saw everything. She could look through every individual's mind, and fathom things beyond a common person's understanding. This responsibility hung heavy upon her, like the numerous beaded necklaces strung round her neck.

If a stranger walked into her throne room, they would have been struck most of all by the sadness of her countenance. Her eyes were dark and expressive, a gorgeous contrast to the pure whiteness of her teeth. Her skin was unblemished, her hands and bare feet soft and delicate to the touch. But nobody touched her, nobody hugged her, and no strangers were allowed into her throne room: not even the other members of what had once been her family. She was caught in a life of utter seclusion.

Soon it would be time to pray. The monks would return, Khumbu at their head, as always. They would bow as they entered, prostrating themselves at her feet, worshipping her presence, always reverential. Then she would eat. Then she would sleep. Then another day would begin, much the same as before. How much longer would this life continue? But the girl already knew the answer to the question. That was another of her burdens. She pushed it away.

Outside, children were playing, chattering to each other. They were careless and joyful. The girl eased herself forward on the throne until she could put both feet on the floor. As she slid off the high seat, the elaborate headdress, which was fixed to her hair with a dozen tiny pins, tilted and almost fell free. She hurriedly pushed it back into position. It would not do to drop the headdress; Khumbu would disapprove. She heard the distant thunder outside, as if giants were calling from one mountaintop to the next, wistful and angry, searching for their lost loves.

The girl was only seven. She had been living in the crimson chamber for three years. Her old life seemed an eternity ago. It was like an old dream. Back then she was just another child among the many of her village, living high up the mountain slopes, unaware how hard her family fought to survive in such an unforgiving environment. It took a special kind of people to cling on here. They required both resilience and acquiescence to the whims of the mountains. The tall peaks were forces of nature, unbound and unbroken by man. You lived among them, but you never conquered them – she knew that now.

The girl sighed.

Since then the room had become her home. She had known what was to come – it was her talent. She knew that something was almost upon them and still there were no answers, no insight and no wisdom to solve the riddle. She had to go on and play out her part. She had to fulfil her destiny. Whatever comes of that, will come, in darkness or in light, she thought. Beyond that, not even I can see. I must be content with that.

She hitched up her ceremonial garb high enough so she could walk without tripping over the hem. Picking her way carefully over the ancient rugs that covered the black-stained floorboards she walked to the doorway of glass and wood that led out on to the balcony. Her left hand clasped the heavy golden handle and twisted it, pushing against the door. After resisting her temporarily, it opened with a sigh. The girl stepped out of the room, thick with incense and dust, into the cold autumn air.

A riot of aromas filled her nostrils. Meats and spices fought with animal dung and burning wood for precedence. Beneath the balcony was a quadrangle, filled by the monthly market. Merchants and farmers, from villages on the mountain slopes, made the trek up to the citadel, bringing their crops and belongings to sell or exchange. Children ran excitedly between the makeshift stalls and carts, while beasts were fed and watered in a quiet corner of the stone courtyard, straw laid down beside the trough for them. I wonder if my family is among them, the girl thought? Should I even know them if I saw them? Her parents had been present at the ceremony to confirm her as the chosen one, but that was long ago.

The holy men had spent days testing her, asking questions and seeking answers beyond the knowledge of any four year-old. Even when they decided she possessed the required twenty-seven noble virtues, there had been one final trial to undergo.

A dozen buffalo were sacrificed in the courtyard. Their heads were gathered onto a bloody pile. At the urging of the monks, she had walked around the grotesque display, while a man in a hideous mask danced nearby. Somehow, she had not flinched. Perhaps terror kept me still, she thought. It did not matter. Khumbu and his brethren had taken her inside. Their chanting filled the night for hours, calling for the goddess to come down and enter her body.

The next morning she was dressed in the garb befitting her new status and they led her back out into the courtyard. A huge crowd – her family amongst them – watched as she walked across a white cloth, the last rite of passage. From that moment onwards, the monks called her Mukari. But the truth of what was to come had already claimed her. It lived inside her now, a constant companion.

The girl looked down at the quadrangle once more. I see the courtyard as it was, the joyful faces of my proud family, the others applauding and cheering. I see the courtyard as it is now: the running children, the villagers trading goods for grain and bread. I see the courtyard as it will be: blood running along the cracks between the stones, the dead bodies piled like unwanted rags. Beyond that? I see only darkness and sadness and nothing else, nothing more.

She sagged against the wooden rail around the edge of the balcony, her feet nudging a smooth pebble over the side. It fell on the shoulder of a plump man passing below, his arms full of vegetables. Startled, he looked up and smiled, his face coming alive at seeing the girl. "Mukari, Mukari," he called, his voice echoing around the stone walls of the quadrangle. Other merchants and villagers turned towards him. A crowd formed quickly beneath the balcony, dozens of people lifting their hands to the girl in supplication, their sun-bronzed faces creasing into smiles, their narrow eyes sparkling with excitement. Each raised their voice and chanted. "Bless us, Mukari! Bless us!"

The girl waved at them shyly, careful not to let any expression show on her face. You must never smile, Khumbu had told her a thousand times. Never laugh before your people.

Another cry came from inside the chamber of crimson and gold behind her. "Mukari!" It was Khumbu's stern voice. "You should not be out on the balcony. You know it unsettles the people, when you make an unexpected appearance like this. Come back inside please."

The girl sighed and returned to her room, a sudden gust of wind closing the doors once she was inside. Khumbu was on his knees and bent forward to kiss the floor in genuflection. Sunlight filtered through the windows and reflected on his smooth and hairless scalp. The saffron colouring of his monk's robes accentuated his Himalayan tan. He waited until the girl was seated on her throne before looking up. When he did, his sightless eyes stared past her, an admonishing cast about his features. "Please, goddess. You must not look upon your people without protection. These are troubled times. Rumours fly between the villages of Imperial troops that are massing in the valleys below."

The Mukari already knew about the soldiers; how could she not? "Don't worry, Khumbu. I have seen what is to come. I have nothing to fear from my own people. It is the outsiders who bring death to this place. The gates of the Forbidden Citadel shall fall-"

"Never! It is impossible!" the monk protested, before realising the temerity of his outburst. "Forgive me, goddess, I lost control of my tongue. You are all seeing and all knowing, if you say something is true, it must be so. But how can outsiders find the citadel? My brethren and I protect these walls day and night. Only those who have been here before can find the way back, and they would never willingly betray us."

"There is another, one who bears the symbol of the Mukari. The gates shall open. They shall walk inside. When they do, the cataclysm will be almost upon us. The gates of the Forbidden Citadel shall fall and there is nothing any of us can do to stop that, Khumbu. I have foreseen it."

The monk slowly rose to his feet, joints in his legs clicking. He collected a bowl of broth from outside the doorway and carried it to the Mukari, along with a simple ceramic spoon. "I have brought food to soothe your worries away, goddess. You must eat."

The girl shook her head. "I am not hungry."

Khumbu smiled slyly. "Gylatsen will be disappointed, he made it specially for you. There are shiitake mushrooms at the bottom of the bowl, grown on mahogany wood. Gylatsen said to tell you it's what gives the broth its smoky flavour."

The Mukari looked at Khumbu shyly. "He made it for me?"

"Yes, goddess. Please, you must eat."

She took the bowl from him. Among all the monks that were her constant companions, Gylatsen was her favourite. The others were so serious, but he had mischief in his eyes and joy in his heart. She could not help smiling when Gylatsen was around. He made her burdens lighter. The Mukari dipped her spoon into the

steaming broth, careful to scoop some shards of mush-
room up with the liquid. She blew over the spoon's
rounded bowl, then tipped the contents into her mouth.
It tasted just as Gylatsen had said, smoky and warm,
comforting to the body as a blazing wood fire on a cold
winter's day. Before she knew it, she had finished the
broth, eagerly spooning the last morsels into her mouth.

Khumbu smiled as he took the empty bowl away. "I'll
be sure to tell Gylatsen how much you enjoyed that, goddess. He will be pleased."

"Thank you, Khumbu."

The monk dropped to his knees and kissed the floor
again before leaving, pulling the thick wooden door
closed gently behind. Once she was alone, the Mukari
leaned back in the throne and closed her eyes, feeling the
pleasant warmth of the broth spread through her body.
Being so aware, so alive, could be an overwhelming experience. But it was half her lifetime since the Mukari had
known any other way of being. It had become natural to
her.

The Mukari let her spirit escape its mortal cage of flesh
and bone, slipping out through the heavy stone walls to
float effortlessly above the market. Even old Khumbu
could not stop her going outside like this. No one could
see if she was smiling or not. She flew away from the
citadel, through the surrounding clouds and then went
into a dive, her spirit scudding along invisible zephyrs,
passing mountainside villages and ice-covered ravines.
Soon the snow on the slopes gave way to the detritus of
erosion from many millennia. At last she found them, the
killers, the butchers, the bringers of death. To her eye
they were no more than human, despite the terrible
wrath their gathering would bring upon her people.

I pity you, her spirit whispered, the words becoming a
cold breeze from the mountaintops, blowing down to
chill the soldiers' bones and put out their fires. The
Mukari turned away, the approach of a familiar presence

intriguing her. She wanted to get closer, but he was yet beyond her reach. All in good time.

On the throne a frown crossed the girl's face, wrinkling her nose. There was so little time left before the darkness came, and not much of it good.

SEVEN

*"The wheel of fortune spins
faster than a windmill."*
– Russian proverb

"When in residence at the Imperial Palace, Tsar Vladimir Makarov favoured the holding of daily assizes in the Chamber of Judgement. This vast space, with its enormous vaulted ceiling and intimidating architecture, had a seating capacity approaching five thousand people. However, these places were rarely full, except for special events such as the trial of Nikolai Dante in 2668, for allegedly engineering the kidnapping of the Tsar's daughter, Jena. It was this case that helped accelerate the onset of war between the Tsar and the Romanovs. Few trials have had such far-reaching consequences for the Empire at large.

In the Chamber of Judgement criminals ranging from the pettiest thief to the most treasonous of curs were brought before The Ruler of all the Russias to have their case heard, make a plea of mitigation and receive sentence. Such phrases as "due process" and "innocent until proven guilty" had little currency in a court of law. All were guilty in the Tsar's eyes. The only thing in question was finding a punishment to fit their crimes.

Before the war, Count Pyre often acted as chief accuser. After the war, Lady Jena was sometimes used to fulfil Pyre's former function at proceedings. In cases involving matters sensitive to the security of the Empire, the Tsar chose to hold proceedings behind closed doors. Few accused delivered to the Chamber of Judgement in such circumstances ever left it alive."

– Extract from *The Law of the Tsar*
by Johann Grissholm

Zachariah Zhukov was surprised, and not a little disturbed, by the frosty reception he received on returning to the Imperial Palace. Was he not the brains behind the Parliament of Shadows, a covert operation that had successfully accounted for close to a dozen leading dissidents? Had he not masterminded the scheme from the first, persisting with the plan when others had predicted its utter failure? Most importantly, was he not carrying the names of more than a hundred members of the aristocracy, all of them identified as co-conspirators by the Parliament's members before they died?

I must not be too proud, or too demanding Zhukov told himself. I must remember my work has been carried out in secret. He doubted there were more than a handful of people at the Imperial Palace who knew what had transpired beneath the Romanov Necropolis. Once the coup against the plotters is made public, then I shall bask in the adulation of my peers, warm myself with the Tsar's gratitude. Until that moment I must be patient.

The red-haired nobleman had endured endless delays, biting back his temper. For two days he was kept waiting on the ground in St Petersburg, denied a place in the authorised airships that made their hourly visits to the great palace, hovering above the city. Twice he had made it to the front of the queue, but was turned away in favour of others with more urgent calls upon the Tsar's time. Finally, when he had almost despaired of being allowed an audience, Zhukov was summoned to a private landing dock on the edge of the city. Jena Makarov was waiting for him there with a small flyer, a welcoming smile and words full of apology.

"Lord Zhukov, my father wishes me to convey his sincerest regrets that you have been kept waiting so long. He says it was necessary to maintain the deception of your noble house being out of favour, while suspected dissidents were rounded up for interrogation. You understand, of course."

"Of course," he said, allowing a small smile. Just as well I didn't try to throw my weight around and demand an earlier appointment he thought. That would not have gone well with the Tsar. Vladimir Makarov was many things, but a forgiving soul could not be counted among the many facets of his character.

Jena led Zhukov into her private flyer, motioning for him to take the co-pilot's seat. "Don't worry, I'm fully qualified," she said, laughing at the concern on his face. "When the Tsar needs a special envoy to deliver messages personally, diplomatic immunity ensures the least problems."

Zhukov nodded. Wait until the Tsar hears all I have achieved, his rewards should be beyond imagining.

Within the hour Jena led Zhukov into the Chamber of Judgement. He never failed to be intimidated by the vast space, despite it being all but empty. His footsteps echoed up into the high ceiling as he walked to the centre circle where so many had heard their fate pronounced. On either side was a precipitous drop. Nobody knew what lurked in the darkness, as the palace staff were not permitted to speak about it, on pain of death. A handful of Raven Corps soldiers guarded the platform's edges, with long pikes clasped in their gauntlets. Behind them was no railing, just a yawning gap between the platform and the public galleries round the sides of the chamber.

The Tsar floated above the platform in a grand throne, silent thrusters maintaining its magisterial position. He was clad in the Imperial robes of office, a rich mixture of purple and gold fabrics draped round his powerful frame. Zhukov reached the centre circle and dropped to one knee, displaying his obedience. But the Tsar gave no word or signal for the nobleman to rise, so Zhukov was forced to stay on a bended knee.

Jena produced a scroll of vellum and read aloud the text printed in blood red ink. "The court of Vladimir the Conqueror, Tsar of all the Russias, is now in session. Prisoners, do not weep or beg. Undignified signs of weakness or repentance will result only in harsher punishment. Zachariah Zhukov! Prepare to face the judgement of the Tsar."

The nobleman listened to her recitation with growing incredulity. When the Tsarina finished speaking, he could not help but reply. "There must have been some terrible mistake," he protested. "Tsar Vladimir, I came here to–"

"Silence!" the Tsar thundered. "You may speak only when given permission to do so, traitor. Lady Jena, please read the charges against this individual."

She nodded, resuming her recitation from the scroll. "Zachariah Zhukov, you are guilty of conspiring to topple the rightful ruler of the Empire, a treasonable offence. You are similarly charged with promoting anti-Empire ideals, duping others into following your misguided and dangerous notions, and of fomenting insurrection among a dozen noble houses."

"What say you to these charges?" the Tsar demanded.

"Sir, I must confess my confusion at being accused of such crimes," Zhukov began. "I freely admit I am guilty of everything charge as stated–"

"Then there is little more to be said," the Tsar snapped.

"But I committed these acts at your behest!" Zhukov said, trying and failing to hide the panic rising in his voice. "I proposed the Parliament of Shadows as a way of luring dissidents out from the protection of their noble houses. You gave me full permission and every assistance to make this covert mission possible."

"Can you prove that?"

"Can I prove it?" Zhukov spluttered.

"Yes."

"I... I have no documents, nothing official to verify these facts."

The Tsar folded his arms. "Then there seems little hope for you."

"But sir, you agreed to let me pretend I was guilty of treason to establish my credibility with the dissidents. Lady Jena was present at the meeting, she is my witness."

"My daughter, do you recall this meeting the prisoner alleges took place?"

Jena shook her head. "I am sorry, father, I do not. You have so many meetings, I must confess they all blur into one after a while."

"No!" Zhukov cried out, standing up. A cluster of Raven Corps troops surrounded him, pointing their pikes at his torso. "Please, Tsar Vladimir, I do not understand why you are doing this to me." Tears of frustration filled his eyes, the nobleman's emotions overwhelming him.

"Consider it a test of your resolve," the Tsar replied. He motioned to the Raven Corps and they returned to their original positions. Jena smiled at Zhukov, her face showing some compassion again.

"You mean... I'm not on trial?" the bewildered Zhukov asked.

"These charges are a formality," the Tsar replied. "Although the Parliament of Shadows' other members are all dead, some may have told friends or relatives about your involvement before the trap was sprung. So you must be seen to stand trial, just as they have been, otherwise your noble house might suffer reprisals from anti-Imperialists."

"I'm not to be punished?"

The Tsar laughed, a rare sound in the Chamber of Judgement. "Zhukov, if what I hear of your exploits is true, you deserve all our congratulations. Come, give me your report and then we shall deal with these charges against you. I'm sure an amicable resolution can be found."

The nobleman let himself breathe again, the tension slowly melting from his shoulders. It had all been a hoax, so the Tsar could maintain culpable deniability. He was merely toying with him, as a cat plays with a mouse it has captured. Zhukov gave a sigh of relief and then outlined his activities of the past week.

The Tsar listened politely until the name Nikolai Dante was mentioned. "What? You had him in your grasp and you let him escape?"

"I didn't let him escape, sir. I sent him on a collision course with your mission into the Himalayas," Zhukov explained, perplexed by the Tsar's sudden, almost volcanic reaction. "One of the other cabal members, Lady Nikita Zabriski, suggested it. She had heard about you sending a contingent to search for the Forbidden Citadel."

The Tsar's eyes narrowed. "How had she heard this? From you?"

Zhukov shrugged. "I had no knowledge of the mission before she brought the matter up. It was her idea we use Dante's Crest to help locate the citadel."

"And why should his Crest be of any use?"

"Forgive me, sir, I thought you knew all this. Lady Zabriski told us anyone bearing a Romanov Weapons Crest could see the Forbidden Citadel. She even provided an electronic means of tracking Dante via his Crest."

"Do you still have these tracking devices?"

"Err, no," Zhukov admitted.

The Tsar looked across at his daughter. "Did you know anything of this?"

Jena shook her head. "We always suspected the House of Zabriski had close links with the Romanovs. One of our spies suggested Lady Nikita shared intelligence with Dmitri Romanov, that the two might even be lovers. But our operative disappeared shortly before the war."

"We've already purged the Zabriski dynasty, thanks to the efforts of Lord Zhukov," the Tsar growled angrily. "Now we may never know what Lady Nikita could have told us and what secrets she took to her grave."

"Sir, I didn't know," Zhukov said weakly. "I couldn't know."

The Tsar ignored the interjection. "Jena, I want you to make contact with Ivanov's expedition. Warn them about Dante's presence in the mountains and make sure the general knows I want the Romanov bastard captured alive." She departed the Chamber of Judgement, leaving Lord Zhukov to face her father's wrath.

The Mukari was meditating, both legs folded into the lotus position beneath her gold and crimson gown, hands held outwards in supplication. The girl's eyelids fluttered as she communed with the mountains, becoming one with the mighty peaks that were worshipped like herself. She could feel every drop of moisture that fell upon them, sense every breeze and zephyr that caressed their sides, touch every soul upon their surface. But already there were those on the mountains whose presence spoke of the darkness to come.

The girl's nose wrinkled in disgust as she smelled the soldiers, their hatred, their cruel spirits and their harsh, guttural laughter. She did not like these men. That would make what was to come easier, but it offered no comfort. The Mukari was moving her mind's eye elsewhere when a sensation like a squall of daggers invaded her thoughts. Dozens of words and images battered her consciousness, seeking a way past, seeking the soldiers. Somebody was trying to communicate with them, warn of approaching danger.

I cannot allow that, the Mukari resolved. What must be will be, but I cannot allow anyone else on to the mountains – in person or as a message. She brought her hands together in prayer, fingertips almost touching her nose. I will hold back the daggers. Let them fall upon deaf ears.

The Tsar glared down at his double agent. "Well, what do you have to say in your defence, Zhukov?"

"Wh... When the Zabriski woman suggested sending Dante into the Himalayas, I... I thought it was a fool's quest, a doomed errand. The renegade has no knowledge or experience of that terrain. It would be remarkable if he survived more than a day in such a hazardous environment."

"Unfortunately, Nikolai Dante seems capable of surviving almost anything anywhere, despite my best efforts to have him exterminated," Vladimir sneered. "He went alone into the mountains, yes?"

"Not exactly. He had two accomplices with him, vile creatures I doubt could be of much use to him. There was also a woman, a native of the mountains. She was the one who found and captured Dante. Curiously, she was able to read his thoughts. She could even hear what the Crest was saying to him."

The Tsar's brow furrowed. "How did she come by this useful talent?"

"I don't know," Zhukov admitted.

"So, not only did you have the notorious renegade in your grasp and let him go, you also had control of an operative able to read the mind of anyone bearing a Romanov Weapons Crest?"

"Well... yes."

"And you didn't think her ability might be of use to your Tsar?"

"I..." Zhukov looked down at his feet. "It never occurred to me." He could see a vein on the Tsar's forehead was throbbing and his face was a glowering shade of crimson.

"Lord Zhukov, you may be the greatest fool I have ever had the misfortune to encounter. From all you have told me, it is plain Lady Nikita had access to secret information about the deployment and dispersal of my Imperial forces. She also possessed key facts about the Romanovs and even handed you a means of hunting down the survivors of that accursed family. But you have thrown all of this away in a crude grasp for glory and kudos. What did you call this mission taking Dante into the mountains?"

"A... doomed errand, sir. A fool's quest."

"Precisely. But you were the fool, Lord Zhukov, and now the doom shall also be yours." The Tsar snapped his fingers. The Raven Corps on one side of the platform divided, creating a gap in their number. Those on the opposite side advanced on Zhukov, their pikes herding him slowly towards the edge.

"Please, sir, I made a mistake," the terrified nobleman cried out. "Give me a chance to correct that error! I will travel to the Himalayas myself, make amends for my folly."

"The folly was mine, for entertaining your suggestions in the first place. I should have known better," the Tsar snarled. He nodded to the Raven Corps. The scarlet-clad soldiers edged Zhukov ever closer to the precipice.

"Sir, don't do this! I beg of you!" he screamed.

"Never beg," the Tsar replied. At his signal the soldiers sent the still protesting nobleman over the edge of the platform. "If there's one thing I can't abide, it's men who beg."

Zhukov's scream was still audible when Jena re-entered the Chamber of Judgement. The Raven Corps were returning to their positions around the edge of the platform. "Well?" the Tsar demanded.

"I'm sorry, father, but we are unable to get a message to Ivanov's mission. The mountains block out most conventional forms of communication, but there is something else at work. A deliberate jamming signal has been established, blocking all our attempts to bypass it." Jena smiled. "I imagine the general and Dante will get quite a surprise when they find each other searching for the Forbidden Citadel."

"You sound almost pleased as such a prospect, Jena. Perhaps you are happy Dante still lives?"

"His survival means nothing to me," she replied quickly.

"Rest assured, his survival will not continue much longer," the Tsar promised. "Ivanov will take the greatest of pleasure in murdering the Romanov renegade. They have an old score to settle, and it is written in blood."

EIGHT

"The Tibetan Plateau is beautiful and bleak. Shielded by the Himalayas from the rains of monsoon season, the plateau's surface is akin to that of a desert – without the sand. Brown and bare, the vast horizon is littered with glacial rubble from millennia gone by. The forces of nature that created this landscape have, thus far, held back the encroachment of Imperial civilisation. In the most unexpected of places you can still discover ancient scraps of fabric, tattered banners that speak of a religion systematically destroyed in lower regions by outside oppression. Ropes are secured between cairns and nearby crags. From these, the faithful hung their prayers to the gods, written on coloured flags. The effect is a multicoloured kaleidoscope of hope and faith, both cheering and mournful. Cheering because these bright colours lift the spirits in an otherwise barren landscape, and mournful because those who wrote these messages have long since fallen victim to the latest invaders of this noble world, close to the clouds.

Despite the best efforts of the Imperials, small communities survive high on the slopes of the Himalayas, eking out an existence on the roof of the world. They lead a simple life, but one that many would envy. Should you ever have the chance to venture into this remote territory, you can expect to be entranced by the ways of these people and envious of their secret happiness."

   – Extract from *Secret Destinations of the Empire*,
by Mikhail Palinski

"Bojemoi!" Dante cursed, his teeth chattering a staccato rhythm, while sub-zero blasts of air pushed tears from the corners of his eyes. "How can anyone live in this hell-hole?"

Mai glared at him angrily before turning back into the wind, her heels digging into the sides of her yak, urging it onwards.

The four travellers had been left on the Tibetan Plateau the previous morning, their flyer wasting little time before it disappeared over the horizon. Four yaks were waiting for them. Saddling the beasts had proven difficult enough in the finger-numbing cold: riding the creatures was another matter entirely. Dante and Flint-lock had come off at least a dozen times, as their bruised buttocks could testify. Mai had whispered to her yak for several minutes before climbing on its back, the beast offering no resistance to her. Most surprising was Spatchcock's steed. The longhaired mountain ox was constantly trying to nuzzle against his legs and trotted along happily with its malodorous master in the saddle.

"I think my yak likes me," he had said with a smile.

"I think she loves you," Mai replied. "And that's a dri, not a yak. Yak is the male of the species. Your mount has udders."

"Must be the aroma of animal dung and dried urine that does it," Flintlock muttered while trying to climb back on to his transportation. "That creature plainly admires anything that smells as bad as it does."

"Are you talking about the dri or Spatchcock?" Dante asked.

"Take your pick."

More than twenty-four hours later and all conversation between the travellers had long since lapsed. Mai hadn't spoken to Dante since they left the Romanov Necropolis, while Spatchcock was more interested in his new best friend than communicating with Flintlock. They continued their slow progress towards the mighty peaks in the distance. At first, the slopes had appeared deceptively close, waiting for them just beyond the next rise. But the brow of each hill always brought another valley beyond it, and then a further rise to climb.

Dante was beginning to wonder if they would ever reach the Himalayas. "Why didn't the flyer take us closer in?" he shouted at Mai, who was ahead of him.

She didn't look back. "When the Imperials couldn't conquer the mountains, they decided to cut this region off from the rest of the Empire." She dug into her pockets and pulled out a smooth, round pebble. "Watch!" She threw the stone into the air. A flash of blue lightning engulfed the pebble. Once it had been vapourised, a fine dust in the air was all that remained of the stone.

"Sonic disruptors," Dante realised.

This area is seeded with them, the Crest added. *Anything moving more than three metres above the ground is targeted and destroyed.*

"That explains why we haven't seen any birds," Flintlock said. "This place is deader than any battlefield I've been on."

"We should reach the foot of the Himalayas tomorrow," Mai announced. "Another hour's ride tonight, then we can rest. In the morning we release the yaks. They will find their own way home."

"Can't we take them with us?" Spatchcock asked sadly. "I've gotten quite attached to my friend here."

"They'll only slow us down," she replied firmly.

"I doubt my spine will ever recover from riding on these monstrous beasts," Flintlock complained. "I haven't been this black and blue since–"

"Your last visit to Famous Flora's Massage Parlour?" Dante suggested. "You always have a spanking good time there."

"My sexual proclivities are my own affair," Flintlock protested haughtily.

"Proclivities? I thought you liked them to be called your meat and two veg." Spatchcock sniggered. "Least, that's what Flora told me."

"Can the three of you talk or think about nothing but sex every minute of the day and night?" Mai demanded. "Does every comment or conversation have to lead straight into the gutter?"

"Are you suggesting we can only converse in innuendo?" Flintlock asked.

"Innuendo and out the other," Spatchcock added with a throaty chuckle.

"Shut up!" she hissed, twisting her yak round to face the trio of men. "We're in one of the most beautiful places in the world. For once in your sordid little lives, try to appreciate your surroundings."

Shame-faced and embarrassed, the three men mumbled their apologies. Mai pointed a finger at Dante sternly. "And when I turn around, I don't want you thinking about anything except our objective, do you understand? Keep your eyes off my arse and your thoughts on the job in hand, okay?"

"Okay," Dante snapped back. "Can we get on, please?"

"Fine."

"Good." Dante was distracted by tittering from nearby. "Now what?"

"Nothing," Flintlock squeaked, struggling to contain his mirth.

"Nothing at all," Spatchcock agreed.

"It's just… she said… on the job." The Brit lost control of his merriment, and Spatchcock was soon laughing out loud. Dante shook his head despairingly and urged his yak onwards. He caught up with Mai and apologised for such gross behaviour.

"Their hearts are in the right place," he offered. "Well, mostly."

"Shame about the rest of them," she sneered.

"I guess," Dante shrugged. He studied her face, noting the pain etched into her expression. "I thought you'd cope better than any of us with the cold."

"It's not the cold." Mai winced. "Or the yak."

"How did you know I was…? Oh yes, you can read my thoughts."

You have my sympathies, the Crest commented. *His is not the prettiest of minds to experience. I suppose I've gotten used to its sordid little nooks and crannies by now, but they must come as something of a shock to–*

"I'm trying to talk with this woman, Crest. I don't need you butting in with your oh-so-superior observations."

Be like that. See if I care. Before the argument could go any further, Mai slumped forward over her mount. *She's lost consciousness. Get her off that walking carpet, she needs help.*

Dante jumped from his yak and hurried to Mai's beast, lowering her from the saddle to the stone-strewn ground. He stripped off his jacket, folding the garment in half and slipping it beneath Mai's head. Her face was wan, the normally bronze skin blotchy and discoloured. "Crest, what's wrong?"

Rest your palm against her forehead. Direct contact with the skin will enable me to make a more accurate diagnosis.

The others hurried to join them, Flintlock tumbling from his mount in the process. Spatchcock grabbed the reins of both animals so the yaks couldn't wander off in the confusion. "What's the matter with her?"

"That's what I'm trying to find out," Dante hissed. He reached forwards with his left hand, pressing its palm against Mai's skin.

Beginning analysis now, the Crest said tersely. *That's strange. She's...*

Dante waited, but the voice in his head had fallen silent. "Crest? Crest, what's going on? What's wrong with Mai?" Still no reply came. Dante twisted round to look for Spatchcock, but both his travelling companions had disappeared, along with the yaks. "That's impossible. Crest, what's happened to Flintlock and Spatch? Crest?"

All Dante could hear was the wind whistling from the nearby mountains, then even that died away to nothing, leaving an eerie silence.

"What are you doing here?"

Dante realised he was now kneeling on broad wooden panals, his palm resting on the forehead of a beautiful Oriental girl. Surprised, he pulled his hand away. "Sorry," he said quickly. "I was... before, my friend, she was... well, she's not my friend. At least, I doubt she'd call me a friend. Anyway, I was trying to–"

The girl sat and giggled at him. "You're a funny colour!"

"I am?"

"You can't be from the village."

"No, I'm... I'm not sure, to be honest. Where am I?"

"Don't you know?"

Dante shook his head. The girl stood up and gave him a quick kiss on the cheek. "Don't worry. You'll see, in time." She ran away from him, fading into nothing. Dante was still looking for her when a harsh voice cursed at him.

"How much for this one?"

A massive figure loomed nearby, the rancid stench of body odour filling Dante's nostrils. He couldn't make out his face, but somehow knew he must not speak.

"I said how much for this one, old man?"

"Twenty."

"For used goods? Ha! Eight and no more."

"Twelve?"

"I said eight, and that's being generous."

A hand reached down and grabbed Dante by his hair, yanking him on to his feet. Fingers probed expertly, feeling his teeth, searching for imperfections. On impulse, Dante bit down, snapping his jaws together. Blood coated the inside of his mouth, the smell of iron in his nostrils and screaming fury in his ears. The blows came quickly, one upon another, snarling and savage. "You'll pay for that."

After another blur, Dante was sitting on a dirt floor, the pounded earth beneath his hands dry and firm. Animal hides lined the walls, insulating the hut from the bitter winds outside. A man clad in black from head to toe walked in and only his hands and eyes were visible. "You will kill for us. You will become us..." Then he, too, faded away, shimmering into nothing like a ghost.

"Dante? What are you doing here?" The voice was Mai's but Dante could not find its source. He twisted round and round, searching his surroundings. The hut melted away to reveal a snow-covered slope, its whiteness tinted mustard yellow by the setting sun.

There you are, a voice said inside Dante's thoughts.

"Crest? Where am I?"

Inside Mai's subconscious. When you put your hand on her forehead, it opened a long dormant pathway into her thoughts. I was drawn inside and your mind must have followed.

"I don't understand."

Hardly surprising. Interpreting the workings of the human subconscious has kept entire professions gainfully employed for more than a millennium.

"Am I inside one of Mai's dreams?"

Not a bad analogy, but these visions are a blend of her past, present and future. A better question is how can she see her future, even at a subconscious level? Perhaps telepathy is only one of Mai's psychic talents?

Dante watched as the mountains changed colour, each vision darker than the last. The sun was now almost hidden beneath the distant horizon. As it disappeared, a line of shadow crept up each slope, swallowing the mountain. Above that line the snow turned ever more orange, before its shade reddened. Soon only the tips were catching the sun, the light staining them a sinister hue, as if the peaks were covered with blood red. Dante shuddered.

"Don't touch me!" a girl's voice screamed. She ran past him, terror filling her face. Behind her ran nightmare monsters, their faces devoid of eyes, grabbing hands flailing at the wind, mouths howling in hunger. The creatures ran through Dante, startling him but not touching, wraiths of the mind.

"I've seen enough, Crest. How do I get out of here?"

Silence.

"Crest, can you hear me?"

Dante was colder since the sun had gone down. His hands shivered. He sank to his knees in the snow and hugged both arms round his chest to retain heat. Around him the wind whispered then screamed, its gusts a dozen different voices. Dante could hear words echoing around the mountains, growing louder and louder.

What are you doing here? Don't touch me! You'll pay for that. You'll see... I don't understand. How did I get here? Don't touch me! I don't understand. You'll see... Where am I? How did I get here? Crest...? Crest...?

The voices grew louder, until Dante felt himself being consumed. Another noise began to overtake it, a low rumbling from above. At first it sounded like thunder in the distance. Then the rumble became a roar, forcing him to look up. The night sky was turning white again. It was an avalanche. *Dante, evasive action…*

Dante yanked his hand away from Mai's forehead, his lungs sucking in air as if he were a drowning man suddenly pulled back to the surface. "What happened?"

You disappeared, the Crest replied. *The moment you placed your hand on Mai's forehead, I lost all contact with you.*

"What do you mean? I talked with you inside her subconscious."

Not to the best of my knowledge.

Dante could see Spatchcock and Flintlock staring at him, their faces confused and afraid. "The Crest says I disappeared."

"Your body didn't go anywhere, but as for the rest of you…" Spatchcock replied.

"You were in some sort of trance," Flintlock added.

"What about Mai?" Dante asked.

"What about me?" She opened her eyes and looked at the three men standing over her. "What's going on?"

"I wish I knew." Dante explained what had happened.

Dante believes we conversed in your mind, the Crest told Mai, *but I have no recollection of such an event.*

She sat up, stroking her temples with one hand. "Last thing I remember was my headache suddenly getting worse. Then my vision blurred and after that… nothing."

"How do you feel now?" Spatchcock asked.

"As if my head wants to split open. It's been pounding like a drum since we landed, but I thought that would pass. Instead the pain keeps getting worse."

Dante recalled the images that had flooded his mind. Mountains were the recurring motif, peaks becoming an ominous blood red. "The closer we get to the foot of the Himalayas, the greater the pain in your head?"

"Yes," Mai agreed. "Why, do you think there's a connection?"

"I wish I knew," Dante said. "It'll be dark soon. We need to find shelter for the night. Spatch, Flintlock – scout ahead for the nearest place we can stop. I need to talk with Mai."

"Gotcha," Spatchcock nodded, climbing deftly into the saddle on his yak.

Flintlock remained standing, his arms folded resolutely. "I refuse to get back on that creature," he pouted.

"Have it your own way," Spatchcock replied. He trotted off on his hairy steed, leaving Flintlock to run behind, dodging the odd spurt of yak manure. Dante waited until both men were out of earshot before speaking.

"How long is it since you've been home, back to these mountains?"

"I can't remember," Mai said sadly. "My childhood is a blur. If I try to focus on it, I start getting a migraine. After a while, I stopped trying to remember. It was less painful."

"So what's the first thing you can recall? Without pain?"

"Waking up inside a bamboo cage, on a dais in a market. Slave traders were selling me. 'Himalayan beauty, never been touched.' Those are the first words I can remember hearing. I was twelve or thirteen at the time."

"How can you be sure?"

Mai gave Dante a withering glare. "A woman knows."

"Oh, right."

"That was six or seven years ago, before the war. I can clearly recall every moment, every experience I've had since then – but nothing before." She faced the mountains, the snow-covered peaks turning yellow in the setting sunlight. "Until now, that is. I'm getting glimpses of growing up in these mountains, of playing with my brother in the snow round our family's hut."

Dante frowned. "If you couldn't remember anything before you were sold, how did you know about your brother?"

"He tried to rescue me from the slave traders." The snow-caps were turning a shade of ochre, then a deeper orange. "My brother was the only link I had back to my childhood. And you killed him."

"Was he fighting for the Tsar?"

"The Tsar?" Mai cursed in a tongue Dante didn't recognise. "My brother would never fight for that bastard." She stood up, refusing Dante's help. "If you'd killed him because he was one of the enemy, I could understand that. But he was one of your own men. You killed one of your own soldiers. That's not an act of war, that's murder." Mai strode off in the direction taken by Spatchcock and Flintlock.

Dante watched her go, the mountains in the distance blood red at the peaks. He realised that it was just like in the vision. That must have been a glimpse of the future. But what else had he seen in Mai's head that had yet to happen? What clues had he witnessed without realising?

He retrieved his jacket and put it back on. "Crest, can you still access the Imperial Net?"

Not without a relay or external power source.

Dante glanced round the barren landscape, darkness rapidly engulfing him. "The sonic disruptors – could you use them as a booster?"

That could work, the Crest decided. *I will try hacking into their control systems, siphoning off a little residual power. What do you need?*

"There's more to Mai than meets the eye. She claims to have no memory of her life before the age of twelve. Check her story, see if it stands up."

Consider it done. Anything else?

"Yes. Why was I sucked into Mai's subconscious when I touched her forehead? Nothing like that happened when I grabbed her wrist at the Parliament of Shadows' HQ. If something important is locked in her mind, we need to know what that is and how to access that knowledge."

I shall investigate further. Of course, many Asian and Oriental faiths believe gods and holy individuals have a divine, third eye set into their forehead, enabling the bearer to see through every individual's mind, and fathom things beyond a common person's understanding.

Dante set off after the others, not wanting to be separated from them for the night. "Get the feeling that you're out of your depth, Crest?"

No.

"Good. So hacking the Imperial Net shouldn't offer a challenge, should it?"

NINE

"What matters is not who you are at birth,
but at death."
– Russian proverb

"The Imperial Net is among the Empire's most remarkable achievements. This vast artificial intelligence is a gestalt entity, collecting every available scrap of data and interrelating this with the ever-shifting zeitgeist of contemporary culture. The net was inspired by a Twenty-first Century phenomenon wiped out in the AI holocaust of 2027. The Imperial Net uses alien technology to achieve similar results, but has liquid media and bioorganic circuitry as its support mechanism. All the user requires is a power source, some access codes and the ability to interpolate the ebb and flow of raw data. What could be simpler?"
– Extract from *The Smirnov Almanac of Fascinating Facts*, 2672 edition

Dante. Dante! The Crest's voice woke its host from sleep before dawn, drawing him out of a dream involving three shape-shifting alien masseurs and a bathtub full of strawberry-scented lubricants.

"Five more minutes. Just five more minutes…" he murmured, sulkily.

DANTE!

"Diavolo!" Dante exclaimed, sitting bolt upright. "Crest, there's no need to shout. I was waking up. I simply wanted to savour the last, lingering delights of my dream." He smirked, one hand rasping through the stubble on his chin. "Some of the things those shape-shifters could do... They ought to be illegal."

Most of them are. You forget that I am privy to your dreams as well as your waking thoughts.

"Yeah," Dante said. He shivered in the cold morning air, briskly pulling on his jacket. The four travellers had found shelter beneath a rocky overhang, using the slumbering yaks as a windbreak. Spatchcock's snoring had kept the others awake for hours, until one by one they drifted off to sleep.

Dante pulled on his boots and crept out of the shelter, stretching and yawning. "So, why did you wake me, Crest?"

While your subconscious has been busy performing indecent acts, I've been scanning the Imperial Net for any mention of Mai Tsai.

"And?"

There is only one.

"One? That's all?"

I was very thorough.

"I know, but... How many times am I mentioned?"

The running tally is fast approaching one point four billion, the Crest replied dryly. *You seem to exert a fascination for young ladies of a certain age. There's an entire sub-genre of romantic fiction about your exploits. Appropriately enough, it is known as Dante slash fiction.*

"Really? Hot stuff, is it? Could you read me some?"

No. Your self-image is already far enough out of proportion with your ability to satisfy any woman. It does not require further inflation. Besides, you asked me for facts about Mai, not an exercise in stroking your ego.

"Yeah, yeah. Spit it out then."

There is no mention of Mai before the war. She does not exist in any Imperial records, on any census or forms. Nor does she appear to have any documentation issued in her name. Before you ask, I also ran images of her through facial recognition software and image search facilities. Still nothing.

"So what *is* this one mention?"

Eighteen months ago, a clandestine criminal group known only as the Tong of the Red Hand broke cover and issued a rare public statement denouncing Mai. The Tong put her picture on the Imperial Net and said she had turned from the noble ways and traditions of the organisation. Dante, they marked her for death.

The Imperial Black had been advancing on the mountains for three days. A heavy carrier brought all one thousand members of the regiment to the foot of the Himalayas, using an official override code to escape the cordon of sonic disruptors. Once the soldiers were on the ground, they were brought to order by the Enforcer and began their slow ascent. Flight paths recovered from Dmitri Romanov's former pilot had narrowed the search for the Forbidden Citadel to three peaks, but nothing more was known about its location.

Ivanov was proud to lead his men from the front. He couldn't abide armchair officers who preferred to let their men do all the hard work. Ivanov would never ask any soldier to attempt more than he was prepared to do himself. Besides, it was far quicker to make decisions from the front. Then they did not have to be relayed through a dozen intermediaries. Of course, when night fell upon the mountains – and it fell with unusual severity – the general happily retreated to his private tent. This had the benefits of heat pads beneath the ground sheet and a force barrier round its exterior to keep out the cold. Ranks must bring some privileges, Ivanov believed.

The regiment had been ascending since dawn of the previous day. There were paths and tracks, but these only allowed three men to walk abreast in many places. That had slowed progress considerably, as did carrying all their equipment. The Imperial Black had a proud tradition of self-reliance that was proving an extra burden in this challenging terrain. With winter so close, the hours of daylight were limited. Continuing at night was beyond question in this unforgiving environment. Ivanov had responded to these difficulties by leading his men at dawn each morning.

Ivanov reached the top of a rise and called for a halt, his order being passed back through the column behind. A snap of the general's fingers and the Enforcer was at his side. "What does that look like to you, major?"

There was a cluster of huts and enclosures ahead, clinging to the mountainside on a narrow plateau. The buildings were simple structures, with thick walls and low ceilings, dug into the side of the slope. Wisps of smoke rose from most of the chimneys and beasts of burden could be seen waiting inside the narrow compounds. Steps led to the settlement, the centre of each stone worn down by centuries of use. The path continued past the village and up the side of the mountain, eventually disappearing into a halo of clouds.

"A village, sir. Little or no defences. No apparent threat to us."

"Exactly. I doubt they get many visitors." The general smiled. "That should make our arrival all the more of a surprise. If this accursed citadel is nearby, the villagers should know where."

"It's doubtful they shall willingly surrender such knowledge."

Ivanov's eyes narrowed. "Then we shall have to persuade them."

. . .

"When were you planning to tell us about the Tong of the Red Hand?" Dante demanded, glaring at Mai. He returned to the rocky overhang to find the others awake and preparing for the day's trek.

"I wasn't. What I did before joining the Parliament of Shadows is no concern of yours," she said curtly.

"Funny, isn't it?" Dante said to Spatchcock and Flintlock. "She can rant about what I allegedly did to her brother, but we're not allowed to ask what she did during the war."

"I killed for the Tsar," Mai whispered.

"What?"

"I killed for the Tsar," she repeated. "We all did. The Tong of the Red Hand was employed by the Tsar to act as his secret police, hunting and executing dissidents within Imperial ranks."

"You said slave traders sold you—"

"To the Tong. I was inducted into the Red Hand, trained in its ways. I learned a hundred different martial arts. I could kill you a thousand times over, if I wanted, and you wouldn't have a chance. But I promised Lady Nikita you would remain alive until the Forbidden Citadel was found and the weapon secured."

Dante shook his head, hollow laughter catching in his throat. "And you didn't think we should know any of this?"

Mai stepped closer to him, struggling to keep her temper under control. "What difference would it make? I'm not proud of what I did during the war, but I had no choice. I tried to tell myself that by killing the Tsar's men, I was hurting the Imperial war effort. But I knew that was self-delusion, even then. Killing is killing, nothing more, nothing less. All it provided was carrion for the crows that plagued the battlefields during the war."

Dante frowned. Had he not once thought much the same thing? He pushed aside the notion to concentrate on what Mai was telling him. "Once you join the Tong, you join for life. Obey all orders from your sensei or die at his hand. Death is the only way you can ever leave."

"She's right," Spatchcock said quietly. "I had a few dealings with them before the war. Not the most cheerful band of assassins you'll ever meet."

"I dared to desert their ranks when the war was over, so my brothers and sisters in the Red Hand marked me for death."

"Why did you quit?" Dante asked.

"Because of you," she snarled. "The last Imperial I killed worked in counter-intelligence. He was reviewing an Imperial Black report on events from the Battle of Rudinshtein. I had been instructed to make the man's death look like an accident, so I suffocated him. You have to hold the victim's mouth and nostrils shut for ten minutes to make sure of total brain death. While I waited, I read the field reports he was reviewing. One talked about an attempted breakout by a group of civilians from the governor's mansion. I recognised my brother Rai from a description of the soldiers involved. You murdered him."

Dante shook his head. "You don't understand. You weren't there."

"Make me understand! Explain to me how you justified killing my brother!"

"I can't," he admitted.

"You're pathetic," she hissed. "To think I spent months searching for you after the war, searching for vengeance. I fled the Red Hand to hunt you down. I heard a whisper that the House of Zabriski had links with the Romanovs, so I confronted Lady Nikita. She persuaded me to become an operative for the Parliament of Shadows, gave me sanctuary from the Red Hand. I swore to help the cabal overthrow the Tsar and his regime. He's the only living person I hate as much as you. Lady Nikita gave my life a purpose beyond getting my revenge on you. Now I have to make sure you stay alive! I can't decide whether to laugh or cry." Mai spat into Dante's face, then stormed out into the dawn.

That explains why she hates you so vehemently, the Crest observed.

"Thanks," Dante snapped. "I had figured that much out for myself."

Sonam pushed the bubbling mixture of curds back and forth inside the broad pot, his strong hands using the flat sides of the wooden churn to keep the liquid moving. Beneath the pot burned a fire of yak dung, the year-old manure giving off a steady heat while filling the hut with heady aromas. A bag of cured yak hide hung on the wall, awaiting the hot mixture to be poured inside, but Sonam knew the curds needed another hour before they were close to becoming cheese.

His three youngest children were asleep on the bed, dozing fitfully in their brightly coloured clothes. The two girls were different ages, but the resemblance to Sonam was unmistakeable in their oval-shaped faces and dark hair. The boy took after his mother, chubby around the cheeks and with gentle eyes. She had died giving birth to him, five winters ago, leaving Sonam to raise the children alone.

A distant cry made him pause, his hands faltering at their task. Sonam listened for another scream. Perhaps Dukar was hitting his wife again. She would stay inside her hut for days at a time, eventually emerging with the shadow of a bruise still evident over one eye, or wincing in pain as she bent over a fire. Sonam had warned Dukar about this conduct. It was not fitting, not when they lived so close to the goddess. Dukar always apologised, blaming the barley beer, or some fault of his wife, Namu. "I am headman of this village," Sonam had told him last time. "I say you are lucky to have a wife. Treat her as you would treat the goddess herself." Dukar promised to hold his temper, and he had kept that promise for five months. Was he now lapsing back into the bad ways of old?

The cry came again, more of a scream and it was closer, but Sonam knew Dukar's wife had not made it; the cry came from a man. Sonam lifted the churn from the pot, then shifted it off the flames so the curd would not burn. He pushed aside the heavy curtain from the door of his hut and stepped outside to see who was crying for help. Another scream penetrated the air, drifting up from below the village. Sonam shielded his eyes to see what was happening.

A man was racing up the stone steps that led to the village, one hand nursing a red smear across his face. No, not a smear, Sonam realised, it was a cut. The man was Dukar and he had been sliced across the face with a knife or blade of some sort. Perhaps his long suffering wife had finally suffered enough and fought back, as everyone knew she would one day. If that was the case, why was Dukar running towards the village and not away?

Movement below Dukar caught the headman's eye. A black swarm was surging up the slope, like ants, consuming the hillside. Sonam had lived on this mountain for all his forty-seven years, having next to no contact with the world beyond these slopes, but even he recognised soldiers when he saw them. There was a flash of light from the front of the swarm and it was followed by the sound of a gunshot. The effect upon Dukar was startling. His hands flew out sideways and his face showed surprise, before all life left his eyes. The wife-beater's body slumped forwards.

Sonam ran to the highest point within the village, a stone cairn with a massive bronze bell mounted beside a wooden shrine to the goddess. The headman snatched up a rock and smashed it against the bell, again and again. A deep, booming sound resonated out over the village and then on down the mountain-side, towards the valley far below. "Soldiers!" Sonam bellowed between strikes of the bell. "Soldiers are coming!"

. . .

"Why didn't you tell her what happened in Rudin-shtein?" Spatchcock was crouching by Dante, trying to talk some sense into him. "Flintlock and I saw the whole thing from the wall of the Governor's mansion. You had good reason for doing what you did. She'll understand if you explain to her."

"She won't understand," Dante replied bleakly. "We all know what serpent-wire does to a person, we saw enough of it during the war, but Mai didn't. Besides, maybe I don't want her forgiveness."

Flintlock shook his head. "You want her hating you? Why, as some sort of punishment? Rai volunteered for that mission. He knew the risks, we all did. What happened to him wasn't your fault."

"I pulled the trigger."

"It was a mercy killing!"

"Mai doesn't see it that way."

"Then I'll make her understand," Flintlock said, but a popping noise in the distance stopped him. "What was that?"

"Gunfire!" Dante was already running with his Hunts-man 5000 clutched in one hand. Spatchcock and Flintlock followed him. Mai stood in the open, peering at the nearest mountain.

"It came from up there," she said. "Wind can carry sound for miles."

The four of them listened intently, waiting for another gunshot. Instead they heard a bell chiming, each strike low and resonant on the breeze.

The strikes are not in any pattern or rhythm, the Crest noted. *The clustering of chimes suggests panic more than anything else.*

A second shot was heard and the bell stopped ringing. After that nothing was audible beyond the whistling of the wind.

Dante slung his rifle over one shoulder. "We knew the Imperials were ahead of us, but we didn't know how far – until now. If we want to overtake them, we'll have to travel light. Gather any essentials we need from the yaks, then release the animals. From now on we go by foot, at speed. Any questions?" Nobody spoke. "Good. Remember why we're here." He made eye contact with Mai. "Nothing else matters at the moment. We leave in five minutes."

Sonam's hand was a crimson mess from the shot, blood seeping from the cloth he had wrapped around his gaping wound. The bullet had passed through his palm and excited out the other side. The pain was excruciating, but not fatal. Dukar had not been so fortunate. His body lay beside the path to the village, forgotten already and growing cold. Sonam hadn't had time to do anything about his dead neighbour. Indeed, he was still tying a makeshift bandage round his hand when the black-clad soldiers dragged him down the slope to join the other villagers. Hundreds of the invaders surrounded the settlement, their weapons trained on the terrified people. A broad-chested figure was barking orders to the troops, his features hidden behind a black facemask.

Soldiers ran from building to building, searching for anyone who may have been hiding. The wind had died with Dukar, so when the women and children were dragged out into the icy morning, their sobs hung in the air as clouds of steam. Another terse command from the man in the facemask and the villagers were forced into three groups – men, women and young children. Once this was achieved, the soldiers formed themselves into groups of forty, each unit taking a position around the village. The officer, whose voice had commanded them with such authority, turned to a single figure and saluted. "This is all of them, general."

"Very good, major. I want eight units deployed above, and eight units below the village, to make sure we are not disturbed. Anybody else on the mountain will have heard that damned bell, so we may yet have visitors."

"Yes, sir."

Sonam watched the major mustering his well-drilled men. These soldiers looked like professionals: skilled, disciplined, deadly. The ease with which Dukar had been despatched was ample evidence of that, along with the speed of this latest manoeuvre. But it was the glee in the general's eyes that worried Sonam most. He looked at the villagers the same way Sonam's young son looked at his toys. We're playthings to this man, nothing more and nothing less. He will keep us alive as long as we amuse him or have something that he wants. After that, we'll be cast aside. Sonam shuddered at the thought of his son's broken, discarded toys, imagining a similar fate for the village and its people.

"You, the one who was ringing the bell. What's your name?"

The headman realised he was being addressed. "Sonam. My name is Sonam."

The general smiled genially. "Call me 'sir', when you address me."

"Yes... sir."

"That's better. Now, Sonam – you showed remarkable forethought in ringing that bell, alerting the others to our arrival. Are you their leader?"

"I am headman of the village, as my father was before me."

"Sir."

"Sorry, sir."

"Don't forget again, will you?"

"No, sir."

"Very good." The general walked slowly among the villagers, studying their faces, gently patting the heads of the children, nodding to the women. All the while he continued talking to Sonam, as if passing the time of day. "You're probably wondering why we've come to your little corner of the world. Well, I will be completely honest with you, and I hope you'll extend me the same courtesy. We are here on a mission from Tsar Vladimir Makarov, Ruler of the all the Russias, and leader of the our glorious Empire." The general paused in front of Sonam. "Your people know you are governed by the Empire, don't you?"

"Yes, sir. But it leaves us in peace so…"

"Good." The general strolled to a position up the slope from the villagers, where he could look upon all of them simultaneously. "First of all, I suppose I should introduce myself. I am a general in the Tsar's forces and proud to lead the men around you. They are a regiment known as the Imperial Black, a thousand of the finest warriors ever to walk this planet. My name is Vassily Ivanov, but some of you may know me by another name – Ivanov the Terrible." He smiled. "Any questions so far?"

Nobody spoke. Sonam glanced at the faces of his neighbours. Most were too scared or bewildered to challenge the invaders. A few saw what had happened to Dukar, as everyone had heard the shooting. Guns were not permitted on the mountain, as the monks had labelled them a blasphemy against the goddess.

Ivanov raised an eyebrow, intrigued by the silence. "Very well, I shall get to the reason for our rather abrupt arrival. The Tsar has sent us here to find the Forbidden Citadel, a fortress hidden within the Himalayas. We have good reason to believe it is either on this mountain, or one of the peaks either side. Winter will soon engulf this region, so it is imperative my men and I find the citadel before the weather closes in. You will help us locate it, or suffer the consequences. Do I make myself clear?"

Still nobody spoke. Nobody replied to him. Sonam knew that the mood among the villagers was one of shock and fear. But he also knew his people would never willingly surrender the location of the Forbidden Citadel. Most of them had been within its walls and thus could see it from outside, but they were sworn to protect the goddess – with their lives, if necessary. That vow had never been put to the test until now. Sonam was confident his people would not be found wanting. They owed everything that they were and everything they had to the Mukari. Without her, they would have been swept away by the capricious peaks, their village obliterated by avalanches generations ago. But she protected them from such forces of nature.

They must do the same for her, whatever the cost.

The general's face darkened. "I asked you people a question... Do I make myself clear?" The villagers remained silent, even the youngest child refusing to speak out. Ivanov folded his arms. "I will give you one last chance to spare yourselves. I did not acquire the name Ivanov the Terrible without good reason, and those who helped me earn it paid the cost in blood. Now, who will volunteer the location?"

Sonam took a deep breath and stepped forward. The general smiled at him. "That's better. I was beginning to think none of you had the sense to save yourselves. Where is this legendary fortress to be found, headman?"

"None of us will tell you," Sonam replied. "From birth we are taught to keep this secret close to our hearts, to carry it with us to our graves. You can threaten us, you can torture us, you can murder us – it will make no difference. We shall not tell you, we shall never tell you. Better you leave the mountains now, lest our goddess smite you down."

Ivanov pursed his lips. "Does this goddess have a name?"

"None that I would tell to you."

The general nodded. "I see." He gestured at his second-in-command. "This man is a major in the Tsar's forces but, like me, he has acquired another name during his time with the Imperial Black. He is known as the Enforcer." The major stepped out of formation and snapped to attention. "He is a most observant individual, for whom the tiniest detail can offer a wealth of information. For example, at no time during my latest exchange with your headman, did he address me as 'sir'. I gave him two warnings against failing to show me the proper respect, as dictated by my rank. The Enforcer will have noticed this blatant challenge to my authority. He will also have observed the threat veiled within your headman's suggestion that I leave these slopes." The general smiled at his second-in-command. "What do you suggest I do about that, Enforcer?"

"Give him to me for an hour," the major snarled. "I will teach him respect."

"A capital suggestion," Ivanov agreed. "What is your name, headman?"

"Sonam."

"And do you have a dwelling of your own here?"

Sonam pointed at his nearby hut.

"Very good. Enforcer, take Sonam into his hut and teach him respect. Sonam, while you are suffering at the hands of the Enforcer, I want you to listen carefully to what is happening outside your hut. My men can be a savage mob when unleashed, prone to take what they want without indulging in social pleasantries. These one thousand men are a gathering of the Empire's worst murderers, rapists and torturers. While you are being given individual attention from the Enforcer, your neighbours will be used and abused by my soldiers. They will start with the men, then move on to the women and, finally, the children. If at any time you wish to stop the screaming you hear from outside your hut, you need only volunteer the location of the Forbidden Citadel. Do I make myself perfectly clear?"

Sonam nodded, his eyes sliding toward the bewildered faces of his three children. Goddess, protect them from the coming storm, he prayed. Take them from this life if you must, but let them come to no other harm.

The general rubbed his hands together, a broad smile spreading over his features. "Good, then that's settled. To make sure nobody else spoils our fun, I will have each man, woman and children partially gagged. They may cry out or scream, but none will be able to speak. That privilege is reserved solely for Sonam. He will take responsibility for the suffering of everyone else in the village and only he can stop that suffering." Ivanov nodded to the Enforcer. "Begin."

The Mukari's body was slumped to one side on her throne. She had known what was coming for the village and its people. She had carried that knowledge since the moment she was crowned as living goddess of the mountains. Again and again, the girl had wished she could warn those who worshipped her and tell them to flee before the black swarm, to surrender the location of the Forbidden Citadel when asked. But that would not change what was to happen, what had to happen. It was inevitable, as inescapable as the darkness that would engulf the citadel; that would lay waste to the heavy gates, and, which would bring doom inside this very chamber.

Carrying such knowledge, hidden deep inside her, had been burden enough. Now that destiny was becoming reality, it was all she could bear. The redeemer was coming, but they needed time to reach the citadel. The death of the village would create that time, however horrific the price to be paid. The Mukari felt herself weeping, but the tears seeping from her eyes were made of blood, the blood of those dying in her honour.

I must help them, she decided, however little good it will do in the end.

The girl's body went into convulsions for a few seconds, then lay still. Her spirit escaped from its earthly domain and floated through the thick walls, out into the early morning air. She did not feel its cold, and her mind was filled instead with the pain and terror of her subjects. A blink of light and she was standing inside Sonam's hut. The headman's body was broken and bleeding, but his eyes lit up at seeing her again. "Goddess, be with me," he whispered.

The Enforcer stood over Sonam, stripped to the waist, his body wet with crimson stains. "Where is the Forbidden Citadel?" he demanded, the same question he had asked dozens of times in the past hour while administering slow, meticulous and brutal torture.

Sonam's head lolled to one side, his tongue hanging uselessly between purple lips, light slowly draining from blackened eyes. "Mukari, have mercy on us."

My mercy shall keep you all of your days, she replied, speaking her thoughts inside Sonam's mind. *Be at peace now.*

"Thank you, goddess."

The Enforcer grabbed Sonam by the hair and shook his head vigorously. "Nobody dies without my permission, do you hear me? Not until I say you can."

Sonam, there is one more thing you must do for me.

"Yes…"

Listen carefully, and then repeat after me…

"Where is the Forbidden Citadel?" the Enforcer hissed, his facemask almost pressing against Sonam's face. A cloud of doubt passed over the headman's features, before being replaced by understanding.

"I… I will tell you," Sonam gasped. "I will tell you how to find the citadel."

"At last," the Enforcer said triumphantly. "Wait until I get the general–"

"No. She says I must tell you…"

"Who says?"

"The citadel is near the top of this mountain, on a west-facing tor. But you cannot reach it from below," Sonam said slowly, long pauses between his words, his breath was little more a rasp as it escaped his lips.

"What do you mean?"

"To find the Forbidden Citadel, you must cross an ice bridge over a mighty chasm. That is your only way..."

"What else?" the Enforcer demanded.

"When the time comes, you shall see what you seek..." Sonam's voice faded to nothing, the muscles in his face slackening.

The Enforcer shook him again, but the headman did not respond. The torturer tore off his helmet and face-mask, then pressed his ear against Sonam's chest, listening for a heartbeat. He could hear nothing beyond the terrified screams and sobbing of those villagers still alive outside the hut. A curse passed the Enforcer's lips, his ugly face contorted further by rage. He retrieved his helmet from the packed earth floor, brushing dirt from the facemask before replacing it on his head. As he did the figure of a girl was momentarily visible in sunlight that seeped into the hut.

"Who are you? What are you doing here?" the Enforcer demanded.

The Mukari stepped back, startled at her spirit form being seen by an outsider. She concentrated and was gone, her essence taking flight back to the citadel.

I lingered too long in his presence, but it was necessary. Sonam's suffering is over and the general will leave the others in peace – those that are still alive. I hope they survive beyond the darkness.

TEN

"War does not cure, but butchers."
– Russian proverb

"The weapon known as the 'White Death' was first used in the early Twentieth Century during a conflict hopefully dubbed, 'war to end all wars'. The fact that this conflict subsequently became known as the First World War is ample proof that hopes and reality are infrequent comrades in the arena of human conflict. The White Death was among the most feared weapons used in the battle for the Italian Alps. The name referred to thundering avalanches deliberately caused by enemy cannon fire. These massive falls of snow and ice consumed everything in their path, much like the war itself. Subsequent generations have rediscovered this terrible weapon, which turns nature upon the unsuspecting victim."
– Extract from *The Files of the Raven Corps*

Dante and his comrades made speedy progress from the foot of the mountain to its steeper slopes, aided by Mai's expert guidance. They were within sight of Sonam's village only hours after Ivanov and his men had departed. Mai gasped as she crested the same rise where the general had stood that morning, surveying the settlement ahead. "I recognise this place," she said in wonder.

"Why? Is that where you come from?" Dante asked.

"I'm not sure," Mai replied. "But I have been here before, I'm certain of that."

Spatchcock caught up with them, struggling to find his breath. A lifetime of vice and dubious pursuits had not prepared him for such a punishing ascent, nor for the thinness of the air at such a high altitude. "Doesn't look too lively," he said between gasps. "No smoke from the chimneys, no movement round the huts."

"Crest, can you detect whether the Tsar's men are still in the village? Whoever's in charge of the Imperials probably doesn't know we're behind them, but they might have left a rear guard to cover their flank."

There is no obvious Imperial presence. I detect a handful of life signs, several quite weak.

"But I can see dozens of huts," Mai cut in. "A village of that size is normally home to a hundred people."

"The Tsar's men don't leave many witnesses," Spatchcock said bleakly. A wheezing, groaning sound preceded the arrival of Flintlock. The Brit was even less suited to this challenging terrain than the others, thanks to an aristocratic upbringing and a lifetime of indolence. Flintlock's face was crimson and white; his armpits were soaked with sweat and his hands quivered with fatigue. He collapsed at the crest of the rise, flopping listlessly to the ground.

"I don't... think I... can go... much... farther..." he puffed and panted.

"Tough," Dante replied, pointing to the village ahead of them. "We think that's where the gunshots we heard this morning came from. Get your breath back and then join us over there. If the Tsar's men have been through this area, the villagers are going to need our help." He strode purposefully towards the settlement, Mai and Spatchcock close behind.

"I say, Dante," Flintlock protested feebly. "What if any of the Imperials are still lurking round here?"

"Then the sooner you get your bony arse moving, the better."

Spatchcock thought that the village looked like a charnel house. He had witnessed all the horrors of war while fighting with the Rudinshtein Irregulars, but still found himself unprepared for the butchery that had been visited upon the tiny mountain-side settlement. The ground was stained red from the blood shed by those who had lived here until a few hours earlier. A wet carpet of crimson tainted all snow, grass and gravel.

A pyre of corpses had been made in the centre of the village – whether by the invaders or the survivors, Spatchcock could not be sure. The local men had been the first to die, judging from the position of their bodies at the bottom of the pile. Some had been blinded, whilst others were missing fingers or limbs. The woman were the next to suffer: hair crudely hacked from their heads, fingernails torn out and their glassy eyes a mute testimony to the other indignities that they had witnessed. Spatchcock felt his stomach turn at the sight of dead children atop the pyre. But at least they were put out of their misery now, he thought.

The survivors were not so fortunate. A dozen people remained: eight children, three women and a man. Not long after Dante and the others arrived, the last man died, coughing blood and sobbing noises of pain. His tongue had been torn out and apparently fed to him by the soldiers, who laughed when their victim nearly choked to death. Two of the women were too traumatised to speak, cowering against a hut and clutching shredded clothes. The children had survived by fleeing when it became clear what was happening. Eight of them escaped the soldiers' wrath, unlike their friends and families. After the soldiers departed, the children had come back to search for loved ones among the dead and dying. The one woman capable of describing what had happened said her name was Namu. "My husband was the first to die. He was shot while trying to warn us the soldiers were coming."

"I'm sorry," Mai said.

"Don't be," Namu replied emotionlessly. "He wasn't much of a husband and he hit me whenever something went wrong. I'm glad he's dead. But as for the others... They didn't deserve what happened to them."

Mai and Spatchcock listened while the woman talked about the villagers' ordeal. Dante and Flintlock gathered the remaining corpses and added them to the pyre, beginning with the remains of Sonam from the headman's hut. Spatchcock called Dante over after hearing Namu's description of the officer leading the soldiers.

"Tell him what you told us," Spatchcock urged.

Namu pushed a strand of hair from her heart-shaped face. Both her eyes were blackened and she had several teeth missing, but Namu had not given in to the soldiers without a fight. Several of them would be walking bow-legged for days, she proudly told the newcomers. "I can't remember the officer's name. He said he was a general. He was fifty, maybe older – he had no hair, so it was hard to tell. He enjoyed watching us suffer, I could see it in his eyes. Dukar looked the same when he used to beat me, but the general didn't join in. He watched; that seemed to give him the most pleasure. He liked it if you screamed. Maybe that's why I'm still alive. I refused to make a sound, even when they took off my gag. I didn't want to give them the satisfaction of knowing they had broken me. The general got bored when I wouldn't cry, so he left me to the soldiers. The general's second-in-command interrogated our headman, Sonam, while we were tortured outside his hut. The Enforcer, that's what the general called his interrogator. He wore a mask on his face."

"What do you think?" Spatchcock said.

"Sounds like the Butcher of Rudinshtein and his flunkey," Dante said. "You can't remember his name?"

"No, but I know the name of his regiment," Namu said. "I'll never forget that, because of the colour of their uniforms. The general called his men the Imperial Black."

Dante's face darkened. "Ivanov. Vassily Ivanov."

"Ivanov the Terrible," Spatchcock murmured.

"He told us to call him Ivanov the Terrible," Namu said. She stood, using Mai's shoulder as support to rise. "I'll fetch butter for the fire," Namu said, hobbling away into one of the huts.

Mai watched the beaten and bruised woman go before rounding on Dante. "You know this Ivanov? Friend of yours, is he?"

"Anything but," Dante replied, glaring back at her. He opened his mouth to say more, but walked away instead. When she moved to follow Dante, Spatchcock grabbed her by the arm.

"Let go," she demanded.

"Shut up and listen," Spatchcock snarled.

When she refused, he softened his grip on her wrist. "Please?" Eventually Mai sat down opposite him.

"You think you know what happened to your brother, but you weren't there. You hate Dante, you blame him for Rai's death, but what are you basing that on? An Imperial report? Who do you think wrote that report? Ivanov, or one of his officers. It was propaganda, lies to hide the war crimes his regiment committed. You want the facts? Ask somebody who was there. Ask somebody who saw what happened!"

"How can I? My brother's dead and that's Dante's fault!"

Spatchcock laughed bitterly. "Dante killed your brother to save him."

"What the hell are you talking about?"

"You want the truth? Here it is: yes, your brother got caught in no-man's-land trying to save a group of civilians, but Rai volunteered for that mission. Ivanov and his men were torturing Rai when Dante intervened. The general was using serpent wire on Rai. Have you ever seen what serpent wire does to the human body?" Spatchcock demanded.

Mai nodded numbly.

"We could hear your brother screaming from our position in the Governor's mansion. Flintlock and I saw the whole thing from the barricades. Dante had led a diversionary attack against the Imperial forces, in the hope of giving Rai's group a chance to escape. When Dante saw what Ivanov was doing to Rai, the captain did the only decent thing. He shot your brother to save Rai from any more of that torment. I'd have done the same myself, if I wasn't such a coward." Spatchcock shook his head. "That wasn't murder – it was a mercy killing."

"But after the war... why did Dante flee Rudinshtein?"

"You think he had a choice?" Spatchcock gestured at the bodies, the blood strewn around them, the blank-faced children left behind by the Imperial Black. "Look what Ivanov and his men did to this village in a few hours. After the war, that bastard was given Rudinshtein as his private plaything. For three years the Imperial Black have been doing this to the province and its people – murder and rape, looting and pillaging. If someone in Rudinshtein dared say the name Nikolai Dante, they were tortured and publicly executed. Every crop was burned, every treasured possession stolen, every whisper of resistance crushed. The general doesn't soil his own hands, of course. He lets his men do the dirty work. They've got a major, called the Enforcer, who carries out the executions personally. He's almost as sick as his master." Spatchcock locked eyes with Mai's, trying to make sure she realised the importance what he was saying. "Rudinshtein was poor before the war, but its people were happy when Dante was in charge. Now the province is a bankrupt police state, thanks to the general and his underlings. Do you know how many times Flintlock and I have had to stop Dante from going back to Rudinshtein to attack Ivanov?"

"Why? Why did you stop him?"

"Dante is one man – he's larger than life, but still only one man. How can one man hope to stand against an army and hope to win? You've seen how he attacks first and thinks last. Going back to Rudinshtein would be a suicide mission. Dante wouldn't last a day. So, he stays away while thousands suffer because he isn't there to defend them, but knowing that tens of thousands would be summarily executed if he tried to intervene. Have you any idea of the guilt he carries for what's been done to Rudinshtein in his name?"

"I didn't know," Mai murmured, her face coloured by shame. "How could I?"

Spatchcock glared at her sad but beautiful features. "Next time, try getting your facts straight before you start making accusations. Dante's no saint, but his heart's in the right place."

"He said the same thing about you and Flintlock."

"Well, I never said he was a good judge of character." Spatchcock looked across at Dante heaving the last corpse on to the pyre. "Now Ivanov and Dante are on the same mountain, both looking for the Forbidden Citadel. If one of them leaves here alive, it'll be a bloody miracle."

Namu emerged from her hut carrying a large bowl, steam rising from it. She spoke quietly to the cluster of children and they ran to the other buildings. Within a few minutes each of them emerged with similar bowls. The smallest child carried a burning taper, with a flame dancing around its end. Once all of them were ready, the solemn procession approached the pyre, Namu leading the way. She emptied the contents of her bowl over the pile of corpses, then stepped aside and motioned for the children to follow her example. Spatchcock and Mai had joined Dante and Flintlock to one side of the pyre, watching as each child poured viscous liquid over the dead villagers.

"What is that?" Flintlock asked.

"Yak butter," Mai replied quietly. "The animals provide much of the essentials for life here: wood, meat, skins, cheese. But they also provide something essential for death. The butter is fuel for the funeral pyre. We do not bury our dead, we burn them."

"I say, is that wise?" Flintlock worried. "The Imperials are bound to see the smoke rising from the fire. It might warn them that we're coming."

"Let them see," Dante muttered.

The last child threw her taper on top of the pyre and the flames quickly spread, engulfing the corpses and belching black smoke into the sky. Namu beckoned Mai to join the other villagers and handed her a broken tree branch.

"What is it?" Mai asked.

"Juniper. The white smoke from its burning creates a road between the earth and the sky, so the spirits of the dead may find their way."

Mai closed her eyes and whispered to herself before adding the juniper branch to the funeral pyre. She watched intently as pale clouds rose, mingling with the darker fumes from the fire. Around her the children were singing a sad lament.

Further up the slope, the Enforcer noted the plume of smoke and alerted Ivanov to it. The general waved away suggestions of sending a squad down to investigate. "We're close to our quarry, major, and you want to go backwards? That is why you shall never attain my rank or status. The bold soldier always goes forwards, no matter what the cost or consequence!" Ivanov continued leading his regiment up the vertiginous slope.

The Enforcer remained where he was, studying the column of black and grey that swayed in the air currents that flowed around the mountain. If what the headman had said was true, they could not be far from the ice bridge. Cross that, and the Forbidden Citadel was within reach. Behind his facemask the major frowned, still per-turbed by the vision of that ghostly girl he had seen in the hut. The sooner this mission was behind them all, the better.

It was mid-afternoon by the time the funeral pyre's flames started to die down. Spatchcock had been busy keeping the children entertained with suitably censored tales of his adventures, assisted by a less enthusiastic Flintlock, while Mai helped Namu tend to the other survivors. Dante stayed by the fire, staring into the burning mass of bodies, as if transfixed by it. Even the Crest was unable to tear him away from the grim spectacle.

It was Mai who suggested the time had come to resume their quest for the citadel. Spatchcock and Flintlock agreed with her but Dante remained unmoved. Mai joined him in front of the pyre, watching the reflection of the flames in Dante's eyes. "It doesn't matter how long you stare at those bodies, Nikolai. You can't bring them back. None of us can. What's done is done."

He frowned. "Spatchcock told you what happened to Rai, didn't he?"

"Yes. Why didn't you?"

"Would you have believed me?"

"Probably not," Mai conceded.

"Besides, your hatred made you stronger, drove you on. We needed that anger. We still do."

"Don't worry, I have plenty of anger, more than enough to keep going. And I have a new target for my hatred." Dante grimaced. "Ivanov."

"Yes. Spatchcock thinks it unlikely you and the general will leave the Himalayas alive."

"Spatch is smarter than he looks."

"Are you going to let your hatred for Ivanov cloud your judgement?" Mai asked. "Spatchcock told me what the general did in Rudinshtein after the war."

"Don't worry," Dante replied. "I know where my priorities lie. We've got to reach the citadel before Ivanov. If that butcher gets holds of the weapon, whatever it is... the consequences don't bear thinking about."

"Then it's past time we moved on. Once we're gone, Namu will lead the other survivors off the mountain. There's another village where they can take refuge. If the Imperials come back this way, the survivors will be safe from them."

"Good."

"Namu says the village headman was tortured for an hour to get the location of the citadel. She overheard the Enforcer telling Ivanov they should climb up this slope, then cross an ice bridge to reach a tor on the western side of the mountain. Namu has never been to the citadel, but she knows that it is located somewhere on that tor."

"Then we know what path to follow–"

"No," Mai cut in. "She says it is quicker to climb down for an hour from here, then take a smaller path that leads up the side of the tor. Namu believes the headman deliberately sent the soldiers by the longest route."

"Why? He couldn't know we were coming."

"Not him – the goddess of the mountain."

Dante raised an eyebrow at Mai. "Excuse me?"

"My people believe each mountain is a goddess, just as they believe each lake is sacred. But this mountain is home to a living goddess. Namu says the goddess knows we are coming, as she knew the soldiers were coming. She knows the past, the present and the future."

"Sounds like a woman after your own heart, Crest," Dante commented.

A living goddess? This will be fascinating.

Mai pointed at the sun dipping towards the distant horizon. "We must get moving if we are to find the new path and suitable shelter before darkness falls."

"Agreed." Dante smiled as she moved away from him. "So I'm not on your list of those marked for death anymore?"

Mai stopped abruptly. "Keep thinking about my body like that and I'll be perfectly happy to castrate you free of charge." She marched away, muttering under her breath darkly.

Mai may not want you dead anymore, the Crest said, *but you would do well not to antagonise her needlessly.*

"I'm keeping some spice in our relationship," Dante replied. "Nothing worse than a love affair that's gone stale."

Love affair? The two of you have never even kissed. That's hardly a relationship, even by your rather limited standards.

"But she's thought about it. Any woman who protests that loudly about my appreciation of her backside must fancy me, right?"

Did you ever think Mai might not want to be seen as a sex object?

"No."

I rest my case.

"Can I help it if my libido overwhelms my better judgement sometimes?"

Sometimes?

"Alright, frequently."

Dante, your libido has gotten you into more trouble than your mouth and fists combined. In matters of the heart, your groin always takes precedence.

"You say that like it's a bad thing."

Spatchcock whistled from the other side of the village. "Dante, time to go!"

The renegade gave the funeral pyre a final look. "You will be avenged," he vowed before hurrying to join the others.

Dusk was approaching by the time Ivanov and his men reached the ice bridge. During their ascent, the soldiers had marvelled at the mighty chasm that opened up between the mountain they were climbing and its secondary peak, to the west. The tor was covered in snow and ice, but its slopes were considerably steeper and more challenging. At the highest point was a jagged stab of snow that resembled a broken tooth against the darkening, blue horizon.

Ivanov studied the terrain with interest, his inner doubts silenced by what he saw. The headman was right to send them this way. The general had harboured suspicions about the directions, but getting so many men up to the tor would have been almost impossible over such terrain. Of course, that was before Ivanov saw the way over the chasm that plunged between the two peaks. Such a crossing gave pause to any sane person.

The ice bridge was two metres wide, at most. It was difficult to tell how deep the accumulation of ice was, perhaps a metre and a half. Certainly, it should be sufficient to sustain the weight of the regiment crossing the precipitous chasm, if not all the soldiers at the same time. Ivanov called for the Enforcer and together they calculated the various factors.

"The men will have to go in two's," the Enforcer surmised. "The chasm is some three hundred metres wide at this point. Allow a metre between each row to spread the weight evenly, and we should be able to cross the divide before nightfall. Those who go first can begin establishing our shelters for the night."

"Very well," the general replied, satisfied with these calculations. "I will lead the first group of two hundred across. When we reach the other side, you may bring the remaining men over."

"Sir, let me go first," the Enforcer suggested. "This ice bridge is an exposed position from which it is impossible to quickly escape – the perfect place for an ambush. If an enemy should choose to strike against us–"

Ivanov waved aside such notions. "You saw how weak those villagers were, no fight in any of them. Are you seriously expecting some secret army to be hidden in these mountains?"

"No, sir, of course not. But I would prefer–"

"Your preferences are not my concern," the general warned. "I have given an order and it is to be obeyed without question. Do I make myself clear?"

"Yes, sir."

"Very well. Assemble the first group by the ice bridge. In the meantime, I will test the crossing on my own." Ivanov marched briskly to the edge of the ice bridge and peered into the looming chasm below. He could see where the snow ended and the rocks began, but one slip would certainly be fatal. Such were the perils of leading from the front, Ivanov reminded himself.

He stepped out on to the ice. Its surface was wet and slippery, but not impassable. The general stamped on the bridge several times, gradually putting more and more weight on the crossing. Satisfied with its solidity, he strode out on to the ice. Ivanov waited until he was halfway across before calling back to his men.

"As you can see, the ice bridge is perfectly safe. However, as a precaution, you shall begin crossing in sections of two hundred, with no more than three sections on the bridge at any time. I will see you men on the other side!" He continued his journey and reached the tor's slopes within a minute. The first section of two hundred was already halfway across, with the Enforcer leading a second section on to the ice bridge. Soon there would be nothing to stop the thousand-strong Imperial Black regiment from finding the Forbidden Citadel.

Gylatsen smiled as he entered the Mukari's throne room. He was one of the few monks allowed to visit her on a daily basis. Most of his brethren were serious men, their faces heavy with the burden of responsibility and sacred duty. But Gylatsen had never forgotten the joy of being a child and he always tried to share that joy with their deity. Yes, the Mukari was their living goddess, but she was also a seven year-old – a child who needed to play and have fun. So Gylatsen let his natural exuberance shine through in her presence, never remonstrating with her for smiling or laughing as Khumbu was prone to do.

After completing the ritual bowing that was required of all those who came into the throne room, Gylatsen approached the Mukari's throne. "Goddess, I am preparing the evening meal. I understand you enjoyed the broth I made. Perhaps you want something similar?"

"I'm not hungry," the girl replied. To Gylatsen's surprise she was standing by the windows. Normally the black-haired monk instinctively knew her position in the room, even though he was blind. But his goddess was fond of teasing him by projecting her spirit out of her body. She could be quite the trickster when the mood took her, yet the sombreness of her tone belied any tricks.

"But, Mukari, you must eat," Gylatsen insisted, swivelling to face where her voice had come from. "Going hungry is not good for you."

"I do not want for food," she said quietly.

Gylatsen could hear a gentle sobbing. "Goddess, are you crying? What saddens you?"

"I saw the villagers dying and I could do nothing to protect them. They were beyond my power to help."

"What villagers? Forgive me, Mukari. I do not understand."

"I know, Gylatsen." She walked gently towards him and rested one small hand against his rough, calloused palm. "I shall show you."

And Gylatsen saw what the Mukari had witnessed and the light went from his face too. After he had seen enough, the monk pulled his hand away. "Forgive me, Goddess. I did not know."

"Gylatsen, I need you to stand guard outside the throne room," the girl said, her voice devoid of feeling. "Let none enter, not even Khumbu. I must concentrate now, and any distraction will undo that."

"Yes, goddess." He bowed deeply, then withdrew. Though he was blind, the vision of what the soldiers had done repeated itself endlessly in Gylatsen's mind's eye, hammering at his heart.

Inside her room, the Mukari remained still, her breathing becoming increasingly shallow, all her energies concentrated inwards. Finally, when she felt in complete control, the girl clapped her hands together – once, twice, three times. The sound they made grew louder, echoing around the walls of the throne room, building relentlessly. With the final collision of skin upon skin, a mighty rumble joined the sounds, as if the mountain was grinding against itself, harsh and abrasive. Still, the noise got louder, the echoes repeating. The Mukari was oblivious to the cacophony building around her, not noticing the paintings falling from the walls, the candles and small statues toppling over.

In the corridor outside Gylatsen kept his back to the door, both hands clamped over his ears to block the booming sound leaking from inside. Khumbu and several of his brethren appeared, bellowing to be heard above the cacophony, but Gylatsen refused to move from the door. He pushed away any hands that tried to pull him aside. The citadel walls were vibrating: floorboards rippled and shuddered beneath their feet. Whatever was happening, it threatened to tear the fortress apart unless unleashed.

In her room the Mukari smiled, picturing what was about to happen, seeing its effect. She should not rejoice in this, the goddess told herself, but it was no more than they deserved. Content with her choice, she steered the noise to the balcony doors. They were flung open and the noise escaped into the dusk, searching for a target, bouncing from peak to peak in the mighty mountain range. The Mukari nodded and the noise buried itself in the eastern side of the tor. The throne room's balcony doors swung gently shut and the cacophony was audible no more. But its effects were about to reveal themselves with terrifying ferocity.

Ivanov stared into the sky, trying to locate the source of the noises, which were booming overhead. It sounded like a barrage of distant cannon fire. The noise abruptly died away, not even an echo remaining in the air. Ivanov was determined not to be distracted from the task in hand. The first unit of two hundred men had safely crossed the ice bridge, and the Enforcer was already two-thirds of the way across with the next section. Beyond him a third section was resolutely following in their footsteps, while a fourth was stepping on to the ice bridge. Another few minutes and all of the Imperial Black troopers would have crossed the chasm.

It was the Enforcer who first saw what was coming. He gave an order for his men to run across the bridge. The general saw this and demanded an answer from his second-in-command, but the Enforcer did not reply, pointing at the sky instead. Ivanov looked up and staggered back a step. Under the cover of darkness he could see only white and grey, as if the mountain was tumbling towards them. The first wave of ice and snow struck seconds later, punching through the ice bridge like fists, smashing the structure into fragments. Hundreds of soldiers were crushed to death in an instant. More fell to their doom, screaming in pain and fear. Ivanov hugged the side of the mountain, bracing himself for the moment when the avalanche claimed him, too.

Flintlock had been happy to lead the others back down the mountain path, but soon lagged behind when they took the side path that led up the adjoining peak. His whining was alleviated solely by his shortness of breath and the thin air. "Please... Can't we stop... for the night?" he whimpered. Further up the slope, Mai paused at a small plateau in the shadow of an overhanging cliff face.

"Remind me, what talents does Flintlock add to your gang of three?" she asked Dante tersely. "You have the Crest and all it adds to your capabilities. Spatchcock proved himself an adept pickpocket on the *Okiya*, and his body odour is no doubt a useful weapon in unarmed combat. But what does his lordship do?"

Dante smirked. "He makes the rest of us look good."

Not an easy task in any circumstances, the Crest added.

Spatchcock opened his mouth to speak, but was drowned out by a thunderous noise in the sky. He and Dante tried to see what had caused the cacophony, but Flintlock was already running for the concave space beneath the cliff. As the sound died away, he screamed at them to hurry.

"Why?" Dante asked. "There's nothing up there to worry us, it's a clear blue..." His words petered out as he glanced upwards once more. "Hey, the sky's turned white."

That's not the sky, that's an avalanche. Dante, evasive action – now!

"An avalanche? But..." He realised Spatchcock and Mai were hurrying towards the safety of the overhang. "Diavolo!" Dante sprinted after them, the first falls of snow and ice already slamming into the mountainside around him.

ELEVEN

"A caress is better than a fist."
– Russian proverb

"The Dante campaign is perhaps one of the most famous advertising extravaganzas of the pre-war era. Over a period of months the same image of the notorious Romanov renegade were plastered across billboards, airships and almost every other imaginable space. The picture showed Dante stark naked, but for a pair of underpants incongruously positioned atop his head. On either side of him were two curvaceous women, subsequently identified as prostitutes from the infamous House of Sin brothel. Dante was apparently unaware the image of him was being captured, otherwise he might have arranged for his genitals to have appeared larger or in a more flattering arrangement.

Most industry commentators believed that Tsarist sympathisers, who were using Dante to make the House of Romanov look ridiculous by association, funded the relatively harmless campaign. But to this day rumours persist that it was the Tsar's daughter, Jena Makarov, who paid for the campaign from her own allowance. Whatever the source of its funding, the picture of Dante's flaccid groin remains one of the most remembered images from the pre-war era. Despite the amazingly unimpressive genitalia displayed, the notorious rogue continues to exert an attraction for an inordinate number of women who simply should know better."

– Extract from *Nikolai Dante: A Character Assassination*, various contributors

Dante got within a metre of the cave and dived the rest of the way, throwing the Huntsman 5000 in front of him. He narrowly escaped being crushed by a massive section of the shattered ice bridge as it thundered into the ground where he had been standing moments before. Spatchcock and Flintlock helped Dante to his feet while Mai watched the spectacle outside, both hands over her ears to block out the deafening sound.

The avalanche continued, the area beyond the cliff's overhang resembling a waterfall of snow and ice. The utter whiteness was broken by bodies flying past, the familiar all-black uniforms leaving little doubt of their origins. Most terrifying of all was the noise, as if the mountains themselves were roaring, threatening to crush them alive. Wave upon wave of debris kept hurtling past until, finally, the sound and fury abated.

Dante smiled bleakly. "That was a demonstration of why we keep Flintlock around. He has a particularly strong sense of self-preservation."

"Dante's right," Spatchcock added. "If there's danger nearby, chances are his lordship is already running in opposite direction."

"I resent that remark," Flintlock protested.

"You resemble that remark, more like."

"Now see here, you vile little guttersnipe. I am a lord of the Britannic realm and I am not to be addressed with such crass insensitivity!"

"Former lord of the realm," Spatchcock reminded him. "What did you do to be deported from own your country, exactly?"

Rolling her eyes in exasperation, Mai pressed a hand against the wall of snow and ice that covered its entrance. Dante joined her, extending a cyborganic sword from his left fist and plunging it as far as he could into the mass of solid white. "Crest, can you analyse how deep this wall of snow and ice is?"

At least twenty metres. Unfortunately, you were near the bottom of the mountain when the avalanche happened.

"I'm not complaining. It gave us enough time to get out of the way. The Imperials weren't so lucky."

True, but the snow and ice stopped when it reached the bottom of the mountain. Everything that fell from above accumulated outside your impromptu shelter. It will be weeks before the debris melts and you will never dig your way out.

"According to the Crest, the good news is we survived the avalanche," Dante told the others.

"And the bad news?" Flintlock asked warily.

"We'll starve to death before a thaw enables us to escape," Mai replied.

Spatchcock picked up the discarded rifle. "Can't you shoot a way out?"

"It's a rifle, not a cannon," Dante said. "The weight of snow would fill any hole the bullets created." He withdrew his cyborganic sword from the white wall. "Maybe those soldiers we saw were lucky. At least they died quickly."

Further up the tor, Ivanov was assessing his losses. More than half his regiment was still crossing the ice bridge when it shattered beneath the avalanche. Fortunately, the Enforcer had reached this side of the chasm before the avalanche hit. But close to seven hundred members of the Imperial Black had been taken in less than a minute, the greatest single loss of life in regimental history.

"Most of the men are in shock," the Enforcer told Ivanov. "They have lost comrades, brothers-in-arms. They need time to mourn."

"They are soldiers in the Imperial Black, they will do their duty," the general retorted. "Don't tell me what my men need!"

"Forgive me, sir. I did not mean to second guess you, I merely–"

"Stop," Ivanov commanded. "There is nothing to forgive, major. You were thinking of the men, as any good second-in-command should." The general rested a hand on his second in command's shoulder. "Night is almost upon us, we can go no further tonight. Tell the men to make camp as best they can. Once that is established, you and I will go among them, giving what comfort we can. If a regiment's officers do not support the rank and file at such a time, we do not deserve their support in battle."

"Yes, sir." The major hesitated before speaking again. "Sir, how do you rate our chances of success after so grievous a loss?"

"We still have over three hundred men. I believe they are more than enough to deal with whatever awaits us."

"I know the men will follow you into hell if they have to," the Enforcer agreed. "But that avalanche... it was almost as if the mountain was guarding its secrets."

Ivanov snorted derisively. "Superstitious nonsense! In the morning we will press on. I do not believe an entire fortress can remain hidden from us, no matter what mystical force may conceal its location. The Imperial Black shall prevail!"

Spatchcock was failing to start a fire, much to Flintlock's chagrin. "What's the point of doing that?" the Brit asked despairingly. "Even if you manage to get that puny pile of twigs and moss to burn, we haven't any fuel to feed the fire. Besides, where is the smoke going to go? Had you thought about that?"

"If you've got a better idea for keeping us warm then spit it out, your lordship," Spatchcock hissed back.

"I didn't say I had a better idea, I was merely–"

"Pissing all over mine!"

"Could the two of you be quiet for more than a minute?" Mai pleaded, her face drained of colour. She was pacing back and forth in the cramped cave, fingertips urgently massaging her temples. "My head feels like it's about to split open and listening to the pair of you is not helping!"

One big, happy family, the Crest observed pithily.

"Don't you start," Mai snarled at Dante.

"Hey, I didn't say anything," he protested.

"Well, try not to think so loud," she replied. "Better yet, try not to think at all. That shouldn't be hard for someone like you."

Charming.

"You said it," Dante agreed. He was sat with his back against a rock wall. "Strange, it must be dark outside, but it's still light in here."

The rocks are rich with a luminescent ore, the Crest explained.

Mai stopped pacing to glare at Dante. "Have you any idea how annoying it is to be constantly bombarded with the know-it-all comments from your Crest?" The beautiful Himalayan swayed slightly on her feet. "Just shut up, will you? Just–" Mai's eyes rolled back into her head.

"Bojemoi!" Dante dived forward as her legs crumpled, catching her lithe body in his arms as she fell. He eased her gently to the ground.

"Is it the same as before?" Spatchcock asked.

All the symptoms appear the same.

"We need to know what's causing this," Dante said. He pressed one hand against Mai's cold, clammy forehead. "Nothing's happening. I can't–"

Dante blinked, but when he opened his eyes the surroundings were different. Spatchcock, Flintlock and the cave were gone. Mai was still lying in front of him, but now she was a young girl, perhaps five years old, lying on a floor of broad, black-stained wooden beams. Around them wafted scents of cinnamon and hot butter. She opened her eyes and smiled. "Hello. Who are you?"

"My name's Nikolai. Nikolai Dante."

The child giggled. "You're silly."

"Why do you say that?"

"You look so pale," the girl replied. "Don't you ever go out in the sun?"

Dante took his hand away from Mai's forehead. Beneath where his palm had rested was a third eye, red against black. The girl was dressed in a simple white robe that made her bronzed skin tone even more apparent. She was right, the difference in their pigmentation was noticeable – his pale pink, her skin the rich brown typical of those raised in the Himalayas.

Mai gestured at the room around them. "This is my new home. If I pass my last test, the monks will make me the Mukari."

"The Mukari?"

The girl giggled. "Goddess of the mountains. Don't you know anything?"

Apparently not.

"Crest?" Dante glanced around the red and gold chamber. "Is that you?"

I am a Crest, but not the one with which you are bonded.

"I don't understand. What is this place? Where am I?"

"In my room," Mai replied, playfully punching him in the arm. But her face was changing: cheekbones became more prominent, while the rest of her body blossomed into that of a young woman. "Nikolai, what's happening to me?"

"You're getting older," he realised. "You're becoming a woman..."

The girl screamed, clutching at her abdomen, face contorting with pain. "It hurts," she gasped through gritted teeth. "Make it stop – please!"

"I can't. It's called growing pains."

Mai grabbed his hand, her fingernails digging into the skin. "Don't let them take me. Don't let them touch me!" A pool of blood appeared on the floor, seeping out from beneath her.

A door was shoved open behind Dante, and three men in saffron robes burst into the room. All were blind, their eye sockets hollow, yet they stared accusingly at Mai on the floor.

"She is bleeding," one of the monks announced.

"The goddess has left this earthly vessel," another intoned.

The monk who had opened the door regarded the girl coldly. "Her time is passed. She is nothing to us now – less than nothing. Her mind must be emptied. She must be cast out forever. She must be purified before the next Mukari can be chosen."

"Purified," the other monks echoed.

The three monks advanced on Mai. "Let the cleansing begin," their leader said. The trio walked though Dante as if he was a phantom.

"Don't let them do this Nikolai," Mai pleaded. "Not again."

Dante flailed at the holy men without effect. The monks surrounded Mai, trapping her in the centre of the room, their lips muttering a language Dante could not recognise. As the trio touched the screaming Mai, she faded to nothing.

So it was for her. So it is for all the Mukari and has ever been thus.

"What did they do to her?" Dante demanded.

What they believed was necessary.

"Who are you? Show yourself!"

"Show yourself!" Dante shouted, his hands bunched into fists. Spatchcock was holding him back from attacking the wall of ice and snow. He stopped fighting and let his anger subside.

"Who were you shouting at?" Spatchcock asked. "You were ranting and raving at thin air. His lordship got in the way and you nearly knocked him out cold."

Dante saw the blond Brit sprawled on the rocky floor of the cave, one hand clasped over a bloody nose. "Flintlock, I'm sorry. I didn't realise..."

The supine figure acknowledged the apology. "I'll survive – just."

Mai stirred on the ground, her eyes fluttering open. Dante crouched beside her, resting one of his hands atop hers. "Don't worry. You passed out again."

She winced. "The closer we get to the citadel, the closer my headaches appear too."

"I saw inside your mind again," Dante said.

"I know," Mai nodded. "I saw what you did this time, as if I was watching everything through your eyes. Thank you for trying to defend me."

"For all the good it did."

"But you tried." She stroked the side of Dante's face. "That means more than you know."

He noticed the others watching them, so Dante recounted what he had witnessed. Afterwards Spatchcock looked at Mai with a new respect. "You were some sort of living goddess?"

"The Mukari, yes. It's a religious tradition that stretches back many, many centuries in this part of Asia."

Dante had been thinking about the vision's implications. "Crest, the gaps in Mai's memory – could they be man-made?"

Psychic blocks to stop her recalling her time as this goddess? It's possible. But that would require telepaths of unusual strength and ability, to say the least.

"That might also explain the headaches," Flintlock observed after the Crest's words had been relayed. "They could be a defence mechanism, to stop Mai from returning to the citadel or even from trying to remember her childhood."

The others looked at Flintlock, all equally surprised.

He folded his arms sulkily. "I'm not a complete moron, you know."

"There's still one thing I don't get," Spatchcock said. "If that wasn't your Crest in the vision, whose was it?"

"One of the other Romanov Crest's, I guess, but what would they be doing here?" Dante shrugged. "Crest, can you identify others like you?"

Of course. Each of my kind has a specific signature, like a fingerprint. I know all the other Romanov Crests as you would know your own siblings.

"So, which one of my noble family is nearby?"

The Crest in Mai's vision was not one I recognised. It was distinctly different from all the Romanov Crests, and much more powerful. Whoever is bonded with it possesses a weapon of formidable force.

"That must be the secret hidden inside the citadel," Mai realised. "The Mukari must be bonded with a Crest – that's what makes her a living goddess."

"But how is it transferred from one Mukari to the next?" Spatchcock asked.

"Good question," Dante agreed. "The Romanov Crests bond with their host for life. When the host dies, the Crest does too. This Crest must be different."

"There's only one problem with all of this," Flintlock pointed out testily. "We may know what the citadel's secret weapon is, but we're still trapped in this bloody cave, aren't we?"

Dante blew between his hands before rubbing them together. "We're exhausted too, we need to get some sleep."

"How?" Flintlock protested. "We'll freeze."

"Then we'll have to sleep together, share our body warmth." Dante regarded his three companions in the cave. "I'll bunk down with Mai. Flintlock, you can snuggle up with–"

"Never!" the Brit protested. "I'd rather freeze to death than spend a night in the arms of this vile, repugnant and malodorous streak of urine!"

Spatchcock smiled. "Is he talking about me?"

"Yes, and not even behind your back," Dante replied. "Fine, if you two want to become human ice blocks, be my guest. Mai, you're welcome to choose another sleeping partner if you want."

She looked at the three men in turn before pointing at a grinning Dante. "But remember," she warned, "if I feel your hands wandering anywhere they shouldn't in the night, you'll lose all sense of touch before morning. Permanently."

"Fine by me," he agreed hurriedly, already unrolling the bedding from their few possessions. Dante let Mai get between the blankets first, then clambered in behind her, pressing against her back. He wrapped one arm around her in a hug, trying to still the sudden warmth in his groin. After much grumbling and griping from both men, Flintlock and Spatchcock agreed to share bedding for the night. They settled down together, the Brit insisting he face away from Spatchcock to avoid death by suffocation.

Dante closed his eyes and left himself drift off, trying not to inhale the sweet scent of the woman pressing against him. Within minutes he could hear snoring from the other side of the cave, and Mai's breathing settled into a deep, steady rhythm. Despite his best intentions, Dante could not help wondering what it would be like to know her better. Perhaps when this mission was over...

"I suggest you put that rifle to one side," Mai whispered, surprising him.

"I though you were asleep."

"I was, until you starting digging that thing into my back. I'll never get any rest while that's in here with us."

"The Huntsman 5000 is over there," Dante said sheepishly, pointing at the nearby weapon.

Mai sighed. "Then what's sticking into my–" Her words stopped abruptly. Dante could feel her squirming away, but the bedding kept them locked together. "It's no good, we'll have to turn over. That's safer for both of us."

Dante reluctantly did as he was told. Soon Mai was curled into his back, her thighs pressing against the back of his legs, her breath warming his neck, her pouting breasts creating two circles of warmth either side of his spine. Fuoco, this is going to be a long night, he thought.

Concentrate on the sound of Flintlock snoring instead, the Crest suggested. *You often say his voice could put anyone into a coma. Perhaps his snoring will have the same effect?*

Dante gasped as a hand closed around his groin. "Tell your Crest I'm trying to get some sleep too," Mai whispered. "If he doesn't shut up, I'll squeeze what I'm holding until your eyes pop out. Is that clear?"

"Understood," Dante squeaked quietly.

Dante snapped awake to find the hairs on the back of his neck standing up. His eyes searched the cave, but could see no obvious cause. Spatchcock and Flintlock were engaged in a mutual snoring contest nearby, while Mai was lying beside him, her face serene and beautiful in sleep. I must have turned over during the night, Dante realised. Temptation got the better of him and he leaned closer to steal a kiss. To Dante's surprise Mai responded warmly, her lips moving against his, her tongue sliding into his mouth. One of her hands slid across his body. Slowly her eyes opened and she smiled.

"I thought you hated me," Dante whispered. "You wanted to murder me."

"I changed my mind," she responded with a mischievous glint in her eyes. Mai kissed him again, her hand now sliding down his chest.

"You should always give someone a second chance," Dante agreed, his hands slowly, deliciously exploring her body. "I like to think that–" He stopped abruptly.

Mai paused, her face displaying confusion. "What's wrong, Nikolai?"

He hushed her with a finger over the lips, before craning his head to look at Spatchcock and Flintlock. The two men were watching them intently, lascivious expressions on their faces.

"I say, don't stop on our account," Flintlock exclaimed.

"That's right," Spatchcock urged. "Nothing I like better than a good peep show. Warm the cockles of my heart, and the heart of my–"

Dante, I'm detecting a presence nearby, the Crest interjected.

"I'm aware of that. It's two presences and both of them are in trouble."

I wasn't talking about your disreputable travelling companions, I was–

Suddenly the cave was ablaze with brilliant white light. A girl was floating in the centre it, her legs and arms folded into the lotus position. She was wearing a rich gown of red and gold, while long black hair spilled from beneath an elaborate headdress. In the centre of her forehead was a third eye, vermillion against a black background. She smiled at the surprised group benevolently.

I was trying to tell you about her, the Crest concluded.

When the girl spoke, her voice was audible in their minds, not their ears. *Your Crest is correct: you are not alone here. You are never alone on this mountain, not while the Mukari sits on the holy throne. But a day is upon us all when the reign of the living goddess ends forever – unless you intercede. A blackness is coming, when the snows of this peak will run red with blood.*

TWELVE

"Winds erode mountains, words rouse people."
          – Russian proverb

"In the ranks of the Imperial Black, many crimes and misdemeanours, which would never be permitted within other regiments bearing the Tsar's emblem, are tolerated. Rape, murder, looting – all are perfectly acceptable behaviour for these troops, once the commanding officer has given his men leave to indulge their baser instincts. However, there is one crime that even the worst elements within the Imperial Black consider beyond redemption: cowardice. General Vassily Ivanov makes it known to all new recruits that any soldier who runs from the enemy can expect to be executed by their own brothers-in-arms. Such ferocity of will has created an army that never turns away, never backs down and never surrenders, no matter how overwhelming the foe or how uneven the odds in any conflict."
          – Extract from *The Files of the Raven Corps*

Dante used a hand to shield his eyes from the Mukari's blinding apparition, squinting at her through a gap in his fingers. The ghostly girl floating inside the snow-bound cave looked similar to Mai, but her features were sharper and her eyes less hooded. This must be the current Mukari, Dante decided, projecting her spirit into here from the Forbidden Citadel.

I am doing all I can to hold back the darkness engulfing my realm, the Mukari told Dante and the others. *But I cannot contain the forces sent against me much longer. You must reach the citadel soon, or else all is lost.*

"How can we?" Mai asked. "The avalanche entombed us in this cave."

There is another way, faster than climbing the side of this mountain. The girl clapped her hands three times, and a cracking sound tore the air. Flintlock and Spatchcock scrambled to safety as the rock wall behind them split apart, releasing a cloud of dust into the air. When this dissipated a stairway was revealed, its steps winding upwards into the heart of the mountain. *Climb the stairs,* the Mukari said, *but hurry. Even I cannot sustain them indefinitely.*

Dante was first to his feet, hastily gathering his possessions. "Get your things together," he told the others. "Now!"

You shall not need bedding or spare clothes where you are going. All will be provided for you. Bring only your wits and your weapons.

"Flintlock'll be travelling light then," Spatchcock cackled and received a clout round the ears.

Dante shoved his two comrades towards the staircase, then stood aside for Mai to go next. "After you?"

"Better if you're in front," she replied. "That way you'll focus on the job in hand and not on my arse."

"But it's such a nice ass," Dante said, smirking.

The Mukari cleared her throat, glaring at him pointedly.

"Sorry, force of habit," he replied before taking to the stairs.

Mai lingered in the cave briefly, staring at the girl's apparition. "You look like me – when I was your age." She strode to the staircase and began climbing upwards, taking two steps at a time. The doorway in the cave closed behind her.

. . .

Khumbu pounded his fists on the throne room door. The Mukari had sealed herself inside the chamber for hours, not allowing anyone to enter since the previous sunset. Back then, the citadel had trembled at the noises emanating from behind this door, noises that triggered a massive avalanche outside. Gylatsen had refused to allow anyone into the throne room, enraging the head monk. In retaliation Khumbu had banished Gylatsen to guard duty at the citadel gates. The young monk was too familiar with the Mukari, in Khumbu's opinion. A living goddess should be treated with reverence, not as a friend.

Despite sending Gylatsen away, Khumbu had still been unable to get into the throne room. The door remained sealed shut and the Mukari did not respond to the voices of her disciples. At midnight Khumbu had retreated to his cell for prayer and meditation, hoping these might offer him solace and guidance. But calm proved elusive and sleep as hard to find.

It was dawn – long past time for the goddess to eat. Khumbu had warmed a bowl of Gylatsen's broth and brought it to the doorway. He called to his goddess, but she did not respond. "Mukari, why do you keep us out? Have we offended you in some way? Tell us how to deserve your forgiveness. We will do whatever you ask. Please, Mukari – let us in!" He tried the handle once more, but it remained resolutely still.

Khumbu leaned his back against the door and let his old, weary legs fold together, sliding slowly down to the floor. Tears of frustration were pricking at his eyes, anger knotting his chest. Why was she treating him this way? Had he not devoted his life to her worship, kept alive the customs and traditions held sacred by the monks for generation upon generation? What more could she ask of him? I'm a fool, Khumbu realised. It is not for mortals to question the ways of the goddess. I am a disciple of her will – nothing more.

A thick clunk sounded behind Khumbu and the throne room door swung slowly open. The old monk got to his knees, bowing at the entrance before moving inside. He could hear the Mukari. She was sitting on the throne, her breathing shallow but steady. "Goddess, forgive this intrusion. Are you hungry?"

"No," she replied quietly. But after she stopped talking to him, Khumbu's keen ears could hear her lips and tongue still forming words. He had witnessed this phenomenon once before, when a previous Mukari had taken to projecting her spirit beyond its mortal shell.

"My apologies, goddess. I shall leave the chamber and stand guard outside, to make sure you are not disturbed again. Forgive my intrusion, my goddess."

"Thank you, Khumbu," she replied.

Ivanov had tasked the Enforcer with rousing the men at dawn. A roll call of the survivors found their number to be three hundred and twenty-seven, not counting the general or his second-in-command. Ivanov inspected the troops as best he could on the difficult terrain, before addressing them from a rocky outcrop a few metres up the mountainside. His breath formed into vapour in the cold air, each phrase becoming another small cloud in the still atmosphere.

"I know the events of yesterday were a shock to you all, as they were to me. Losing so many comrades so quickly was a blow, but one from which we must recover quickly. Do you want their loss to stand for nothing, their sacrifice to have been in vain?"

"No!" the soldiers shouted back in unison.

"Will you still follow me, even if our mission should lead into hell itself?"

"Yes, sir!"

The general nodded, a grim satisfaction evident on his face. "Very well. Today shall be an end to our endeavour, for better or for worse. The top of this peak is not far above us, and the Forbidden Citadel must be close by. We shall make a systematic search of the mountain. If this legendary fortress is here, we will find it, and we will take it!"

The troops responded with a roar of approval, brandishing their weapons.

Ivanov waited until the noise subsided before speaking once more. "When the Enforcer and I received our briefing for this mission, we were told the citadel is guarded by a religious sect blessed with special abilities. These holy men possess a secret weapon so powerful any man who looks upon it goes blind. Are you afraid?"

"No!" the soldiers shouted back.

"You are the Imperial Black, the most feared, the most notorious, the most dangerous regiment in the Tsar's forces. If anyone should be afraid, it is these monks, for they know what terror we bring. Are you with me?"

"Yes!"

"I said are you with me?"

"YES!"

The general nodded, satisfied with their response. "Before another sunset, we shall hold the Forbidden Citadel in our grasp, we shall take this mighty weapon for our own. And then every army, ever regiment in the Empire will tremble at our name. We are the Imperial Black and we shall be victorious!"

"Did you hear something?" Spatchcock asked. He and the others had been climbing the stairs inside the mountain for more than an hour, their backs aching from the effort.

"Only my stomach rumbling," Flintlock replied sourly.

"No, it was more like shouting – hundreds of men shouting." Dante leaned against the curved wall that encircled the staircase. "Crest, can you detect any unusual sounds through the mountain?"

Nothing distinct, it replied. *The last noises audible from the rocks did sound man-made, but I could find no pattern or rhythm to them.*

"The Mukari said she could not hold back the forces sent against her much longer," Mai recalled. She paused below the others on the staircase "We know that the avalanche killed many of Ivanov's men, but the survivors cannot be far from the citadel. We must press on."

"How do you know the soldiers are close to the fortress?" Flintlock asked. "How do we even know this citadel is near the top of the mountain?"

"Why else would the Mukari be helping us up the mountain, except to defend her?" Spatchcock replied, shaking his head. "What did you think she was inviting us for? Tea and bloody crumpets?"

"Don't mention food," Flintlock protested. "I feel like I haven't eaten in days." The former aristocrat yelped in pain, jumping up two steps at once. He spun round to find a grinning Dante wielding one of his cyborganic blades. "You stabbed me in the arse!"

"Anything to get you moving," Dante said with a smile. "Now get climbing again or else I'll carve my name into your backside!" Flintlock scurried up the steps, pushing his way past Spatchcock to take the lead.

Ivanov's men searched every square metre of the tor above where the ice bridge had been, but could not find any evidence of the Forbidden Citadel. The general reacted angrily, raging at his second-in-command, at the mountains around them, even the sky. When his fury had passed its peak, Ivanov demanded the major repeat every word uttered by the village headman. "There must be some clue among what he told you, some hint to where we shall find this fortress!"

But the Enforcer was looking past Ivanov, pointing into the sky. "General, look..."

Ivanov twisted round to see what was so important. The surviving soldiers were all doing the same, staring dumbstruck at what was looming over them. It was a massive, translucent skull floating in the air, thirty metres tall. Scraps of flesh and skin hung from its bleached white bones. An eyeball floated within each socket, but they had no lids or lashes. The mouth of the skull opened and shut soundlessly, its words spoken directly into the mind of each man on the mountain. *Why have you come to this place, outsiders? Speak now or I shall send another avalanche to smite you from my holy mountain!*

Ivanov stepped forwards, puffing out his chest and clasping his hands together behind his back. "My name is Vassily Ivanov and I am a general in–"

I know who you are, fool. I asked why you came here!

"We were sent by the Ruler of all the Russias, Tsar Vladimir Makarov, on a peaceful mission to find the Forbidden Citadel. Our leader wishes to open a dialogue with those who live inside the citadel."

You lie, the skull retorted coldly. *You wish to steal and you would kill my people to get what you want. That is the truth.*

"You are mistaken. Since you can speak into our minds, you can probably read our thoughts too. Look deep into mine and witness the truth there!"

I know your truth all too well, Ivanov the Terrible, Butcher of Rudinshtein. You have killed women and children, murdered and tortured thousands for your own pleasure. Even here, in my sacred mountains, you have spilled the blood of dozens solely to make one man speak. You are the worst of creatures and I will not weep at your death later today!

That last remark caused a stir among the soldiers, the general could hear them muttering to each other. "You are mistaken, whoever you are! I will not die today, nor shall any of my men," he shouted at the ghostly skull.

You do not believe me?

"Why should any of us believe the lies of a creature that hides behind this elaborate illusion, a creature that lacks the courage to face me in person, a creature so weak and feeble it dare not even reveal its name?"

My name is death and this mission shall be yours, Ivanov. I shall let all of your men see their own deaths. Close your eyes and bear witness, mortals!

Ivanov felt his eyes closing, despite trying to keep them open. Then his mind was filled with a vision of his body bleeding to death on a black floor, his throat run through by an unseen blade, his legs brutally severed at the knees. Ivanov shuddered at the vision that replayed itself over and over in his head, the same few seconds, the same excruciating pain lancing through his body in sympathy with the injuries.

Perhaps I can't stop myself seeing this, Ivanov decided, but that will not still my voice.

"No, this is a lie," he bellowed. "I deny this future, it is a falsehood designed to frighten the weak and feeble. I deny this future and say it is a lie!" The general shouted to his men. "Imperial Black, repeat after me: 'I deny this future and say it is a lie.' Say it!"

"I deny this future and say it is a lie," the nearest soldiers repeated.

"Louder!" Ivanov shouted. "I want to hear every man, every voice!"

"I deny this future and say it is a lie," the soldiers shouted, more of them joining in, the chant becoming stronger and more powerful.

"Again!"

"I deny this future and say it is a lie!"

Ivanov forced open his eyes and glared in triumph at the apparition. "Listen to my men. They reject your falsehoods! We shall find you and we shall destroy you, pretender! Ivanov the Terrible shall rule this mountain!"

Not yet, butcher. And not all your men agree with you. See for yourself. The general realised dozens of his soldiers were fleeing down the mountain, scrambling over the snow-covered rocks, terror etched on their faces.

"Cowardly scum!" Ivanov snarled. "No soldier ever disgraced the uniform of the Imperial Black by fleeing a battle or an enemy. Enforcer!"

"Yes, sir!" the major responded, snapping to attention.

"You know what we do to deserters in this unit."

"Yes, sir." The Enforcer produced a weapon and began executing those fleeing, a single bullet exploding the head of each soldier. His shots rang out, one after another, until close to a hundred men lay dead on the slope below. The blood from their wounds drained into the snow, staining it crimson. Once the slaughter was concluded, Ivanov folded his arms and glared at the ghostly skull.

"I broke no opposition, be it the running coward, or the supernatural spectre. This fortress will be found and it will be mine!"

In her throne room the Mukari cried out, her concentration broken by the deaths of so many terrified men. She collapsed to the floor, hands struggling to keep her elaborate headdress in place. "Forgive me," the girl whispered. "I have failed."

Outside, the translucent skull glowed brightly for a second, then disappeared. Ivanov heard a gasp from one of his soldiers. "General, look!" Above them, a white fortress appeared, clinging to the side of the mountain. Its outer walls were ten metres high, with a pair of mighty gates built into them. Inside the wall were wide white buildings and windows dotted across their upper levels, each structure topped by a golden pagoda roof. The Forbidden Citadel was visible, at last.

"We searched that area, I know we did," the Enforcer hissed.

"Our eyes were deceived," Ivanov said quietly. As he spoke the citadel faded away once more, leaving no trace of its presence. "Our eyes are deceived once more, but our brains know the truth now. The fortress of our enemy is but a hundred metres above this position. Enforcer, I believe the time is right for you to don the exo-skeleton. Forward, men! Destiny awaits us."

THIRTEEN

"Amens alone won't ward off evil."
– Russian proverb

"The exo-skeleton is among the more formidable weapons available to members of the Tsar's armed forces. It is a lightweight suit of body armour panels that can be wore over any uniform, without impeding the user's movements. Indeed, the exo-skeleton significantly enhances the physical power of whoever wears it. Activated by a hidden control button on the chest plate, the suit generates a force field around the user, simultaneously protecting them from harm and enhancing their strength by a factor of ten. A single blow from a normal soldier's fist can break bones and glass. A single blow from anyone wearing the exo-skeleton can smash through walls with ease."
– Extract from *The Files of the Raven Corps*

Dante's legs ached, his muscles weak and giddy. He and the others had been climbing the steps within the mountain for what felt like an eternity. At long last, there was a glimmer of daylight above them. Flintlock saw it first and gave a feeble hurrah of relief, before quickening his pace. Spatchcock followed suit and Dante hurried to keep up with them, Mai close behind. Finally, all four stood at the top of the stone staircase, where a landing broadened out into a hollow space. Sunlight poured in the cave's mouth, dazzling the four after so long in the near dark.

"Let's give ourselves a minute to rest," Dante said. "We don't know who or what is waiting for us out there, or how close we are to the Forbidden Citadel. We need to be ready for anything."

Flintlock pulled a sidearm from the holster beneath his left armpit and a dagger from the inside of his right boot. Spatchcock produced a vial of purge juice – a pernicious concoction of his own making that reduced its victims to violently vomiting, diarrhoea-stricken wrecks. "This should make the Imperials sorry they came to the mountains," he muttered happily. His other hand dug inside his trousers and removed a tiny pistol.

Flintlock arched an eyebrow at this revelation. "Since when did you have a gun concealed beside your crotch?"

"I've always had this," Spatchcock replied. "It only fires six shots, so I've kept it for emergencies. Nobody ever searches my groin thoroughly enough to find it."

"I wonder why," Dante said dryly. He removed the Huntsman 5000 from its usual position, slung across his back, and went through the ritual of checking the long-barrelled rifle. Beside him, Mai unwrapped a cloth bundle to reveal two short-bladed swords and a bandolier laden with dozens of throwing stars. She secured the bandolier diagonally across her chest, slotting one sword into a sheath that hung down over her left hip. The other sword she clasped in her right hand.

Dante admired her weaponry. "Sure you've got enough there?"

"I don't have the luxury of cyborganic swords," she replied testily.

"Hey, I was only saying…" Dante began, but then saw Mai swaying slightly. "Bojemoi!" He caught hold of her as she swooned, gently lowering her to the cave floor. Before passing out, Mai grabbed his hand and pressed it to her forehead.

∙ ∙ ∙

An old, bald monk was looming over Dante, his eye sockets hollow and empty. "We must empty her mind, brothers, tear out every memory of her time here. She must never recall this place, never return here. When that is done, I will take her down the mountain." There was a murmur of assent from unseen voices. The monk leaned closer to Dante, his orange robe falling forwards, his breath thick with yeast and honey. "Forgive me, but what must be, must be done." Dante felt hands touching his body, fingernails clawing at his mind. He screamed in pain and terror, but the voice he heard cry out was that of a girl – Mai's voice. Then he knew only blackness, swallowing him like a cold ocean.

When his senses returned, Dante shivered. He was sitting cross-legged inside a cage, clad in a simple white robe. Hard bamboo canes dug into his legs and he felt hungry, prying eyes staring at him. "How much for this one?"

A massive figure loomed over him, the rancid stench of body odour filling Dante's nostrils. He couldn't make out their face, but somehow knew he must not speak. They would kill anyone who spoke out of turn.

"I said how much for this one, holy man?"

"Twenty." Dante twisted round in the cage to see who had responded. It was the same monk as before, but now he wore heavy winter clothing over his robes. The monk was bartering with Dante's life, selling him like a yak or a goat.

"For used goods? Ha! Eight and no more."

"Twelve?"

"I said eight, and that's being generous!"

Another blur and Dante saw a face he recognised staring at him. It was a man, a Himalayan with the familiar brown skin and dark hair. Something about the features reminded him of another face – but whose? "Farewell, daughter. We are so proud of you. This is the greatest honour any of us can imagine."

"Please, don't leave me here," Dante pleaded, but this time the voice was that of a child, young and afraid.

The man smiled benevolently. "Nothing bad will ever befall you here, daughter. Besides, we will see you for feasts and holy days. We love you, all of us. Never forget that, will you?"

"No Father, I will never forget," Dante whispered. He opened his eyes to find Spatchcock and Flintlock staring at him quizzically.

On the cave floor Mai sighed and looked up, her face free of all pain. "My headaches. They're gone," she said. "I can remember what happened. I remember everything."

The last psychic block in her mind has collapsed, the Crest said. *They must have been what caused Mai such pain. Her subconscious has been fighting them all these years, battering against the walls somebody else built in her mind.*

"How do you feel?" Dante asked.

"Better than I have in years," Mai replied. She got back to her feet, retrieving the short-bladed sword that had fallen from her grasp. "Let's go." Mai led the way out of the cave, followed by Dante and Spatchcock, with Flintlock nervously bringing up the rear. The four emerged into blazing sunshine, the sky a vast canopy of brilliant blue. The tor's snow-covered peak was visible a few hundred metres above them. The Mukari's staircase had brought them out on to a plateau within striking distance of the summit.

"So where's this bloody fortress?" Spatchcock asked. "After all we've been through to get here, I thought it would be right outside."

Flintlock's shoulders sagged. "We climbed all those stairs for nothing?"

Dante stared at his travelling companions, amazed. "Can't you see it?"

In front of them stood the Forbidden Citadel, its white-washed walls rising from the snow as if hewn from the mountain. Beyond the wall stood the citadel buildings, wide structures with golden roofs and dozens of rectangular windows studding their sides. The fortress had an unearthly quality, as if it had been standing on this mountain for centuries beyond measure. Barring the entrance were two massive wooden gates, each inlaid with panels of gold.

"It's incredible," Mai whispered, her voice awestruck.

"You see it too?" Dante asked.

"Yes," she smiled. "It's like coming home."

"Do let us know when you've finished pulling our legs," Flintlock said petulantly, folding his arms. "I don't think it's clever, trying to make fools of us."

"We've got bigger problems than that," Spatchcock warned, pointing down the mountainside. "Look!" Soldiers were swarming below them, ascending the mountain like an incoming, inexorable tide. One of the Imperials saw the foursome and shouted, his voice alerting others.

"I take it all back," Flintlock said hurriedly. "If you two can see a citadel round here, now would be a good time to get all of us inside it."

Ivanov was leading his men to where the fortress had briefly appeared when an advance scout spotted four figures emerging from a concealed cave in the mountainside. "Sir, there's somebody else up there, ahead of us!"

The general pulled a pair of binoculars from a pouch on the side of his uniform. When he saw who was leading the new arrivals, Ivanov spat out a curse. Of all the people that should suddenly appear, here and now… "Send for the Enforcer!" he barked. Within a minute his second-in-command was at the general's side, standing to attention. The black regimental uniform was partially hidden by blue body armour, while matching gauntlets encased his hefty fists. "Major, if I believed in fate, I would say it was playing a trick on us. Look at the four people on that plateau and tell me who you see."

The Enforcer focused his attention on the area Ivanov was pointing at. "Nikolai Dante! What in the Tsar's name is he doing here?"

"No doubt he, too, is trying to secure the weapon inside that fortress," the general snarled. "But I very much doubt he is doing it in the Tsar's name."

The Enforcer had already drawn his weapon and was taking aim at the Romanov renegade. "Do you want me to kill him, sir?"

"No," Ivanov said, his lips forming a cruel smile. "That's one pleasure I shall reserve for myself. Tell the men that the three people with Dante are fair game, but the so-called Hero of Rudinshtein is mine."

"Yes, sir!"

Dante pushed against the citadel gates, but they did not move. He shoved his shoulder into the wood and strained with all his might, but still could not shift them. "Open up!" he demanded. "In the name of the Mukari, open these gates!"

Mai was observing the advancing soldiers below. "Hurry, Dante! The Imperials are almost within firing range."

"Hey, I'm doing my best. I don't notice anybody else offering to help," he snarled. Spatchcock and Flintlock looked on with bemused expressions.

"It's like one of these things you see in parks, where they don't talk," Spatchcock said, scratching his stubble.

"A memorial garden?" Flintlock offered.

"No. You know, the actors who don't say anything."

"Oh, mimes!"

"That's the one," Spatchcock agreed, pointing at Dante. "He looks like one of those mimes, pretending to push against an invisible wall."

Dante swore at them. "It's not invisible, you fools. *You* just can't see it!"

"Sounds like an invisible wall to me," Flintlock decided.

Dante swore again, before another thought occurred to him. "Crest, can you do anything to open these gates?"

If they were controlled by some computer or electronic circuitry, yes. But these gates are simply blocks of wood, albeit of a density and size so great you have no hope of ever moving them.

"In other words?"

For once, I'm of absolutely no use to you.

"Fuoco," Dante muttered. Bullets flew past his face and thudded into the gates, several ricocheting off the golden panels. Mai hastily retreated from the edge of the plateau, Spatchcock and Flintlock following her example. "I guess we're now in firing range," Dante noted sardonically.

Mai stepped back from the gates and shouted something in a tongue Dante did not recognise. She repeated the phrase with added urgency in her voice. Moments later the mighty gates began to open inwards, a gap appearing between them. Spatchcock stared at the gates, open-mouthed.

"Where did those come from?" he spluttered. Flintlock shared his bemusement, momentarily forgetting the bullets flying past both of them.

"How did you...? Where were those...? I don't..."

Dante rolled his eyes. "At least we're all on the same page now. Don't just stand there, get inside!" He shoved the two men through the gap between the gates, while aiming his rifle towards the advancing soldiers. Mai took position beside him, extracting a handful of throwing stars from her bandolier.

"Ready?" she asked.

"I guess. What was that language you spoke?"

"Nepalese, I think. It was the common tongue in these mountains for centuries. The people inside the citadel must still recognise it."

"When did you learn Nepalese?" Dante asked, his finger tightening round the Huntsman's trigger.

"I must have always known it, but the blocks in my mind suppressed that knowledge."

The first line of the Imperial Black reached the edge of the plateau. Mai's left arm cut an arc through the air, flinging throwing stars at the soldiers. Each went down screaming, slices of metal embedded in their face or throat, blood spurting from the wounds. "Makes me wonder what else I'll recall."

Dante took out the next wave of troops with a dozen shots from his rifle. "You go inside. I'll keep them back."

"We both go in," Mai replied. "The Mukari brought us here to protect the citadel, not to die outside its gates."

"Ladies first," Dante replied, taking out a trio of soldiers.

"Age before beauty," Mai said, hurling another handful of throwing stars.

"Tell you what, let's go in the same time," he suggested. "On the count of three. Ready? One... Two... Three!" The duo retreated backwards through the gap before bumping into Spatchcock and Flintlock, both of whom were standing with their hands in the air.

"Out of the frying pan..." Spatchcock hissed.

"...and into the bloody fire," Flintlock added.

A phalanx of blind monks in saffron robes blocked the way, their empty eye sockets crackling with purple electricity. All too aware of the Imperials rapidly approaching the citadel, Dante stepped towards the monks and smiled broadly.

"Hi! My name's Nikolai Dante," he began.

Oh yes, that always wins people over, the Crest sighed.

Dante maintained his smile. "Perhaps you've heard of me? Hero of Rudinshtein, bastard offspring of a noble dynasty..."

The monks said nothing, their silence a stark contrast to the sounds of gunfire and boots crunching on rock and snow outside the gates.

"Anyway," Dante continued, "we've been sent here to save you from a regiment of the Tsar's most vicious soldiers, who plan to storm the citadel and probably slaughter you all. The good news is we got here before the soldiers, thanks to your Mukari's intervention. The bad news is, well..."

"The citadel is ours for the taking, men," a voice bellowed from outside the gates. "Prepare yourselves for glory!"

Dante shrugged. "You can probably guess the bad news for yourselves. My point is that now would be a good time to close the gates again, yes?"

As one the monks raised their hands and pointed at Dante. Purple energy shot from their fingertips to engulf him, sending his body into spasms so that he danced like a rag doll in the hands of an angry child. Mai cried out in Nepalese, gesturing for the monks to stop. The holy men lowered their hands and Dante collapsed on the cobbled path, his limbs still twitching.

Another monk emerged from a side door in the nearest building, his face kinder and friendlier than the others. "Forgive my brethren. They were told the defend the gates with their lives!" The new arrival crouched beside the unconscious Dante, his hands rummaging inside Dante's clothing for injuries. "He will quickly recover, his..." The monk's words stopped when his fingers reached Dante's left arm. "Can this be true?"

Spatchcock peeked out through the gap in the citadel gates. Dozens of Imperial Black soldiers had formed a line on the plateau outside. They were waiting for something or someone, their weapons aimed and ready to fire. "Whatever you're doing, I'd make it snappy," he advised.

The monk peeled back Dante's top, exposing the upper left arm to reveal the double-headed eagle symbol of the Romanovs, the mark of the Crest. "Brothers, this man bears the sign of the Mukari! He is one of us!" The other monks murmured amongst themselves.

Mai knelt on the other side of Dante. "You should tell them to shut the gates. If the soldiers get inside, the citadel will fall within minutes." The monk nodded. He sent eight monks out to face the Imperial Black and told the other four to close the gates once their brethren were outside. "They'll be slaughtered," Mai protested.

The monk smiled sadly. "I know. But all of us vowed to die for our goddess. We live to serve her, should we not perish in the same cause?"

By the time Ivanov and the Enforcer reached the plateau, the fortress gates had closed and more than three-dozen soldiers lay dead or dying in the snow. But the Forbidden Citadel was no longer hidden from them. It stood directly ahead with eight elderly men guarding the entrance. Their frail bodies were clad in saffron robes, their eye sockets hollow.

"Stand aside or suffer the consequences," the general shouted, but the monks did not move. "Suffering it is, then. Major?"

The Enforcer called forward three ranks of men, twenty in each row. Those at the front lay on the ground, the middle row dropped to one knee and the rear rank remained standing. "Take aim!" the major bellowed, and all sixty soldiers choose a target from among those blocking the gates. The monks raised their hands, purple electricity crackling at their fingertips. "Front rank – fire!"

A volley of shots rang out, but none reached their targets. Instead the rounds slowed to a halt in mid-air, then fell to the ground.

The Enforcer's face darkened. "Middle rank – fire!" Another fusillade of gunfire, but the result proved the same. "Rear rank – fire!" By now the monks were slowly moving toward the soldiers, still untouched by the invaders' weapons. With each step they took, a bolt of purple lightning would leap out and electrocute several troopers. The Enforcer drew his own sidearm. "Independent firing – fire at will!" In an instant all the soldiers were shooting.

Such was the volume of ammunition being fired at the monks that it was forming a wall in the air where each bullet met the psychic force-field. "Keep firing," the Enforcer bellowed to his men. "They can't keep this up forever!" He shot at the holy men and was surprised to see the bullet pass through the barrier, although it missed his intended target. "It's working, they're tiring," he shouted triumphantly. "Keep firing!"

More bullets began punching through the faltering force-field. One hit a monk in the shoulder, jerking him sideways. Another passed through a hand before embedding in the same monk's chest.

As he sank to one knee, the barrier weakened further and the deadly blasts of psychic energy from it ceased. Another bullet among the many penetrated the barrier, then another, the latter wounding a second monk. After that it took less than a minute for the force field to collapse completely and the eight monks to be left bleeding to death on the plateau, soldiers still pumping bullets into the crimson-stained corpses.

"Cease firing!" Ivanov shouted, taking charge from his second-in-command. A thick cloud of cordite filled the air, mingling with the dying moans of the last monk. The general drew his sidearm and silenced the final defender with a bullet to the brain. "So much for their much vaunted special abilities," he sneered. "Major?"

The Enforcer snapped to attention. "Sir!"

"I want those gates open. Now."

Dante regained his senses as the sound of gunfire died outside the gates. "Wh... What happened? Wh... Where am I?"

"The Forbidden Citadel," Flintlock said. "We made it."

"Now we have to save it from Ivanov and his bastards," Spatchcock added.

"I wish I hadn't asked," Dante admitted, sitting up with help from Mai. He noticed the friendly-faced monk at his side. "I don't think we've been introduced. My name's Dante, Nikolai Dante."

"Gylatsen," the monk replied with a smile. "I shall take you to Khumbu, he will want to see you. It is too long since a Romanov visited us."

"I'm not a–" Dante began, then checked himself. "Sure, take me to your leader. But Mai comes with us."

Gylatsen shrugged. "If you wish that, Master Nikolai."

"Call me Dante, okay? I'm nobody's master."

The monk pointed at Spatchcock and Flintlock. "What about the smelly one and his lover? Are they not your servants?"

"Servants?" Spatchcock laughed.

"His lover?" Flintlock protested simultaneously.

"Not exactly," Dante said, getting to his feet. "We are travelling companions." He approached Spatchcock and Flintlock, who were arguing with each other about Gylatsen's descriptions of them. "Will you two stop bickering? I need you to stay here, help the monks keep Ivanov and his men out for as long as possible."

Spatchcock jerked a thumb over his shoulder. "Those gates won't last long against an Imperial assault. It sounds like the monks outside have already been finished off."

"Do your best, okay?" Dante pleaded. "I'm not asking you to commit suicide, just slow them down. Every minute gained gives me and Mai the chance to find this weapon. Then we can use it on Ivanov."

Flintlock clutched his sidearm in one hand and his dagger in the other. "Alright, but the second those gates start going, so do we."

"Master Nikolai, we must go!" Gylatsen called. The monk was already leading Mai into the nearest building, one hand waving for Dante to follow.

Khumbu felt the last of his brethren die in the snow beyond the citadel wall. The old monk lit a yak-butter candle for the fallen soul, the eighth such flame that he had created in the last few minutes. How many more must die to keep our secret, he wondered? Could the outsiders be stopped, or would this day be the last time a living goddess resided upon the sacred mountain? The sound of hurried footsteps was getting closer. Khumbu rocked back from his knees on to his feet, then rose to a standing position, his joints creaking at the effort.

Knocking resounded at the door of his cell. "Brother Khumbu, it's Gylatsen. There is someone here to see you. He is one of the Romanovs and he bears the sign of the Mukari."

"Praise be to the goddess!" Khumbu whispered thankfully. "Bring him to me, Gylatsen. Bring him in." Khumbu heard the young monk usher in one person, then another, before entering the small stone chamber himself. "I hear three sets of footsteps. Who is my other visitor?" Khumbu was shocked when he heard a female voice, and even more shocked by what she had to say.

"I am known as Mai Tsai, but you called me by another name, didn't you?" she said quietly. "Once you called me goddess."

The Imperial Black had tried everything within their power to open the citadel gates. The brute force of two-dozen men had made no difference. Shooting at the gates was no more effective, every bullet bouncing back at them. Even explosives made little difference, beyond charring the wood and blackening the gold panels. Finally, Ivanov nodded to his second-in-command. The Enforcer punched the concealed control button on his chest, powering up the exo-skeleton. Artificial energy surged through his body, tendons of power creating junctures between the adjoining plates of body armour. Satisfied the equipment was working, even in such cold conditions, the major charged head first at the gates.

The effect was remarkable. A single blow knocked the two huge slabs of wood out of shape. His second blow destroyed whatever mechanism was locking the gates together. A third blow shattered them completely, reducing most of the wood to kindling. From within came a volley of gunfire and bolts of purple electricity, but both sides knew this battle was nearly over.

The Enforcer stood aside and bowed to his commanding officer. Ivanov smiled gratefully, then commanded his troops to return fire against those within. "The citadel is ours, men. Forward to glory! Forward to victory!"

"This is impossible," Khumbu protested. "What is she doing here? It is forbidden for one of her kind to return to this place!"

"I do not understand," Gylatsen said, looking to Dante for guidance.

"Mai used to be the Mukari, your living goddess," he replied.

"How can this be?" Gylatsen wondered. "Brother Khumbu?"

The old monk pointed at Mai with a wavering, bony finger. "She must leave, now! She will bring doom upon us all!"

"If it's doom you're expecting, it has already arrived," Dante said. "There are three hundred Imperials smashing their way into the citadel right now, led by the cruellest, most sadistic man on the planet – excluding the Tsar."

"Khumbu probably runs both of them a close third," Mai spat angrily. She glared at Gylatsen. "Do you know what your leader did to me, him and his brethren? Once they'd decided I was no longer fit to be the Mukari, they cast me out of your little paradise. But that wasn't enough for them. No, they invaded my thoughts, tore every memory they could from my brain. Khumbu and his holy men raped my mind, over and over and over. It wasn't enough to steal away the experience of having been a living goddess – they also gouged out memories of my family, my parents. Then, once they had finished with me, the noble Khumbu took me down the mountain and sold me to a slave trader for eight roubles. I was worth less to him than a pound of salt. That's how your precious leader treats his goddess, Gylatsen!"

"Brother Khumbu, is this true?"

The old man shook his head. "I did what I did for the good of us all..."

"What about my good? What about my rights?" Mai demanded furiously. "Is that how you reward someone who was your living goddess for eight years – by ravaging her mind, by filling it with such pain and torment she cannot bear to come back here, so she can never discover the truth? Tell me I'm wrong, Khumbu! Tell your brethren I'm wrong!"

"You are not wrong, sister," another voice replied. "Khumbu cast you out of this hallowed place, as he casts out all Mukari once they reach the age of womanhood. As he would have cast me out, in time." A young girl walked into the crowded chamber, one hand holding up the hem of her red and gold robes to stop from tripping over them. As she spoke, Khumbu and Gylatsen dropped to their knees, bowing before her, their hands clasped together in supplication.

"Goddess, you should not be away from the throne room," Khumbu urged.

"Perhaps not, but I wanted to see more of the citadel, while I still could. The end is upon us, but we all have our parts to play."

"Does she always speak in riddles?" Dante wondered out loud.

That girl has the power of a goddess, the Crest interjected. *You would do well not to anger her.*

"You must be Dante," the Mukari said. "Your Crest is as bossy as mine."

"You can hear it too?"

I also bear a Crest, the girl said inside Dante's thoughts, *but mine has a different purpose than yours. A purpose that will become clear all too soon.*

A series of thunderous noises boomed through the citadel – once, twice, then a third time. The Mukari listened to them, her face filled with sadness. "The gates have given way before the Imperial onslaught. The blackness is upon us, and death follows close behind. It is time I went back to the throne room. Khumbu, you choose to come with me."

"I choose, goddess?"

The girl hitched up her robes again, preparing to leave the stone cell. "This is what will happen. You can stay here if you wish, or go with the others to launch a counter-attack against the invaders."

"No, I will guard you in the throne room," Khumbu decided.

"The choice is made, as it always was," the Mukari said. She smiled at the others. "I will see you soon enough." Then she was gone, Khumbu hurrying after her.

"Weird," Dante commented. "It's like she knows what is going to happen, before it happens."

"She has always known," Gylatsen said. "That is her burden as the Mukari, to know the future as you know the past. To her the past, present and future are one and the same. What must be, will be – it is inevitable."

"So what do we do now?"

Mai pulled a fresh handful of throwing stars from her bandolier and strode to the doorway. "We launch a counter-attack, of course. Coming?"

FOURTEEN

"War loves blood."
– Russian proverb

"A typical Himalayan monastery or holy palace is divided into three levels. The ground floor is devoted to places of worship and functional rooms such as kitchens. The middle level is given over to individual cells for each of the monks or priests that reside within the structure. Finally, the top floor is reserved for the holiest individual of all, with various adjoining antechambers and places of meditation."
– Extract from *Secret Destinations of the Empire*,
by Mikhail Palinski

Spatchcock ran as fast as his stubby legs could carry him. He had become separated from Flintlock in the chaos caused by the sudden implosion of the citadel gates. Both men had decided that staying alive was more important than trying to hold back the Imperial Black's inevitable advance. Spatchcock shouted at the four monks guarding the entrance to follow his example, but they remained in place, their psychic energy keeping the soldiers at bay temporarily. "Well, we tried," he called over his shoulder to Flintlock. But the blond Brit had already fled inside, so Spatchcock did the same.

He sprinted through a room filled with burning candles and religious icons, resisting the urge to pocket what looked like a gold statue. There was a time for looting and a time for saving your own skin. Spatchcock was not a religious man, but decided displeasing whatever deities looked after this place probably wasn't the best of ideas.

The next room he entered was a dining hall, with long wooden tables and benches neatly lined up for the next meal. He dodged round these and ducked through a darkened doorway. Beyond was the kitchen, if the smell of cooking oils and spices were to be trusted. Spatchcock squinted to see better, his eyes still adjusting from having been outside in the blazing sunshine. A haunch of cooked meat sat atop a bench, steam rising slowly from it. Can't remember the last time I ate, Spatchcock thought. He searched his surroundings for a knife or any kind of blade. Finding nothing of use, he tore at the flesh with his grubby fingernails instead, saliva dribbling down his jowls. Finally he freed a hunk of meat from the joint and shoved it into his mouth.

"Ahh, that's good," he enthused while masticating furiously, his mouth hanging open. "I haven't tasted anything that good since–"

Out in the dining hall, the wooden legs of a bench scraped across the stone floor. Spatchcock froze, half-chewed flesh hanging from his lips. It could be one of the monks – or it could be one of the Imperials. They'll have finished off the old guys in orange by now, he thought. They could already be searching the building.

Spatchcock saw a shadow in the doorway and threw himself to the floor, retrieving the tiny pistol from inside his trousers. He scrambled across the floor, his eyes watching the doorway. Another bench scraped across the dining room floor and someone cursed. They were close. Any second, any second now...

"Spatch? I say, old boy. Are you in there?"

"Flintlock!" Spatchcock exclaimed, standing up. He walked over to the doorway, pocketing his pistol. "I

almost fired, you stupid bastard! I thought you were one
of the Imperials."

The Brit stepped into view with another figure behind
him, holding a gun to Flintlock's head. Before Spatchcock could react, a second soldier appeared, his weapon
aimed and ready to fire. "Sorry, old boy," Flintlock said
apologetically. "These chaps got the drop on me. Said
they'd blow my brains out if I didn't help them. Haven't
seen Dante, have you?"

"No," Spatchcock scowled. A third Imperial emerged
from the darkness behind Spatchcock and nudged him in
the back with a gun barrel.

"Outside," the soldier commanded, reaching into
Spatchcock's pocket to remove his small pistol. "Our
commander will want to interrogate you personally."

"Your commander?"

"General Vassily Ivanov."

"Ivanov the Terrible," Flintlock said nervously.

"So the avalanche didn't get him?" Spatchcock
enquired. "Shame." He got a rifle butt in the back of his
head that sent him staggering into Flintlock.

"I say," the former aristocrat protested. "There's no
need for that!"

The soldier advanced on him, rifle butt raised and
ready to strike the Brit too. "We decide what is needed
now, not you. Move!"

Dante found a window on the second level overlooking
the broken gates where soldiers were still marching into
the citadel. "Time to even the odds a little," Dante muttered, taking aim with his Huntsman 5000. He began
firing rapidly, knowing his weapon would correct any
flaws in his aim. By the time the Imperials began returning fire, Dante had downed three-dozen of their number
and dived out of view. He scuttled along the corridor,
keeping below the windows, before popping up at the
other end and opening fire again. The soldiers reacted

more quickly this time, his element of surprise lessened, but Dante had still killed another twenty before he was forced out of harm's way. Two more attempts netted a dozen more men in total, by which time the remaining soldiers had made it safely inside the citadel. From now on the fighting would have to be hand-to-hand, Dante decided. He hid his rifle behind a small shrine, then ran to the nearest staircase, his cyborganic swords extruding themselves from each fist.

Mai was waiting at the bottom of the steps. Between her and nearest doorway was an uneven pile of Imperial Black corpses, which had all been killed by throwing stars. Mai was holding a short-bladed sword in each hand, the razor-sharp edges of each weapon not yet sullied by blood. She smiled at Dante. "What took you so long?"

"You know how it is – places to see, Imperials to shoot. You've been busy in my absence. Where's Gylatsen?"

The monk came through the outer doorway at speed, leaping over the pile of dead invaders with ease. "They're coming!" he shouted as he ran past. "I delayed them as long as I could. I'm going to the throne room."

"How many are coming?" Dante called after him.

"Plenty," Mai replied, pointing out the door. At least a hundred Imperial troopers were storming towards them, weapons drawn and ready to fire.

"Good, I've got a score to settle with these bastards," Dante muttered. "For Rudinshtein!" he roared, charging at the oncoming soldiers. Mai was one step behind him, her blades flashing through the air, hungry for blood.

Khumbu paced back and forth inside the throne room, the sounds of death drifting up from below. The Mukari sat on the floor, playing with a wooden elephant, talking to it softly under her breath. At last the monk could stand the tension no longer. "How can you do that now, of all times, goddess?"

The Mukari looked at him with sad eyes. "You always forget, Khumbu. I may be your goddess, but I'm also a child. I like to play with my toys. Besides, this is what I am doing when the soldiers break down that door."

"You've seen that?"

"Of course, how could I not? Did I not prophesise all of this to you? "It is the outsiders who bring death to this place. 'The gates of the Forbidden Citadel shall fall and there is nothing any of us can do to stop that.' I said those words to you in this room, not so many days ago. Now the darkness is here." The Mukari went back to playing with her wooden elephant. "Beyond that I see no further."

"General, we have captured two of the outsiders from the plateau!"

Ivanov heard the soldier's voice and smiled. Excellent. Killing Dante would the culmination of three years' endeavour in that tiresome backwater Rudinshtein, he thought. But before the Romanov whelp dies I plan to extract the maximum amount of pleasure from torturing him. When he is beaten and broken and utterly spent, only then shall I take off his head. Perhaps I shall impale his rotting skull on the tip of a spike and have it paraded through the streets of Rudinshtein, one final indignity to crush any rebellion in the hearts of that lice-ridden rabble.

The general pivoted on his heels to discover his moment of pleasure was not yet at hand. His soldiers proudly clutched the collars of two men, one with an odour to equal any battlefield latrine, the other displaying a haughty, upturned nose that cried out to be punched. "What are these... dregs?"

"They were with Dante when he entered the citadel, sir," one of the soldiers said, his face crestfallen. "We thought you might wish to interrogate them."

"You thought? You thought?" Ivanov raged. "Since when did I encourage my men to think? If I wanted a regiment of philosophers, I would not have recruited a thousand of the Empire's worst scum to fill my ranks, would I?"

"No, sir."

"I wouldn't sully the heel of my boot on these pieces of excrement! Get them out of my sight. Now!"

"Yes, sir!" The soldiers snapped to attention, then bundled the prisoners away, eager to put as much distance between them and the general as quickly as possible. "You made us look bad," one of the soldiers hissed at Spatchcock and Flintlock. "You'll pay for that."

"What a shame," the Brit replied cheerily. "And I was so looking forward to having a chat with the mighty Ivanov the Terrible."

"Me too," Spatchcock agreed. "I was going to tell him about that bag of gold coins I hid down the front of your trousers."

Flintlock looked at his companion as if he were insane. "Spatch, old boy, what are you talking about? There's nothing down the front of my trousers."

"You can say that again."

"Shut up and keep moving," a soldier warned, shoving his rifle butt into Spatchcock's back.

Dante cut a swathe through the first five Imperials that crossed his path, his cyborganic blades severing hands, arms and even the head of one unfortunate soldier. Mai was just as effective, the shorter blades of her weapons enabling the Oriental assassin to stab as well as slice her targets. Together the duo fought the Imperial onslaught to a standstill, using the soldiers' own numbers against them. The battle was taking place in a narrow corridor, so only three or four men were able to take on the duo at once. Those in front blocked anyone behind them from shooting at Dante or Mai, while the close quarters combat made rifles all but useless.

Realising the folly of their frontal assault, a veteran soldier shouted to his comrades to use bayonets and other blades against the enemy. Dante smiled at the order. That's right, he thought. Fight us on our own terms. He leaped atop the corpses of the fallen Imperials, using their bodies to gain superior height over the next wave of soldiers. Several troopers charged at him, bayonets fixed to their rifles, a war cry on their lips. *Dante, evasive action!*

"Don't worry. Mai and I can handle this," he told the Crest.

Dante jumped nimbly over the thrust of the bayonets, but landed awkwardly on top of the soldiers. "Fuoco!" he cried out, before plunging to the corridor floor in a tangle of Imperial arms and legs.

You were saying?

"Mai! A little help here!" Dante shouted, elbowing one of the soldiers in the face while kneeling on the crotch of another.

The Himalayan woman came flying over the pile of corpses, her leading leg smashing into the chest of an onrushing soldier. He tumbled backwards, knocking over several of his colleagues. Mai landed neatly on the floor, using her left blade to decapitate an Imperial before they could stab Dante. Her right sword plunged into another soldier on the floor, severing his spinal column in one devastating movement.

Mai helped Dante back to his feet while delivering a swift kick to the head of the nearest trooper. "We're getting bogged down here," she said. "We need to fall back, before they outflank us."

Dante flashed his blade through the air, disabling another four Imperials with a single movement. He could see soldiers running past the end of the corridor, looking for another way up into the heart of the citadel. "You're right," he conceded. "Head for the throne room. I'll see you there."

Mai nodded and flung herself over the pile of corpses in a compact somersault. Dante dodged a stabbing bayonet that was aimed at his head, then drove the point of his right sword through the hand of his attacker. "You should be more careful," Dante said, cheerfully twisting his blade. "You could have somebody's eye out with that."

The soldier spat blood at him. "You'll die here, Romanov scum!"

"The name's Dante – Nikolai Dante. Remember that!" Dante ripped his sword out of the soldier's hand, slicing off four fingers in the process. He smiled at the remaining Imperials. "Sorry to loathe you and leave you, but I'm required elsewhere." Dante dove over the corpse pile and rolled into a somersault as he hit the floor on the other side and came up running.

Mai was racing up a stone staircase to the citadel's top level when she heard a voice sneering at her from above. "Quite the little hellion, aren't you? The Imperial Black has a fearsome reputation, but such strength is borne of numbers, not skill. How would you cope with an adversary worthy of your talents?"

She slowed her advance, creeping to the top of the steps, tensed for the inevitable attack. "I've killed more men than I can remember," Mai hissed. "Another one will make little difference to me."

"Brave words, but such bravado is wasted on me."

Mai searched the landing around the top of the staircase. It was a wide corridor, with half a dozen doors leading away, all of them ajar. The source of the taunts was not obvious, hidden amidst echoes and stone walls. She dropped into a crouch, a short-bladed sword in each hand, ready for action. "If you're so invincible, stop hiding in the shadows and show yourself."

"Very well." The mighty figure of the Enforcer emerged from the nearest doorway, his black uniform glistening wet and crimson, blood splashes staining the blue plates of his exo-skeleton. His face remained hidden behind the blankness of his mask, Mai seeing only her own reflection on its burnished surface. "How much do you want to die?"

"Yours will be the death here," she said evenly.

The Enforcer folded his arms. "I ask because there is no need for me to kill you. Surrender or run, either will keep you safe. Engage me in combat and there can be only one outcome. In this exo-skeleton I am invulnerable, whereas all you have to defend yourself are two puny blades and those clothes."

"Before my brother was killed on the orders on your master, I was an assassin for the Tong of the Red Hand," Mai snarled. "I know how than a hundred ways to kill and I will need only one to finish you."

"Then we fight to the death, warrior against warrior. So be it." The Enforcer bowed gracefully to her, his shoulders higher than the top of her head. "Begin."

Dante was fighting a running battle through the citadel's lower levels. Every time he reached a staircase, half a dozen Imperials had already occupied the way up. He sliced them apart, his superior agility and speed enabling him to escape each skirmish unhurt. But another half dozen would be waiting beyond the first, forcing him into a tactical retreat. Sheer weight of numbers was driving Dante sideways, stymieing his progress.

"Crest, I need to find another way to the top level," he whispered, pausing to catch his breath behind a stone pillar. "I don't suppose they're got an elevator in this place by any chance?"

Dante, this is an ancient stone citadel dating back hundreds, if not thousands, of years, built on the side of a mountain in one of the world's most remote regions.

"You're telling me no, aren't you?"

Your knack of stating the obvious does you credit – even if little else does.

"Any other easier methods of reaching the throne room?"

None, unless you plan on climbing the citadel's exterior.

"Thanks for the help," Dante sighed. He ran along a stone corridor and found one last set of steps leading upwards. Curiously, there were no Imperials blocking his path. "Call me old fashioned, but this looks too inviting."

Plainly, this is a trap. You must find another way, the Crest insisted.

"There are no other ways," Dante replied.

Nevertheless, you cannot–

The Crest's words were drowned out by a mocking voice, its words drifting down the stone steps. "That pip-squeak I hear talking to itself below – I wonder who it can be? Perhaps a rat has wandered into the fabled Forbidden Citadel, searching for cheese. Run away, vermin, there's nothing for you here."

"Ivanov," Dante snarled.

"Why, the vermin recognises my voice. Perhaps it is not a rat after all. Is somebody else down there? The so-called Hero of Rudinshtein, perhaps?"

"What do you want, scumbag?"

"A little respect will do for a start," Ivanov replied. "Call me general."

Dante spat an obscenity at the taunting voice.

"Such language! And I thought the Romanov family was taught proper manners, like every other noble house. But then, there's nothing noble about you, is there? Niko-lai Dante, bastard offspring of a disgraced dynasty and a sea-hag, who murdered women and children to line her purse!"

"That's rich, coming from a butcher who's raped and murdered most of a province," Dante retorted. "During the war there was a rumour you could only achieve sexual climax by violence. What's the problem, Vassily? Can't get it up unless somebody's bleeding in front of you?"

"Sticks and stones may break my bones," Ivanov snapped back.

"But at least they'll give you a hard-on."

"The Hero of Rudinshtein reveals his true colours: a foul-mouthed guttersnipe excreted by some ocean-going whore too lazy to have an abortion. Of course, what could I expect from a coward who fled his own kingdom, who left his people to die while he went adventuring across the Empire? What kind of hero does that? You could have come back to save your precious province, tried to rescue the scum you claim to love. But you didn't have the balls."

Dante's face twisted with anger and fury as he moved closer to the stone steps. *Don't do it,* the Crest warned. *Ivanov is trying to goad you into making a mistake.*

"I don't need his goading to make those," Dante said bitterly.

Perhaps not, Nikolai, but even you must see sacrificing yourself to silence him will achieve nothing.

Dante paused. "Did you call me Nikolai? You never call me that."

Anything to get your attention, the Crest said. *Or save you from yourself.*

"Sorry to interrupt your schizophrenic small-talk," Ivanov called down. "Are you coming up or do I have to send down my men to fetch you?"

Dante smiled. "Come and get me, general."

Ivanov had sent down a dozen soldiers to capture the Romanov renegade, but they had not returned. He waited three more minutes with the rest of his men, listening to the sounds of fighting, then the sounds of pain, then the sounds of dying. After that, all was silent below. "How tiresome," the general said to himself. From the fifty soldiers still at his disposal, he sent another twenty down to pursue Dante while taking the rest up to the citadel's top level. It was time to secure the secret weapon, whatever it was. If must be here, otherwise why would Dante fight so hard for this place?

Mai flung herself sideways, avoiding another killing blow from the Enforcer. He was surprisingly fast, despite his bulk. She knew it would only take one direct hit from those hyper-powered gauntlets to finish her. Blue energy rippled between the joints of his body armour, maintaining a force shield around him that was almost impossible to penetrate. Mai had danced around him for more than ten minutes, somersaulting gymnastically from one point to another, flailing at him with her swords. But each thrust bounced away harmlessly. If there was a weak spot in the Enforcer's exo-skeleton, she would not find it from this distance.

I'll have to get inside his guard, she realised, and turn his size against him. Yet in the moment it took her to grasp this, he was already upon her. A mighty fist clutched at the air where her head had been. The Enforcer missed, but caught her long black hair, yanking Mai back in mid-air. She stabbed one of her swords into his chest with all her strength, but the blade broke off at the hilt and flew to the wooden floor beams. Mai tried to cut through his fingers with the other sword. However, he snapped the steel blade in two and tossed it aside as if it was a child's toy.

The Enforcer gripped her throat below her jaw, and held her up in the air at arm's length, examining Mai's pretty features. "You fight with great courage and skill," he said. "But you are no match for my power."

"You triumph without honour, letting your exo-skeleton fight for you. A true warrior would not need its power against me."

"Perhaps you are right," he conceded. "But I am not so foolish as to switch it off now." The Enforcer held up his free hand before Mai's face. "Such is the power of this suit, a single jab of my fingers would push your eyes out through the back of your skull. Does a quick death meet your wish for honour?"

"There is no honour in murder," Mai retorted.

"Of course, I could slap your face like this," the Enforcer said, his free hand swiping across her face like a thunderclap of pain. "To me that felt like the lightest of touches, but it almost took off your head. How much punishment can you take before the brain damage becomes permanent? Before it claims your life?"

A trickle of blood spilled from Mai's mouth, running down her chin on to the gauntlet round her neck. She lashed out with her feet, kicking desperately at his chest, trying to inflict some pain, however hopeless the attempt. This brought a laugh from the Enforcer, the futility of her actions amusing him. "And still this vixen fights back! You have a spirit that does you credit, but it shall not save you. I shall close my gauntlet around your neck and crush the bones within. It will not be the quickest of deaths, but your pain will soon be over. Goodbye."

Dante, this is foolhardy at best and potentially fatal if you fall from this height, the Crest warned. *The odds against an unskilled, inexperienced individual like you successfully free-climbing a structure like this are–*

"Never tell me the odds," Dante hissed under his breath. He was hanging from the outside of the citadel's second level, his fingertips clinging to the slightest of handholds. Above him, a wooden balcony protruded, its base supported by thick struts that dug into the side of the building. "You said it yourself, this is the only way to get the top floor without fighting my way through all of Ivanov's men."

Yes, I know what I said, but I didn't expect you to take it as a suggestion. I could count the number of times you've done that on one hand. If I had a hand, that is.

"For once in your precious existence, could you let me concentrate?"

Fine. But on your own head be it.

"That's exactly what I'll land on if you don't shut up!"

Charming. Kill yourself. See if I care.

"Thank you." Dante closed his eyes, preparing himself mentally for the leap to grab at the nearest support strut. On the count of three, he told himself. One... Two... Th–

Which I don't, by the way.

"Diavolo!" Dante cursed, almost losing his handholds on the citadel wall. "Must you always have the last word?"

Not always.

"Good, then shut the hell up!"

I simply prefer to offer the occasional observation in th hope these comments of mine might guide you toward a wiser course of action.

Dante screamed obscenities at the sky, then hurled his body towards the wooden support before his Crest could make another comment. His fingers scrabbled at the strut, clawing, grasping, then finally taking hold of it. He reached up to the balcony and dragged himself over to its edge. Straining mightily, he lifted his head high enough to see past the wooden banisters and through a pair of glass doors. Beyond them Dante could make out Khumbu, pacing back and forth, and the Mukari seated on the floor. This must be her room, he realised.

"Crest," he said, but no response came. "Crest?"

I thought you didn't want me to speak.

"Stop sulking and scan that room. The Mukari said she was bonded with a Crest. Can you detect it inside that room?"

Yes. It is bonded with the Mukari's mind.

"Like you are with mine?"

I cannot be more specific. Her Crest is far more powerful than any other I have encountered before, preventing me from discovering its secrets undetected.

"Then there's no need for subtlety, is there?" Dante asked, clambering up and over the balcony's railings.

You were being subtle?

Khumbu heard the balcony door's opening and swung round to confront the intruder. "Who are you? What are you doing here?"

"It's me, Nikolai Dante," the new arrival announced. "I see Ivanov hasn't got here yet, there's still hope." He crouched beside the girl. She was still playing with her toy elephant, sadness in her eyes.

"Ivanov is looking for a weapon. Is it nearby?"

"Yes," she said evenly.

"Can we use it against the Imperials?"

"Not directly, no."

"But you created the avalanche that swept most of Ivanov's men away."

Khumbu intervened, grasping Dante's arm and pulling the unbeliever back from the goddess. "Show the Mukari the respect she deserves, outsider!"

Dante wrenched his arm free. "Don't you get it, old man? The general will kill everyone and everything in this place to get that weapon. Without it we have no defence against him. Your precious citadel will be levelled and your goddess murdered in front of you."

"I cannot act against the darkness directly," the Mukari said. "That is why I brought you and Mai here, and the others. You are my champions. If you fail, all is lost. But no victory comes without a cost."

Khumbu could hear shouting in the corridor outside the throne room. "That voice, I know that voice…"

"Poor Gylatsen," the girl said, a single tear rolling down her sad face.

Gylatsen had heard the soldiers coming long before they arrived outside the throne room. He pressed his back against the wooden door, preparing himself for what was to come. The Mukari had told him about this moment long ago, how the end would engulf the citadel, how his life would be sacrificed to save hers. To know he would die in such a worthy cause had been a comfort before today. But now the moment was almost upon him, it was no comfort. Gylatsen pressed his palms together, letting all the energy stored within his thin frame gather between them.

Along the corridor he heard the general talking with another man. Ivanov told him to kill the woman and be quick about it. He must mean Mai, Gylatsen realised. She might be still alive – but not for long.

Now the soldiers were marching towards Gylatsen, boots stomping in time with each other on the wooden beams, bringing death with them.

Forgive me, goddess, but I am scared, he prayed. I don't want to die.

Everything dies, the Mukari whispered into his mind. *I am with you, now and forever. I always will be.*

"Thank you," he whispered, swallowing hard.

A phalanx of soldiers surrounded the monk, their weapons aimed at his chest. From nearby a voice commanded them into action. "What are you waiting for? He's one man. Strike him down!"

As the soldiers opened fire Gylatsen opened his hands and let the purple energy escape, electrocuting all those within reach of him. He died, but more than twenty of the Imperials perished with him, screaming in agony.

The Enforcer waited until Ivanov and the other soldiers had passed before turning his attention back to Mai. His fingers tightened their grasp round her neck, until Mai could feel the blood pounding inside her forehead, blackness closing over her vision. A voice entered her head, childlike and soothing, urging her to keep fighting, to lash out with all her might. Mai kicked one last time and felt something give way under her foot, as if she had connected with a small button. The gentle hum of energy from the Enforcer's exo-skeleton faded and then was gone, his grip on her throat slackening at the same time.

"N... No!" he stammered. "You couldn't have known how to do that!"

Mai kicked at him again, this time aiming her blow higher so it caught him under the chin. The Enforcer's head snapped backward and he let go of her, both hands clawing at his throat, choking and gasping for breath.

Mai dropped to the floor, one hand closing over the broken blade of her sword Before the Enforcer could react, she was slicing it across his body, hacking at the gaps between his body armour, blood spurting from the wounds.

He went down before her savage attack, crumpling to one knee, his gauntlets held up to ward off further blows. Mai stabbed the broken blade through one of his hands, pulled it free and impaled his other hand with it. She stepped back, satisfied with the amount of blood the Enforcer was losing. But something about his response disturbed her. Most men would be begging for mercy by now, or weeping in agony. But the Enforcer remained where he was, staring at his pierced hands. Finally, he started laughing.

"What the hell is wrong with you?" Mai demanded.

"Even if you kill me, I won't feel it," he said quietly. "My master had all my nerve centres surgically shut down, to turn me into an unbeatable fighting machine. 'The man who feels no pain almost feels no fear', that's what he told me after the operation." The Enforcer pressed the gauntlet impaled by the broken blade against the floor, gradually forcing the slice of metal through his hand until it fell free.

Mai spun round on the spot, one foot arcing through the air to smash into his head. The impact cracked his helmet apart and the facemask fell free, revealing the ruptured features underneath. They were a mass of scar tissue and ancient wounds, a road map of pain. A chill of recognition ran through Mai. No, it couldn't be, it wasn't possible. She knelt before him, one hand reaching for the broken face. "Rai? Is it you?"

FIFTEEN

"Samovar is part of the Romanov dynasty and widely considered to be the harshest prison colony in the Empire. Nicknamed the Gulag Apocalyptic, it was said no one ever returns from Samovar. I was despatched to this distant outpost in the Starship *Andrei Tarkovsky*, as bodyguard to a distinguished visitor [name deleted]. I subsequently discovered the prisoners were being used as raw material for [remainder of text deleted by an unknown hand]."

– Extract from Nikolai Dante's report on the Samovar Incident, 2667 AD

Dante recognised the smell of burning flesh and the screams of pain coming from outside the throne room door. He had seen what the citadel's monks could do, but Ivanov had too many men to be held back for long. Dante extended the cyborganic swords from each of his hands, stepping between the doorway and the Mukari. He glanced over his shoulder at Khumbu standing by the windows. "If you've got any tricks, old man, now's the time to use them!"

The door smashed inwards, soldiers brandishing their weapons. Dante killed five of them before he was overwhelmed. A soldier gripped each of his arms and held them in check, pistols levelled against Dante's head. Khumbu offered no resistance, his quivering hands hanging at his sides. Once the throne room was declared safe, the general strode in, a broad smile on his cruel face. "Ah, the redoubtable Romanov renegade! I might have known you'd get here first – but it shall do you no good. Your partners in crime are being held captive by my men, while your slant-eyed sidekick is having her neck crushed by the Enforcer. Whatever you came here to do, you have failed."

"Spare me the gloating, Vassily," Dante replied.

"I don't recall saying you were permitted to address me by my first name," the general snapped. "Such impertinence shall be your undoing." Dante did not speak, preferring to make an obscene finger gesture. "And such crudity too. You should be honoured to stand in the presence of such a fine soldier!"

"Honour be damned."

"Rai, what happened to you? I thought you were dead," Mai whispered to her brother. The Enforcer knelt in front of her, his hands dripping blood on the black floorboards.

"I thought I was dead, too," Rai replied, his scarred lips struggling to form the words. "Ivanov and his men captured me outside the Governor's mansion in Rudinshtein. The civilians I was leading to safety, they–"

"Were all slaughtered, I know. Dante said you volunteered to take them."

Rai nodded. "I was young and idealistic, a fool. The general taught me the error of my ways, tutored me in the reality of the world. The reality of war."

"I read a battlefield report about your death, signed by Ivanov himself. He said Dante shot you to prevent his interrogators getting any information about Romanov troop movements."

"Dante fired because the general was going to use serpent-wire on me. He thought the bullet killed me, but it hit

the canister of serpent-wire instead." Rai touched a bloody
hand to his horrific face, caressing the scars as though they
were old friends. "When the serpent wire exploded, I
caught most of it in the face, tiny fragments all fighting to
slice through me. Ivanov's own surgeon worked for eighteen hours to get them out before they reached my brain.
Dante did this to me, but the general saved my life."

Mai shook her head. "That's a warped version of reality, Rai. Ivanov's twisted the facts, turned you into his
slave, his pet torturer."

Rai glared at her. "The general said you wouldn't
understand. He knew how it would be if we ever met,
face to face. He's a great man, Mai. He's been like a
father to me."

"What about our real father? Did you ever wonder
what happened to him?"

"I don't need to wonder," Rai said, smiling bitterly. "I
already know. He was headman of the village we
attacked. I killed him myself."

Mai stared at her brother, disbelieving. "You couldn't...
You wouldn't!"

"The Imperial Black is all the family I need," Rai
smiled. His hands shot forwards, grabbing his sister by
the throat. "That's why I have to kill you, Mai."

Spatchcock and Flintlock were held captive in a latrine
block at the eastern end of the citadel's lowest level,
guarded by four Imperials. When Flintlock complained at
the smell of stale urine, the soldiers laughed bitterly. One
removed his helmet to sneer at the Brit, the insignia of a
sergeant evident on his black uniform. "This place
doesn't stink half as bad as you two."

"My associate may have the odour of a dung heap
while possessing none of its charm," Flintlock replied,
"but I pride myself on–"

"Shut your mouth," the sergeant retorted. "I don't care
if you smell sweeter than the Tsarina's purse. You made

us lose face in front of the general. That's gonna cost you both. Now, how do you intend to pay?"

"I'm not sure I understand your meaning," Flintlock said.

"It's simple. You fill our money pouches with roubles or else we have to find another way of getting our money's worth out of you two." The sergeant grabbed his own crotch and shook it, to the amusement of his comrades.

"Sorry to be obtuse, but I'm still not quite with you," the Brit bumbled.

Spatchcock sighed. "It's simple, your lordship. Either we pay up or else they turn us into their whores."

"Oh," Flintlock said, his mind processing the information. He caught the lecherous glint in the eyes of their captors. "Oh!"

"Don't worry your lily-white ass," Spatchcock continued. "We can pay these boys off with that bag of gold I hid down your trousers."

"Bag of gold?" Flintlock glanced down at his crotch in bewilderment.

"I heard you mention that before," the sergeant said. "Let's see the proof."

"Certainly," Spatchcock smiled, plunging a hand inside his partner's pants.

"I say!"

Spatchcock leaned closer to Flintlock. "Whatever you do next, don't breathe in," he whispered, his hand clasping a small object in the Brit's breeches.

"Whatever you do next, don't squeeze," Flintlock replied.

"Oh... Sorry," Spatchcock said apologetically. He resumed rummaging.

By now the soldiers were growing impatient. "What's taking so damned long? If this bag of gold is going to satisfy all of us, it'll need to be impressive!"

Spatchcock smiled and winked at Flintlock as his search located its target. "Don't worry, boys... I'm sure this will make a big impression on you." He pulled his hand free and flung its contents at the Imperials in a single movement. Glass shattered on the stone floor by their feet and green gas billowed outwards, rapidly engulfing the surprised soldiers. Spatchcock was already running for the door, pulling Flintlock along with him. Behind them were moans of pain mixed with the sounds of vomiting and bowels being evacuated.

"What the devil was that?" Flintlock shouted.

"I hid my supply of purge juice in your pants when the Imperials took us captive," Spatchcock called back, fleeing for his life.

"But what if the vial had broken inside my trousers?"

Shot flew past the two fugitives as the stricken soldiers opened fire.

Spatchcock smiled. "Then you wouldn't be quite so full of sh–"

"Shut up and run!" Flintlock snapped, overtaking him.

Ivanov lashed out, his right fist plunging into Dante's midriff. The prisoner doubled over in pain, air whistling out from between his teeth. The general stepped closer and thrust a knee up into Dante's groin, the impact so hard it lifted him off the floor. Once the captive had finished coughing and retching, Ivanov lifted Dante's head by the hair and spat phlegm into his eyes. "It's time somebody taught you some manners, whelp. A little respect for your elders and betters."

"You might be older than me, but you're no better," Dante replied. That earned him a slap across the face. "Getting warmed up yet? In the crotch area, I mean." Another slap, then another, and another. "I'll take that as a yes, shall I?"

"You'll take it and you'll like it," the general hissed, his breath coming in short, excited gasps. He straightened up, letting go of Dante's hair. "But I have more pressing matters than teaching you how to behave. The Tsar sent me here on a specific mission and now is time for that mission to be accomplished." Ivanov strode across the room to Khumbu. "Where is the weapon?"

"I do not know of what you speak," the old monk replied.

"This citadel houses a powerful weapon, a weapon the Romanovs had planned to use against the Tsar during the war. The Ruler of all the Russias has sent me and my men–"

"What's left of them," Dante interjected.

"–to take possession of this weapon for the good of the Empire," Ivanov continued. "You shall give the weapon to me or suffer the consequences."

"We have no weapon," Khumbu insisted. "We are holy men, disciples of the Mukari, living goddess of our people."

The general looked around the room. "Do you mean this girl?" he laughed.

The monk nodded gravely. "She is our deity, made flesh on this earth."

Ivanov snapped his fingers and one of the soldiers produced a knife, its hilt inlaid with the symbol of the Tsar. "You claim to have no weapon, yet your monks used some form of psychic energy to kill dozens of my men."

"The goddess gives us such ability for her defence, nothing else."

"I was told the weapon you keep here is so powerful, its secret so great, that anyone who looked upon it would be blinded." Ivanov rested the point of his knife against one of the empty sockets in Khumbu's head. "Is that what happened to you and the other monks?"

"No, we blinded ourselves, out of respect for the Mukari's greatness."

"You blinded yourselves?"

"Yes."

The general nodded in admiration. "Your fervour does you credit, no matter how misdirected it might be.

Plainly, you and your men are willing to die in the service of your goddess. Threatening your life would be of little use." Ivanov took his knife away from Khumbu's face. He went to the Mukari and snatched her up, lifting the girl from the floor, his foot kicking aside the wooden elephant she had been playing with.

The general examined her face. "Remarkable. She is quite flawless. Not a blemish, not a mark."

"That is one of the criteria for choosing our goddess," Khumbu said.

Ivanov studied the Mukari closely. "And what are the other criteria?"

"She must be born on the nearby mountain. She must never have shed blood. She must never laugh or smile in the presence of anyone but her disciples. She must–"

"Enough." The general smiled at Khumbu. "I'm sorry to say you may struggle to find a replacement. The nearest village suffered a tragedy recently."

"You mean you had its people tortured and murdered for your amusement," Dante snarled.

"Tragedy or torture, the consequences are the same." Ivanov held his knife close to the Mukari's throat. "So, if I were to slip and accidentally slay this child, you would be without a goddess, yes?"

"If what you say is true, then the holy line would be broken," Khumbu said fearfully, "and everything we have preserved shall be undone."

"Then you have a simple choice," Ivanov replied. "Hand over possession of the weapon or else I gut your goddess like a fish. I will do it too, won't I Nikolai?"

"Yes," Dante admitted.

"I cannot give you what we do not have," Khumbu maintained.

"Then your living goddess shall live no longer," Ivanov vowed, his hand drawing back the knife in the air.

● ● ●

The Enforcer squeezed his hands together, pressing both thumbs against Mai's windpipe, slowly crushing the life from his sister's slender neck. He was surprised how quickly she died, her body falling limp in less than a minute. After satisfying himself she was dead, the major tossed her corpse to one side and marched towards the throne room. Ivanov will need me by now, he thought. I have wasted enough time on the past.

"Killing me will not be necessary," the Mukari said, before Ivanov could plunge his knife into her. "If you want the secret of the Forbidden Citadel, you need only ask. I am the keeper of this legacy, as have been all the Mukari who came before me."

The general relaxed, letting the knife drop back to his side again. "Show me this mighty weapon, so I may look upon its wonder for myself." As Ivanov spoke, the Enforcer strode into the room. "Where is your face-mask?"

"The woman knocked it free before she died."

"Mai's dead?" Dante twisted round to see the new arrival. "I know that voice…" His eyes studied the Enforcer's exposed face, realisation slowly dawning on him. "Private Rai? But I saw you die in Rudinshtein. I killed you!"

"Not quite," Ivanov snarled. "Guards, if Dante speaks again, you have my permission to cut out his tongue. If he tries to resist, you have my permission to kill him. I had hoped to keep that pleasure for myself, but I will not be interrupted again." The general smiled at the Mukari, his eyes glinting with excitement. "Well, goddess – unveil this secret so we can all see it."

The girl brought her hands together as if praying, closing her eyes. The air temperature within the throne room dropped dramatically and the balcony doors were flung open for a moment before slamming shut again. The exotically carved wooden throne flew across the room, narrowly missing the Mukari's head before crashing against a wall. Swirling winds whipped at the white tapestry that hung behind the raised dais where the throne had stood. Silver threads in the centre of the tapestry glowed and pulsated with energy, the subtle design woven into the fabric becoming obvious to all those watching it.

Dante, I'm detecting something else besides another Crest in this chamber – a massive power source. There's something familiar about it...

"The double-headed eagle of the Romanovs," Ivanov said, pointing at the tapestry. "But what is the significance of this?"

The Mukari smiled, blinking once. As she did the glowing white tapestry shimmered out of existence, the wall on which it had hung also disappeared. In their place was a walkway leading towards a swirling globe of alien energy, a vortex some two metres wide. Khumbu dropped to his knees, bowing before the holiest of holies in the citadel.

Dante looked deep into the vortex and shuddered. He knew where it led, the power it represented, and what its existence in this place could mean if the Tsar harnessed that power for himself. Up until now this mission had been merely another adventure in a life full of such adventures. Suddenly, the stakes were much higher he could possibly have imagined. The future of the Empire was up for grabs in this room.

Ivanov stepped closer to the vortex, the Enforcer joining him. "What is it?" the general asked, his eyes filled with wonder.

"A doorway to another world, a bridge to another universe," Khumbu said reverentially. "It is the source of our power. It is the source of all that we are."

"I tire of your riddles and religious babblings," Ivanov snarled. "How do we control this weapon? How do we use it? Tell me!"

Khumbu shrugged helplessly. "I do not tell you because I do not know. My brethren and I are merely the humble disciples of the Mukari. She alone controls the power of the vortex."

"So why am I wasting time talking with you?" The general kicked the old monk in the head, sending him backwards across the floor. Khumbu thudded into the far wall, his bones snapping at the point of impact. Ivanov nodded to the Enforcer, who grabbed hold of the Mukari. Ivanov rested his knife against the girl's left cheek, letting the tip nudge into the soft skin. "Tell me how to use this weapon or else."

The girl did not flinch, did not turn away from the general's maniacal gaze. "What must be, will be," she said quietly.

"She isn't afraid of you," Dante called out.

Anger flushed Ivanov's face. "Guards, I said I did not wish to hear the prisoner's voice again. Cut out his tongue. Now!"

Dante struggled against the Imperials but with his arms pinned, there was little he could do to resist. One of the soldiers forced a knife between Dante's clamped teeth, trying to slice at what was beyond them.

"Hold!" the Enforcer screamed, stilling the soldier's movements.

Ivanov rounded on his second-in-command. "You dare countermand one of my orders, major? You know the penalty for flouting my authority!"

"And I will suffer that punishment gladly, sir, but hear me out. That tapestry had the symbol of the Romanovs woven into it, just as Dante has the same symbol on his left arm: the mark of the Weapons Crest. The girl does not fear death, she will not tell us how to use this vortex's power. But Dante will, as long as he still has a tongue with which to speak."

"And why should he tell us?" the general demanded.

"Because if he doesn't, you cut the girl's throat in front of him." The Enforcer glanced at Dante. "Women and children are his weakness, he never wants to see them hurt. I know – I almost died for his pathetic compassion."

Ivanov smiled, patting the major's shoulder. "You are right. Forgive me for doubting you. There shall be no punishment for your timely intervention."

"Thank you, sir."

The general turned his attention back to the Mukari, sliding the edge of the blade down her face to rest against the girl's neck. He signalled for the guards to remove the knife from Dante's mouth so the prisoner could speak. "Well, will you tell me what you know about this vortex, or shall I cut this child's throat?"

Spatchcock and Flintlock ducked into a darkened doorway, eluding another squad of Imperials still searching the citadel's ground level for them. The pair waited until the soldiers' footsteps faded out of earshot. "It's all clear," Spatchcock decided. Flintlock was already creeping towards the battered gateway. "Where the hell are you going?"

"Away from here," Flintlock replied. "We've done all we can. We're out of our depth here, Spatch."

"Saving your own skin and never mind about the consequences, is that it?"

"If you say so – are you coming?"

Spatchcock grabbed the Brit's collar and hauled him back to the doorway. "What about Dante?"

"What about him?"

"He's saved our worthless hides more times than I can remember. Don't you think we should do the same for him?"

"With what? We haven't got any weapons. He's got the Crest and Mai."

"We can use this," Spatchcock insisted, tapping the side of his head.

"Dandruff? Lice?"

"Our brains, you fool! We've outwitted some of the richest and most important people in the Empire before now, we can outsmart Ivanov too."

"Ivanov the Terrible? The Butcher of Rudinshtein? I don't think so," Flintlock muttered, pulling his collar free of Spatchcock's grasp. A moment later he gasped in dismay as a grubby hand closed around his crotch. "I say, there's no need for that, old boy. I was simply expressing an opinion."

"Good," Spatchcock replied grimly, squeezing a little tighter. "Then you'll be volunteering to help me rescue Dante?"

"Yes, of course," Flintlock squeaked.

"That's better." Spatchcock released his grip. "After you, your lordship."

The blond Brit muttered curses under his breath as he led the way towards the nearest staircase.

"I'm not a patient man," Ivanov warned. "What do you know about the vortex, Dante? Is it why your father, Dmitri Romanov, visited the citadel during the war?"

The general is a borderline psychotic with sado-masochistic tendencies, the Crest observed. *He will carry out his threat to murder the Mukari unless you say what he wants to hear, and he will enjoy the experience.*

"I never knew about this place during the war," Dante replied quietly. "Sorry to disappoint you, but I was a minor part of the Romanov campaign at best: cannon fodder for the Tsar's forces. Why else do you think my so-called family abandoned me in Rudinshtein at the end?"

"If you never knew about the citadel, what are you doing here now?" Ivanov pressed his knife closer to the Mukari's neck, his eyes blazing with hatred.

"I was sent here by an anti-Tsar organisation to secure the citadel and its secret. Like you, they thought it was a weapon, but they knew no more than that."

"Why should I believe you?" the general demanded.

"I would not risk that child's life by lying," Dante said.

Ivanov gestured at the vortex. "What about this doorway to another universe? What is its significance?"

"I have seen something similar once before, on the Romanov gulag at Samovar, before the war. Prisoners were sent to that planet as slave labour. When they were too weak to work, the inmates were sent through the gateway as raw genetic material for those on the other side."

"Raw material... for what?"

Dante hesitated fleetingly and the general pulled back the knife, ready to kill the Mukari with his next movement.

"Raw material for what?"

"Beyond that vortex is another universe where technology like my Crest is commonplace. It was introduced to improve evolution, but instead the technology began transforming the people into creatures more cybernetic than organic. Their society split into two factions, one siding with the technology, one against it. The Romanovs discovered these gateways and forged an alliance with the anti-technology faction. Dmitri sent untainted genetic material to help them preserve their humanity, they gave him Crest technology." Dante's head sagged forward listlessly. "That's it. That's everything I know," he admitted.

Ivanov looked at the vortex with renewed interest. "Your father must have been coming here in the hope of obtaining more Crests with which to arm his troops. Now I control this gateway, I can acquire a Weapons Crest of my own. My men could become the ultimate warriors, unbeatable in any battle. The Imperial Black would soon rival the Tsar himself as the most powerful force in the Empire!"

You humans never fail to disappoint, the Crest sighed. *One sniff of power and it goes directly to your heads.*

"Ivanov was well on his way to madness before this," Dante muttered.

The general smiled at his captive. "Thank you, young Nikolai, a most informative little speech. For once, I believe you were telling the truth."

"I was," Dante insisted. "Now let the girl go, she's no threat to you."

"If only I could believe that," Ivanov replied. "Alas, I cannot suffer a goddess to live, lest her disciples rise up and try to reclaim this weapon as their own." His knife whipped through the air, a flash of blood accompanying the movement. The general stepped back and admired his handiwork. A red line crossed the Mukari's throat where Ivanov's blade had been. For a second Dante thought it was merely a flesh wound, until he saw the distress on the girl's face. The Enforcer released her body and she sank to the floor, her elaborate headdress falling off.

Ivanov held up his knife, smiling joyfully at its crimson edge. "The goddess is dead! Long live the new god of the Forbidden Citadel!"

SIXTEEN

"A multitude of hounds signals death for the hare."
– Russian proverb

"Asphyxiation is when oxygen is stopped from reaching the human brain. If asphyxia is not treated or prevented within a few minutes, it leads to loss of consciousness, irreversible brain damage and, subsequently, to death. The shorter the period of oxygen deprivation, the better the prognosis for recovery."
– Extract from *The Imperial Heath Guide*,
2671 edition

Mai opened her eyes to find Spatchcock crouched over her, his cheeks flushed red and his expression filled with concern. "I think she's coming round," he told Flintlock, who was standing nearby.

"I don't see why you got to give her the kiss of life," the Brit protested. "I've got as much wind-power in my lungs as you, Spatch."

"You gave me the kiss of life?" Mai asked, horrified.

"Don't worry, I didn't slip you the tongue," Spatchcock replied. "Much." He patted Mai on the shoulder. "You've some nasty marks on your neck, but you're lucky whoever was strangling you didn't finish the job."

"It was my brother," she gasped.

"Your brother. You mean…"

"Rai. He's alive," Mai said weakly. "He's the Enforcer."

"Crikey," Flintlock exclaimed.

Spatchcock helped Mai to her feet. "We can't stay here long," he said. "Imperials are everywhere, most of the monks are dead and we can't find Dante."

"The throne room," she whispered. "He'll be in the throne room. That's where Ivanov was going, that's where Nikolai will be."

"She's probably right," Flintlock agreed. "He's got a nose for danger."

"Then it's up to us to get him out of trouble," Spatchcock vowed.

Dante shook himself free of the guards and crossed the throne room to crouch by the Mukari, cradling the dying girl in his arms. Ivanov shook his head, telling the Enforcer to stand guard over them. Then the general summoned the other soldiers to his side. "I want this building secured and a command post set up in the next room. Find and execute any civilians still alive on the premises. Nobody is to get in or out of the citadel without my express permission."

"Yes, sir!" the soldiers saluted in unison. All but one of them hurried from the throne room. The Imperial who remained behind bore a sergeant's insignia on his uniform. "Sir, when will you be contacting the Tsar?"

"Contacting the Tsar?"

"Yes, to tell him what we've discovered here."

Ivanov smiled thinly. "Sergeant, what makes you think I have any intention of contacting the Tsar? The fate of what *I* have discovered here is for me to decide, not some armchair general sat in his palace above Saint Petersburg."

"But, sir, you must see that–"

A single thrust of the dagger Ivanov was holding silenced the sergeant. The Imperial sank to his knees, then toppled sideways, quite dead.

Ivanov looked down at the corpse dispassionately, discarding his dagger. "Enforcer, have someone remove this carcass. I don't want the blood of that fool staining the floorboards of my throne room."

"Yes, sir!"

The general cast a withering glance at Dante. "Keep an eye on the prisoner. He's not as weak and pitiful as he looks. I am going to review the situation elsewhere within the citadel."

"Yes, sir," the Enforcer replied, calling for a soldier to remove the sergeant's body. Ivanov strode out into the corridor, not noticing Khumbu's broken body stirring in the corner. The old monk groaned in pain, his weak sounds attracting the Enforcer's attention.

Dante leaned closer to the Mukari, hugging the girl to his chest, rocking her gently back and forth. "It's alright, everything's going to be alright," he whispered tenderly.

"Do not grieve for me," she said. "Everything happened as I had foreseen it. But now I see beyond the darkness. There will come another, Nikolai."

"Who? Who is it?" But the Mukari had died, her pupils rolling back into her head. Dante shut both eyes, then kissed her forehead. "She's gone."

I am detecting a sudden surge of energy from the gateway, the Crest said urgently. *Whatever was holding it in check is gone. The vortex is unravelling.*

Dante twisted his head to look at the unearthly shape where the tapestry had been. Flashes of energy sparked around the globe, snaking out to the edge of the bridge. "The Mukari must have been controlling it with her Crest. Now she's dead, her Crest is dying too, and the vortex is destabilising."

Perhaps, but the Mukari's Crest is still fully active.

"How is that possible?" Dante wondered. "You've told me before that when I die, you'll cease to function too."

*Yes, but I also told you the Mukari's Crest has signifi-
cant differences to the way I function. It must be able to
maintain an existence without her as host.*

Dante's eyes narrowed. "But that's impossible,
unless..." He glanced at the Enforcer, but Rai was still
focused on Khumbu in the corner. Dante eased up the
dead girl's left sleeve to expose her upper arm – there
was no Crest symbol visible on the skin. He checked the
other arm, but it was also unmarked.

*Her death could have triggered the subcutaneous
defence mechanism.*

"Maybe," Dante agreed. "But I think she was never
bonded with the Crest. At least, not in the same way as
you and me." He noticed the Mukari's fallen headdress
lying on the floor nearby, forgotten amidst the violence.
"Maybe her Crest was housed within something she wore
as the living goddess."

Pain coursed through Khumbu's frail body as consciousness replaced the dark. *One of my legs and both arms are
broken,* the old monk realised. *Something is making it
hard to breathe.* He tried to sit up and fresh stabs of pain
made him cry out in agony. It felt as if knives were shift-
ing inside his chest, their edges gnawing at his core. *No,
not knives,* he decided. *They must be broken ribs, the
jagged ends piercing my internal organs.* Death could not
be far away. Already he could feel a cold numbness consuming his legs.

"Still with us, old man?" a voice asked.

"Who are you?" Khumbu rasped weakly.

"I was once a native of these mountains. I believed in
goddesses and sacred things like you, until the general
taught me to honour only that which you can touch and
see and feel."

"What a hollow, empty life you must lead," the monk
said. He could feel movement on the other side of the
throne room, but was doing his best to distract the figure

crouched beside him. If I keep my tormentor busy, perhaps the others can still escape, he thought. "Have you no faith, nothing to believe in?"

"I believe in the general, his words, his orders. He knows best."

Khumbu smiled. "Too much belief can be as bad as having too little. You must not blind yourself to the wrongs you do. I know that better than anyone." The monk felt a hand closing around his neck. "I am dying already. Killing me will make no difference, except to stain your soul with another life stolen away."

"I have no soul to stain."

"Then you are truly lost," Khumbu whispered with his last breath.

The Enforcer straightened up again, having crushed the life from the old monk. "See what happens to all those who challenge the general, Dante?" But when he swung round to confront the prisoner, only the Mukari's lifeless body remained. It began to glow from within, a blazing white light that flooded the throne room. When that faded, the Mukari's body was gone. Beyond her, the vortex bubbled angrily, errant strands of energy escaping from its slowly expanding outer shell. The Enforcer cursed under his breath and called for help. But it was the person he least expected who entered the throne room.

"You should have killed me when you had the chance," Mai snarled.

Spatchcock watched a unit of Imperials race past, then closed the door. Flintlock was already dragging a piece of furniture across to blockade the entrance. Spatchcock helped him finish the job. Dante stood nearby, staring at the Mukari's headdress in his hands, the girl's blood a red smear across his top.

"You did all you could," Spatchcock said.

"I wish that was true," he replied, "but my gut tells me otherwise. Crest, have you finished analysing this?"

You were correct. It houses the other Crest I detected. That's how each Mukari was able to pass on her abilities to her successor. That's how she controlled the vortex, kept all that power in check.

"What's going to happen now she's dead?"

Left unattended, the vortex will continue to expand, consuming everything in its path. Its hunger will grow exponentially – the more the vortex swallows, the more it wants. In less than an hour it will have consumed the throne room, this floor of the building and then the entire citadel. By sunset most of the mountain will be gone. Unless we find a way to stop it, the vortex will continue expanding until it devours the entire planet: all within a matter of days. When it tries to swallow the sun, that will create a black hole, a cannibal star sucking in solar systems as a child swallows soup.

"What does the Crest have to say?" Flintlock inquired.

Dante smiled grimly. "We're up to our asses in trouble."

"Business as usual, then."

"Not quite." Dante quickly relayed the Crest's doom-laden assessment of events.

The Brit scratched his head thoughtfully. "This is probably a stupid idea," he began, "but why doesn't your Crest bond with the Mukari's Crest? Between them they should be capable of finding a way out of this mess, right?" Dante and Spatchcock looked at Flintlock, then at each other, then back at the exiled aristocrat. "I said it was probably a stupid idea," he protested.

"Flintlock, you're a genius!" Dante said warmly.

"I am?"

"Maybe not a genius," Spatchcock hastily interjected, "but you have your moments, your lordship." Flintlock smiled, a quiet pride evident on his features.

The Enforcer lumbered across the throne room towards Mai, shouting for reinforcements. She somersaulted over him, delivering a swift kick to back of his neck as he passed underneath, sending the bulky figure sprawling to the floor. By the time he was back on his feet, Mai had grabbed up Ivanov's dagger from the floor. A handful of Imperials appeared in the door but the Enforcer sent them to search for Dante. "This bitch is mine," he snarled.

Mai danced inside another clumsy lunge, rapidly stabbing her brother three times in the chest plate, before escaping from his grasping gauntlets once more. "That exo-skeleton is slowing you down," she said. "You would do better without it."

"This exo-skeleton will be your downfall," Rai promised. "It deflects your blows with ease, even when not switched on. Now, when I activate it…" He pushed the hidden control button, but the suit did not respond. He glanced down at the button and noticed three stabs marks in the mechanism, disabling the controls. Mai leapt at him with a flying drop kick, the impact sending him stumbling backwards.

"I wasn't stabbing you," she smiled. "I was disabling the exo-skeleton."

"Very well," Rai muttered, tearing off the body armour panel by panel. "Throw aside your weapon and we shall see who is the superior warrior, sister."

Mai embedded the knife in the floor, then adopted a martial arts stance, ready to parry his next attack. "Take your best shot, brother."

"Crest, what's the best way to establish a link between you and the Mukari's Crest?" Dante asked, still holding the dead girl's headdress in his hands.

It was in close proximity to her brain, so I suggest you do the same.

"Put this on my head?" Dante looked doubtfully at the tiara, with its attached headdress encrusted with stones of crimson and black. "I doubt it'll fit."

All Crests adjust to suit whomever they bond with. I certainly had to.

Dante shrugged. "Maybe, but I'll look ridiculous."

This from a man recently chased through a floating brothel by a dozen enraged Kabuki porn actors while wearing little more than a prostitute's sequinned g-string bearing the legend "Get it here".

"Good point," Dante conceded. He turned to Spatchcock and Flintlock. "Do either of you two want to give me a hand putting this on?"

"If you insist," Flintlock sighed, taking hold of the headdress. He eased the elaborate collection of fabrics, gemstones and finery on to Dante's head. "There you go – pretty as a picture."

Spatchcock whispered for them to be quiet. The heavy footfalls of Imperials could be heard passing outside the room. Dante held the headdress close as possible to his skull. "Crest, are you ready to make contact?"

Initiating inter-Crest communications... now.

Dante screamed in agony before collapsing to the floor, his hands clamping the headdress in place. Flintlock crouched beside him, while Spatchcock hurried to the door, straining to hear if the sudden scream had attracted attention. Within moments soldiers were shouted for the door to be opened, their fists hammering the thick wood. Spatchcock shoved back against the barricade, trying to keep it in place. "Bloody hell, that's torn it," he cursed. "How's the boss?"

Flintlock leaned closer so he could listen to Dante's chest. He sat back on his haunches, his pale face drained of colour. "Spatch, I think he's copped it."

"What the hell are you talking about?"

"I can't find a pulse. He isn't breathing and I can't hear a heartbeat either," Flintlock explained. "Dante's dead."

Rai lunged at his sister, but she easily eluded his attack, darting her slender frame sideways out of his reach. As he passed Mai stabbed her bent fingers into his side beneath the armpit, eliciting a grunt. Rai swung round with a straight arm, but she ducked under it, delivering a firm blow to the solar plexus. Mai jabbed upwards with the side of her hand, intending to chop into his throat, but was surprised to be caught in his grasp.

Rai pulled her closer, his breath hot in her face. "You can dance around all day, but sooner or later I'll wear you down. When I do, this is over."

She responded by ramming a knee into his crotch, followed by a straight arm shove in the chest. Her brother staggered backwards, sucking air in urgently. Mai dropped to the floor and swung one leg round in a sweep kick, taking Rai's legs out from under him. He tumbled over, his head cracking against the broad wooden beams. A dull cry shot from his lips, then he did not move.

Mai moved in to finish the job and was felled by a fist punching in the back of her knee. As she sank to the floor, Rai leapt at her, moving with great agility for someone so big. He closed his hands around her throat and pinned her to the floor, straddling her torso with his legs. "I should have stayed to finish the job the first time," he said. "I won't make the same mistake again."

She flailed at him with her arms, fingernails gouging at his face, her legs kicking uselessly at his back. With her last reserves of strength, Mai sent a spasm of movement up her body, propelling Rai over her head. She rolled away to one side, coughing and choking, gasping for breath. Before she had time to recover, Rai was standing over her again. The knife she had embedded in the floor was now held loosely in his left hand.

The Enforcer grabbed Mai by the hair and lifted her up with his right hand, the blade balanced lightly in his left. "Goodbye, sister." He rammed the knife into her stomach, then gave the hilt a vicious twist inside the wound.

Rai left go of her hair and Mai fell back to the floor, blood quickly pooling around her, her hands feebly clutching at the blade.

The Imperials burst through the door, kicking aside the blockade to get in. Spatchcock and Flintlock were crouched beside Dante's corpse, the Mukari's headdress still stuck on his head. One of the soldiers hurried away to fetch Ivanov, returning with him less than a minute later.

The general studied Dante's body, his face a mask of hatred. "Shame, I was looking forward to killing him myself. Still, you can't expect to get everything you desire in a single day." Ivanov kicked the corpse, but the body merely shuddered in response. "Have these two carry this piece of offal into the throne room. I want them to witness all the indignities I shall inflict upon their master's corpse before I have them slain."

Ivanov marched from the room, smiling to himself. The Imperials saluted crisply as he passed, then turned back to Spatchcock and Flintlock. "You heard the general," one of the soldiers snarled. "Pick up this carcass and take it into the throne room. Now, maggots!"

SEVENTEEN

"Even a bear cowers when taken by surprise."
– Russian proverb

"The out-of-body experience is a post-death phenomenon that has been talked about, debated and discussed for most of a millennia. While there are still those would have you believe that there is nothing beyond the world you can see, touch, taste, hear or smell, the fact remains that near-death events are both common place and well documented. Are they merely the hallucinations of oxygen-starved brains, or is something more fundamental happening? Does the human spirit leave the body at the moment of death in search of the next life? And, if so, what would happen if this spirit did not return when its body was revived?"
– Extract from *The Little Book of Imperial Spirituality*, 2669 edition

Dante opened his eyes and knew something was awry. Around him dozens of smiling Himalayans were clapping and cheering, their eyes alight with joy, their faces beaming at each other. I know some of these people, he thought. They were among the bodies we burned on the funeral pyre yesterday. This must be the past I'm seeing, or a vision of something that never happened. It certainly can't be the future.

Dante was standing in a familiar stone courtyard, surrounded by brown-skinned revellers. They were chanting a name, over and over: "Mukari! Mukari!" Suddenly the chant became a cheer of joy, people pointing into the sky. Dante followed their fingers and realised they were gesturing at the balcony outside the throne room. A small girl was emerging from inside, clad in the red and gold of the living goddess, the Mukari's elaborate headdress on her young head. Khumbu was standing to one side of the child, Gylatsen on the other. The old monk motioned for the people for silence.

"The new Mukari has been chosen," he announced. "Bow before her and she shall bless you all!" As one the people dropped to their knees, clasping their hands together in silent prayer, backs bent forward so their noses almost touched the stone cobbles beneath them. Dante watched as the little girl, the same girl he watched being murdered by Ivanov, waved to the crowd.

"Be happy," she said, "and savour your life while you can."

There were a few confused murmurings from the people in the square, but they accepted her cryptic blessing nonetheless. Gylatsen clapped his hands three times. "Now, let the celebrations begin!"

In an instant the people were up and cheering again. But they faded away before Dante's eyes, becoming wraiths in the wind before disappearing altogether. He stared at the Mukari, who was bleeding profusely from her neck wound – the same cut that had killed her. She also faded away, but her headdress remained, falling down from the balcony into Dante's hands. A voice welled up inside his mind.

So began the reign of the last living goddess, the voice told Dante.

"Crest? Is that you?" he asked.

I am a Crest, but not your Crest. I serve as servant of the Mukari, holding in check the power of the gods.

"You're talking about the vortex. But I thought the Romanovs were the first to have Weapons Crests in the empire."

Not all Crests are weapons, Dante. Just as not all warriors are brave.

He looked round the citadel's courtyard. "What will happen to this place?"

That depends upon you. You hold the future in your hands. Without a Mukari to bear the Crest, all shall be lost.

"So where do I find another living goddess?"

By tradition the living goddess was selected from young, untainted girls of a nearby village. They were taken from their families and made to act as the conduit for the power of the Crest. Over time this process became shrouded in myths and legends, much like the citadel itself. The monks believed their goddess lost her purity when she came into womanhood, so they cast the girl aside and choose a new Mukari.

"But Ivanov's men butchered the villagers," Dante said. "The few survivors – I doubt any are untainted, not after what the Imperials did to their families."

The Mukari must be born of the mountain, but that is all. The rest is dogma, imposed by Khumbu and those like him, who sought to control the power of the living goddess. Strange how so many faiths of this world denigrate and oppress women, even when putting them on the pedestal of godhood.

"I need solutions, not a lecture on religious sexual equality," Dante replied.

You have already been told the solution. The question is whether you have the wit to identify it in time. With that the voice was gone, leaving Dante alone in the courtyard. Above him shards of energy exploded outwards from the throne room windows, showering Dante with broken glass. The vortex was consuming the citadel from the inside out.

Spatchcock and Flintlock carried Dante's corpse into the throne room, his body still wearing the Mukari's headdress. They placed him carefully on the floor next to Mai, who lay in a pool of her own blood. Her face was ashen, while her hands clasped the knife buried in her abdomen.

Ivanov dismissed his guards, then glared with satisfaction at his four prisoners.

"So this is the mighty army sent by the Tsar's enemies to storm the citadel? A Romanov reject, two festering sores from the rectum of humanity, and a slant-eyed whore too stupid to know when she is outmatched. Not what I'd call a fighting force to inspire fear!"

Mai spat an obscenity at the general.

Ivanov moved closer, unable to keep his gloating sneer evident from his face. "My dear, you're in no position to call anyone names. I expect you to bleed to death within the hour, barring some kind of miracle. Since your goddess is already dead, I believe this place is fresh out of miracles, don't you?" He shifted his focus to Dante's corpse. "Why on earth is he still wearing that ridiculous headdress? Enforcer, I want that thing removed and destroyed! No trace of the Mukari or her disciples is to be left here. I plan to make the citadel an impregnable fortress for the new Imperial Black regiment I shall build here."

Rai knelt by Dante's head and tore the headdress free. As he did Dante's eyes flicked open. The general stared in disbelief. "But that's impossible! He was dead a minute ago!"

"Appearances can be deceiving," Dante replied with a smile. He braced his arms on the floor, then kicked his legs up and over his head into the Enforcer's face. Rai tumbled over backwards, his head thudding heavily into the wooden doorframe by the balcony. He slumped to the floor and lay still.

"Enforcer, I command you to get up!" Ivanov yelled, but Rai did not move.

"Guess it's just you and me," Dante hissed at the general, who was climbing to his feet. "No regiment to cover your back, no soldiers to hold your victim down while you torture them. How's that, Vassily – exciting enough for you?" He launched himself at Ivanov, not giving his target time to draw a weapon. The two men slammed into the nearest wall, the impact winding the general. Dante punching a fist into Ivanov's groin, then snapped a knee into his chin. "Spatchcock! Flintlock! Barricade the door!"

"Got it!" Spatchcock replied, already dragging the discarded throne towards the entrance. Flintlock hurried to help him. Together they shoved the heavy wooden chair against the door, wedging it beneath the handle. Within seconds fists were hammering from the other side, but the door remained closed.

Ivanov spat a mouthful of teeth and blood onto the floor. "I don't need my men to beat you, Dante. Any soldier in the Tsar's army could outfight street-scum like you, but they would consider it beneath their honour."

"Honour be damned," Dante snarled. "Where was the honour in murdering innocent civilians during the war? Where was the honour when you herded the women into rape camps? Where was the honour when you tortured anyone who dared speak my name after the war? Where was the honour when you slaughtered a village of people yesterday, simply to get directions?" Dante grabbed Ivanov by the throat and lifted him off the floor, slamming the general's head against the nearest wall. "Don't you dare talk to me about honour, you bastard!"

A burst of blue light oscillated around the room, exploding outwards from the ever-exploding vortex. It had expanded to twice its original size and was engulfing the bridge that led into its ravenous core. Spatchcock pointed at the menacing spectacle, the light bursting from its centre casting strange shadows across his features. "Is that thing meant to be getting bigger like that?"

"Not exactly, no," Dante called back over the noise of soldiers trying to break into the throne room. He noticed movement on other side of the chamber. "Mai, your brother is coming round. Can you deal with him?"

"I'll try…" She grimaced and wrenched the knife from her abdomen, screaming in agony as more blood spurted out. Clutching the wound with one hand and the blade in her other, Mai crawled towards the Enforcer. Rai's eyelids were fluttering and blood dripped from his nostrils. One of his hands opened and closed spasmodically, but he showed few other signs of life.

Mai rolled him over on to his back, pressing the knife against Rai's throat. "Don't move," she warned. "Don't even think about moving."

With Dante distracted, Ivanov used the opportunity to let his hand drop to the sidearm holstered at his waist. He tilted it backwards so the barrel was aimed at Dante, then the general slid his fingers inside the trigger. "You know what I liked most about Rudinshtein?" Ivanov whispered.

Dante, be careful, the Crest warned. *This sadist didn't becoming a general without learning a few tricks.*

"I can handle this sick bastard's taunts," Dante retorted.

"It was the children," Ivanov smiled before pulling the trigger. "The sweet way the children screamed just before they died. It got me so… over-excited." The bullet punched clean through Dante's ribcage, bone, flesh and blood exploded out a fist-sized hole in his back, creating a fine, pink aerosol.

Dante staggered backwards, blood bubbling from his lips. Ivanov fired again, this shot tearing a hunk of flesh from Dante's right shoulder. He toppled to one knee, gasping for air, one hand trying to feebly stop his internal organs leaking out through the hole in his front.

"Dante!" Flintlock shouted, stepping forward to intervene. But he was driven back by the gun in Ivanov's hand, retreating to Spatchcock's side.

"I know a coward when I see one," the general snarled. "You two lack the foolhardy courage of your master. Stay back or share his slow, painful death." Ivanov lashed out with one of his legs, the black boot kicking Dante in the face, knocking him to the floor. "Nikolai, tell your Oriental bitch to unhand my Enforcer."

"Mai does not answer to me," Dante replied through gritted teeth. Mai kept her knife pressed to the Enforcer's throat, holding him down on the floor.

Ivanov stepped on Dante's torso, grinding his heel into the entry wound, winning a scream of pain from the stricken man. "Don't make me repeat myself, boy. Tell her to release my second-in-command or I'll shove this boot through your spine. I doubt even your enhanced healing abilities will recover from that."

"You're welcome to try..." Dante said, his hands coming alive with purple and silver cyborganics, "...but you might find that difficult without any legs!" He ripped a cyborganic sword through the air, slicing clean through both of Ivanov's knees. The general tumbled to the floor, screaming with agony.

Dante rolled over on top of Ivanov, pinning the Imperial Black's leader to the wooden beams. "Now, tell me again how you got off watching children be butchered!"

Ivanov shook his head, refusing to give in. "Damn you to hell, Dante!"

"You first!" Dante stabbed his blade through the general's throat and down into the black floorboards beneath. Dante pulled the sword free and rolled off Ivanov's body. "At least you'll never touch Rudinshtein again, you bastard."

Flintlock and Spatchcock rushed over to him, the shorter man peeling off his jacket and pressing it against Dante's back. "This doesn't look good."

Dante, you've lost a lot of blood, the Crest said. *Ivanov may have been right. I don't think your enhanced healing abilities can repair the damage in time.*

"What about Mai?" Dante gurgled, blood stains visible on his teeth. "Has she finished off the Enforcer?"

"I can't," she admitted. "I know what he has done, but Ivanov brainwashed him. Rai is still my brother, I can't murder him in cold blood."

Mai's bleeding to death, the Crest said. *She's almost as badly injured as you, but she doesn't have a Crest's enhanced healing abilities.*

"She bonded with one before, she can do it again," Dante said.

"What are you talking about?" Flintlock asked, but it was Mai who answered.

"I used to be the Mukari," she said. "I'm too old now."

"You're wrong," Dante whispered. "The Mukari must be a woman born of these mountains, but her age doesn't matter. Khumbu and his brethren made sure only young girls became the Mukari–"

"So they could control them," Mai realised.

Spatchcock was glancing nervously over his shoulder at the vortex. It had now swallowed the bridge and was eating into the floorboards of the throne room. At one edge the glowing globe was consuming the doorway, expanding outwards to attack the soldiers in the corridor. "Whatever you two are planning, you'd better do it quickly. That thing's getting bigger by the second!"

"Put it on," Dante urged Mai, pointing at the discarded headdress. "Once you wear that, you are bonded with the Mukari's Crest."

Mai shook her head. "You don't know what it's like, having the past, present and future all happening simultaneously in your head – coping with knowing all there is to know, being responsible for holding everything together."

"Think what you could achieve with that knowledge," Dante pleaded. "I put on the headdress and it almost killed me, Mai. You're the only one who can do this."

Finally, she nodded. "One of you will have to watch Rai," she said. Flintlock took the pistol from Ivanov's corpse and aimed it at the Enforcer. Mai moved over to the headdress, which was lying dangerously close to the edge of the ever-expanding vortex. Closing her eyes, Mai pulled the headdress into position. Pain stabbed through her features, then she relaxed.

"Is it working?" Spatchcock asked.

Mai nodded. "I can hear the Crest in my head, welcoming me back." She stood, one hand still held over the wound to her abdomen. "The Crest's healing ability, it's repairing my injuries." Mai took her hand away and the gaping hole in her skin sealed itself, leaving just a blood-stained hole in her clothes.

"What about the vortex," Dante cried. "Can you stop the vortex?"

"I'll try," she said, closing her eyes to concentrate.

Suddenly Rai leapt forwards from his position slumped against the wall. He smashed the pistol from Flintlock's grasp, grabbing the startled Brit by the throat. "I'm getting out of here," Rai announced. "If anybody tries to stop me, I'll snap this fool's neck like a twig!"

"Go ahead and snap it. We don't care," Spatchcock replied.

"Spatch!" Flintlock cried in horror.

"I was trying to trick him, you idiot!"

"No more tricks," Rai warned, backing towards the doorway. But the throne room's internal exit had already been consumed by the swirling vortex.

"Don't go any further," Dante said. "You can't get out that way."

"I said no more tricks!"

"This isn't a trick," Spatchcock shouted back. "Look behind you!"

"How stupid do you think I am?" Rai demanded.

"You'll soon find out, but I'd prefer it if you didn't take Flintlock to his doom as well," Dante replied. "He may be annoying, prissy and a royal pain in the arse, but he does have some redeeming features."

"Just don't ask us for a quick list," Spatchcock added.

"Spatch!" Flintlock cried out.

"Only joking."

Dante, the vortex – it hasn't stopped contracting. If anything, it is expanding faster than before.

"Mai, what's happening?"

She was shaking her head, teeth biting her bottom lip.
"I can't do it, the vortex. It's already too strong for me!"
Her legs gave way beneath her and Mai crumpled to the
floor, both hands struggling to keep her headdress in
place.

A scream burst from the other side of the throne room.
Rai and Flintlock were being sucked into the periphery of
the vortex, a crackling tentacle of blue and white energy
wrapped around Rai's left leg, hauling both men towards
it.

"Crest! Any brilliant suggestions?" Dante asked in des-
peration.

If the vortex is already too strong for a single Crest to
control, perhaps two Crests can achieve that task, it
replied.

Dante pushed himself up on to one knee. "Spatch, help
me over to Mai."

"You're the boss," the rumpled runt replied, dipping
his shoulder under one of Dante's arms. Together they
staggered over to Mai, where Dante sunk back to the
floor. He pulled her closer and pressed his lips against
hers.

Beginning bonding process…

Spatchcock glanced over to Rai and Flintlock. Both
men were moments from being swallowed by the vortex,
half a dozen tentacles dragging their writhing bodies into
its edge. "Whatever you're going to do," he urged Dante,
"do it now!"

The vortex retracted for a second, like a wave about to
crash upon a beach, then white light filled the room in an
explosion of light and sound. After that was nothing. A
blank and empty nothing…

EPILOGUE

"Great talkers are great liars."
– Russian proverb

"The blackout of 2673 remains one of the enduring mysteries from the years immediately after the war. Across the Empire every power supply, every light, every candle, every source of energy ceased to function for forty-seven seconds. The cause is still unknown, as is the reason for its abrupt end. It was as if the entire universe blinked and then held its breath, waiting for some great cataclysm to occur. But the cataclysm never came and the universe breathed out again. Some reports suggest the blackout began in a remote region of the Himalayas, an area cut off from civilisation by freakish weather conditions ever since. But that same isolation makes it impossible to prove or disprove those reports."

– Extract from *Unsolved Mysteries of the Empire*, by Danilov Mulderski

Nikolai Dante, with two wounds slowly healing inside him, sat in front of the Forbidden Citadel and thought about life and death.

He could remember little about what happened after he kissed Mai in the throne room. There was a skittering of alien minds within his own thoughts as the two Crests had bonded before attempting to regain control of the vortex.

The inter-dimensional gateway had been like a wild animal inside Dante's head, gnawing, hungry, almost feral. It sensed the Crests coming and launched a pre-emptive attack. Everything after that was a blur of light and fury.

Dante had come to in what was left of the throne room, most of his clothes seared from his body, with Mai's unconscious and equally naked form nuzzled into his. He kissed her and she woke, a quiet joy on her face. Things may have become even more interesting, but for a polite cough from nearby. Spatchcock and Flintlock had been sitting in a corner of the throne room, a few rags hanging from their bodies, observing Dante and Mai's embrace. Spatchcock looked particularly disappointed at being denied a free floorshow, while Flintlock smiled sheepishly.

The cough had come from another corner, where a fresh-faced Himalayan youth was standing. It was Rai, but as Dante had first known him, in the dying days of the war. The horrific scars on his face were gone, and so were all the wounds and injuries he had acquired since.

Lastly Dante had turned to look at the vortex. It too was restored to the way it had been, a glowing ball of energy under firm control. A huge section of the throne room was missing, a gaping void showing how close the vortex had come to consuming them all. But the crisis had been averted – just.

All of that was three days in the past. Since then Spatchcock and Flintlock had busied themselves organising a funeral pyre for the monks killed by Ivanov's men. Mai used the immense power of her Crest to send the few survivors from the Imperial Black back to the Tsar with a warning never to invade or attack the Himalayas again. To underline her threat, she sent every Imperial corpse too, including the remains of General Ivanov.

Dante had spent the three days recovering in Gylatsen's cell, letting his enhanced healing abilities do their job. He emerged much the better for his rest, but still experiencing stabs of pain from where Ivanov had shot him. "Guess I'm not rid of that bastard yet," Dante muttered to himself.

I hope you're not talking about me, the Crest said.

"No, the late, unlamented general. But where have you been hiding the past three days? I expected an endless lecture series on what I should have done differently, but you haven't said a word to me."

I was... preoccupied. The Mukari's Crest required my aid to bring the situation completely under control. Besides, you needed peace and quiet to heal.

"Well, I'm feeling strong enough to leave now," Dante said. "I'm waiting for Spatch and Flintlock to find my rifle, then we can go."

You aren't staying for the funeral?

"I've seen enough death to last me a lifetime."

Mai emerged from the citadel, sitting beside Dante in the autumnal sunshine. "A beautiful day, isn't it?"

"Yes. Spatch, Flintlock and I should make good time down the mountain."

"So you're definitely leaving today?"

Dante nodded. "You're not wearing the headdress. Is that wise? You don't want the vortex–"

Mai rested a finger against his lips, silencing him. Her other hand opened the front of her top to reveal a small, double-headed eagle symbol in the nape of her neck. "I couldn't stand the idea of having to wear that hat for the rest of my days, so your Crest and mine arranged for a more physical manifestation. I can always transfer it back, when the time comes."

"Interesting," Dante said. "Crest, that does mean I can shift you to–"

No.

"But if Mai can do it, why can't I–"

Her Crest is different from yours. Very different.

"We could at least try–"

No.

Mai smiled at their exchange. "Sorry. But at least you can go where you want. I have to stay here on the mountain."

Dante noticed Rai walked past. "Your brother... How much does he remember of his time as the Enforcer?"

"A little." Mai frowned. "I know it was selfish of me, using the vortex to change Rai back to how I remembered him before the war. But I'll need someone to keep me company here in the citadel. Unless I can change your mind..."

Dante shook his head. "Sorry. Your place is here, but I don't belong anywhere – not since the war."

"You could always come back for a visit," Mai offered, smiling impishly. "We never did get to finish what we started in that cave."

Dante was still kissing Mai when Spatchcock and Flintlock appeared, the latter carrying the Huntsman 5000. "Well, we finally found your precious rifle," he said. "Why you decided to hide it behind a shrine I'll never–" A sharp elbow from Spatchcock abruptly silenced the Brit, as Dante and Mai hastily separated.

"Ready to go?" Spatchcock asked, grinning broadly.

"Yes," Dante replied, standing up. He smiled fondly at Mai. "Say goodbye to your brother for us. Tell him... tell him not to worry about the past. The future is more important now."

"I'll do that."

The three men strolled out of the citadel and onto the snow-covered plateau beyond the repaired gates. The trio paused as they surveyed the Himalayas, the majestic peaks spread out around them as far as the horizon.

"You know, I can't help thinking we should get some sort of reward for saving the Empire," Spatchcock commented. "Hell, for saving the whole universe."

"Getting away from you would be reward enough for me," Flintlock muttered under his breath. "What about you, Dante? Do you reckon we should get a reward? Or maybe you think getting vengeance on Ivanov was enough."

"It was a hollow victory," Dante replied. "I can't bring back the tens of thousands he had murdered, or undo the horrors he did in Rudinshtein and other places. All I did was murder a murderer. Where's the honour in that?"

Honour be damned, the Crest said. *There is more to life than honour. You of all people should know that, Dante.*

The three men turned back to see Mai and Rai waving from inside the citadel gates. Beyond them, a column of smoke drifted from the burning funeral pyre, creating a road to the heavens. Dante waved to the siblings, then set off down the mountainside, his travelling companions following him.

"It's strange," Dante commented. "My Crest has been surprisingly busy these past three days, ever since it bonded with the Mukari's Crest."

"What's strange about that?" Flintlock asked.

"When I put on the headdress, I heard the voice of the Mukari's Crest, and it was distinctly female." Dante paused, waiting for a reply from his Crest. "I was wondering if somebody not too far from me has been playing away recently."

A long silence followed.

"Well?" Spatchcock asked eagerly. "What did your Crest say?"

Dante smirked. "Nothing I could repeat in polite company."

"Since when have we been polite company?" Spatchcock asked Flintlock.

"Just shut up and walk," the Brit replied grumpily.

"I dare say Flintlock is right." Dante pulled his coat closer around himself, shivering in a cold wind that blew from the north. "Bojemoi. It's a long hike back to civilisation from here."

ABOUT THE AUTHOR

David Bishop was born and raised in New Zealand, becoming a daily newspaper journalist at eighteen years old. He emigrated to Britain in 1990 and was editor of the *Judge Dredd Megazine* and then *2000 AD*, before becoming a freelance writer. His previous novels include three starring Judge Dredd (for Virgin Books) and four featuring Doctor Who (for Virgin and the BBC). He also writes non-fiction books and articles, audio dramas, comics and has been a creative consultant on three forthcoming video games. If you see Bishop in public, do not approach him – alert the nearest editor and stand well back. Bishop's previous contributions to Black Flame are *Judge Dredd: Bad Moon Rising*, *Nikolai Dante: The Strangelove Gambit* and *A Nightmare on Elm Street: Suffer the Children*.

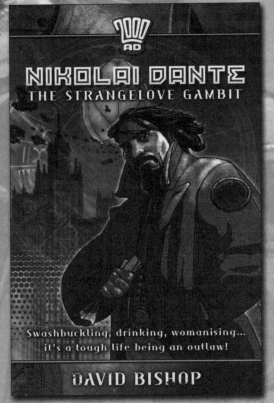